COOKING THE BOOKS

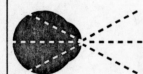

This Large Print Book carries the
Seal of Approval of N.A.V.H.

COOKING THE BOOKS

BONNIE S. CALHOUN

THORNDIKE PRESS
A part of Gale, Cengage Learning

GALE
CENGAGE Learning

Detroit • New York • San Francisco • New Haven, Conn • Waterville, Maine • London

GALE
CENGAGE Learning®

Copyright © 2012 by Bonnie S. Calhoun.
Thorndike Press, a part of Gale, Cengage Learning.

Thorndike Press® Large Print Christian Mystery.
The text of this Large Print edition is unabridged.
Other aspects of the book may vary from the original edition.
Set in 16 pt. Plantin.

LIBRARY OF CONGRESS CATALOGING-IN-PUBLICATION DATA

Calhoun, Bonnie S.
  Cooking the books / by Bonnie S. Calhoun.
    pages ; cm. — (Thorndike Press large print Christian mystery) (A Sloane Templeton novel)
  ISBN-13: 978-1-4104-4794-4 (hardcover)
  ISBN-10: 1-4104-4794-4 (hardcover)
  1. Women booksellers—Fiction. 2. Book clubs (Discussion groups)—Fiction. 3. Older persons—Fiction. 4. Large type books. I. Title.
PS3603.A4387C66 2012
813'.6—dc23   2012012839

Published in 2012 by arrangement with Abingdon Press.

Printed in Mexico
1 2 3 4 5 6 7 16 15 14 13 12

To my longtime spiritual leader,
Pastor Dann Travis of Crossroads
of Life Church, and his wife,
Bonnie Travis, my Best Friend Forever.
Without you two I would not be
on this journey.

ACKNOWLEDGMENTS

First and foremost I want to thank my Lord and Savior Jesus Christ; without you I am nothing. My deepest thanks go to my dear friend Marlene Bagnull and the Greater Philadelphia Christian Writers Conference, where I met Terry Burns, who is not only my agent but a dear friend and mentor. A special thank-you goes to Barbara Scott, and my fabulous editor at Abingdon, Ramona Richards, for having faith in my abilities. You ladies rock! Continued thanks go out to my critique group, the Penwrights; my writing buddy and first reader Wanda Dyson; my personal editor Jennifer Peterson; Officer Kevin Smith; and Detective Robert Harrell. And last but not least, I want to thank my husband, Robert, for always supporting me in everything I do.

PROLOGUE

"Let me go! Why you do this to me?"

"Because you didn't listen." The bald Danny DeVito look-alike stood in front of the chair with his hands in the pockets of his leather jacket.

Sunshine filtered through the grimy window set high in the concrete wall. It angled a dusty ray of light down into the room, casting a shadow in front of the individual tied to the metal chair in the center of the barren space.

Two men entered the room from behind the chair. One remained in the shadows while the other, a Middle Eastern man wearing jeans and a button-down shirt, walked to the bound man. He ran his hand across the man's shoulder as he moved in front of him.

"You no can do this. I give you what you want." The bound man struggled against his ropes, his wrists raw and bleeding from his frantic squirming.

"It's too late." The Middle Eastern man patted him on the shoulder, then moved his hand away. "You've had many chances. You wasted them all."

"No, no . . . I have now. I do now."

The man in the shadows nodded. The Middle Eastern man pulled three hypodermic needles from his shirt pocket, carefully unsheathed the first one, and handed it to the DeVito clone.

The bound man's eyes widened. "I get for you. I give you. I promise."

"Time's up." The DeVito clone ran his fingers along the struggling man's chest searching for the space between his ribs, then plunged in the needle. He gasped with the rush of deadly drugs entering his body. His legs went rigid.

"Madre mía." The words rushed out with his last breath.

1

One month later . . .

The car jerked as though possessed.

I inhaled sharply, holding onto the breath as tightly as I gripped the smooth wood railing with one hand and my garbage bag with the other. I peered down from the landing on the floor below my apartment at the car parked closest to the building.

My heart drummed a monster cadence that pounded on the blood vessels behind my eyes, causing pinpoint stars to float in front of my vision. Was I really seeing this or had I not had enough coffee yet this morning?

Yes. It was no flashback from my days of old. The car still shook.

A warm summer breeze drifted across my skin as I continued to stare down at the vehicle. I shivered. I wasn't cold. It was fear.

What was I, an idiot? I had to will my foot to descend to the next step. At the moment, my feet were apparently smarter than I was. They knew danger. A smart person would turn around and go back upstairs, through the apartment and down the front stairs. But no, I apparently didn't emanate from that smart gene pool. If something could be considered dangerous or reckless, my name was probably attached somewhere.

My dear mom, God rest her soul, always said, "Fools rush in where angels fear to tread."

Yeah, let's not mention that angels must have practiced running for the clouds every time the name Sloane Templeton came up as an assignment. I had a knack for turning them into a bruised and battered little fife-and-drum corps, complete with head bandages and crutches.

A woman's screech echoed from the closed interior of the car.

I gasped and stumbled back against the step, raking my calf on the unyielding wood. I winced. As I tried to steady myself, my left hand lost its grip on the garbage bag I was carrying. It rolled down the rest of the stairs in slow motion and plopped beside the Dumpster.

I stared at it. That's one way to get it down there.

An animal-like howl rolled though the air.

I stiffened.

Lord, help me! She's being attacked.

There was an innocent woman in there. Call the police! Why didn't I think of it five minutes ago? I felt my pockets. No cell phone, just my gun in one pocket, and keys in the other. I must have left the phone downstairs on my desk in the bookstore last night. Figures, I never have it when I need it.

A muffled scream.

Electric fear zipped up my spine. My brain ticked off the options. Up the stairs and down the front. Shudder. Pass the car and around to the front. Either way, to get to a phone was going to take time that might rob this woman of her life. I had to do something now. I was the only one here.

How? Don't be stupid! I have a gun in my pocket. Yeah, but I've never confronted another person with my weapon. This is crazy and reckless. I could be overpowered. They could take my gun and shoot me.

A moan. Banging. Another scream.

No! I have to do something. Now!

With a trembling hand, I pulled the registered .38 from the pocket of my baggy linen trousers. Against my wishes, Mom had badgered me until I accepted her transferring the weapon to me right before her passing. Her excuse was that I needed protection as a store owner in our crime-ridden area. Although I didn't have a clue about what crime she was referring to, I did have a good guess about the criminals. This was a new day, and fear was not going to create any more victims around me than I could help.

As I pulled the gun from my pants, the thumb hammer snagged on the top of my pocket, flipping the weapon out of my shaking hand. I lunged for it. Fingers clawed at empty air. Agh!

I flinched as it hit the step, expecting the gun to discharge and shoot me in my smarter-than-me foot.

The weapon tumbled down two more treads of the wooden staircase, and spun to the edge, hanging there for a split second before continuing its descent. It bounced down another step, spun a couple more times, and came to rest with the barrel facing in my direction. It mocked me as though I was playing spin the bottle. Tag . . . you're it!

A woman's pleading voice resonated from the shaking car.

My first instinct was to leave the gun right where it lay and run away. But my inner warrior wouldn't let me back away.

I ran down the few steps and snatched up the snub-nosed gun. The cool metal was foreign in my clammy fingers. Why in the world did I think I could be like my fearless ma, brandishing a weapon, when I'd never held anything more deadly than nail clippers?

I pulled in a sharp breath to calm my teeth-rattling jitters. If I didn't go now, reason would take over. I charged down the stairs. Vaulting over the garbage bag, I snuck up to the passenger side of the car and yanked on the door handle, almost pulling my arm from its socket. The door didn't yield.

Locked. Great! Now in addition to a skinned leg, I had a throbbing shoulder.

The windows dripped foggy moisture on the inside, masking the interior. I couldn't see a thing.

The woman needed my help. I suddenly summoned an inordinate amount of bravery and slapped my hand on the glass with the same authority Officer Murphy had used on the car Tim Owens and I were in when I was eighteen. "Open the door!"

I stepped back, sucked in a breath, and imagined the worst, waiting for the attacker to launch from the car, and not having the least clue of what I would do. Instead . . .

silence. Nothing. No answer. Touching the side of the car, I could feel the thumping. It imitated pounding feet.

"Let her go or I'll break this window!"

How? By shooting it out? Bad idea. No shooting when you can't see what you're shooting at.

The cries ceased as the vehicle stopped trembling. A hand swiped across the glistening fog inside the window and a wide-eyed female face appeared.

"Are you okay? Open the door." I grabbed for the handle again, then let go. What if some big angry dude charged me?

A lock clicked.

I backed away. The door didn't open.

I tamped down my fear, backed up another step, and raised the weapon like I knew what I was doing. Holding it with one hand cupped in the other, I rested my trembling finger along the trigger guard.

"Open the door now. Let her out."

The door opened a hair.

I lunged and snatched the handle, jerking it open all the way. "Come out with —"

I was staring down at a middle-aged woman with sleep-encrusted eyes and chestnut brown hair haphazardly pulled up in a claw clip.

Her eyes grew wide at the sight of the gun.

16

She wrapped her arms around her head. "Please don't shoot me!"

A whimper escaped her throat as she pulled her feet up onto the seat and tucked her knees against her chest.

I glanced around the inside of the car as the thick moist air clung to my face like a mask. I half expected to see water dripping from the headliner.

The woman was alone.

I lowered the gun to my side. Relief. "It's all right. I'm not going to hurt you. I heard you scream and thought you were being attacked. This neighborhood isn't the safest of places."

The woman dropped her arms. "I'm sorry." She rubbed her hands across her eyes like a little child. "I was having a nightmare."

"Nightmare? Were you in my parking lot all night?" With a solid feeling of averted-disaster relief, I slipped the .38 back into my pocket. The added weight pulled on the drawstring cinched tightly at my waist. I could feel the cool metal against my leg.

The woman's eyes darted around as though she was looking for an avenue of escape. "I was just waiting for you to open, so I could get coffee and do some writing."

"I'm on my way to open the store." I

hesitated. It was not lost on me that she did not answer my question about sleeping in the car all night. I guess that was her business, not mine.

"Come on." Why did I say that? I didn't even know this woman, but she looked like a lost puppy.

While the woman grabbed her laptop case from the backseat, I snuck another look inside, just to be safe.

We crossed the parking lot and walked down the narrow alleyway to the front of the building. Through the wispy leaves of the honey locust trees, I could see the two mega-high-rise buildings jutting out of the low landscape five blocks up Fulton Street. One high-rise building still looked like a tinkertoy creation with its unfinished floors and high cranes. I bit down on my lip. The chaotic intrusion of all this redevelopment made my heart hurt.

I pulled the large, jangling lump of Mom's keys from my other pocket. Sometime soon, I needed to divide these up into more manageable quantities. Forget the gun; the keys could be considered a lethal weapon in most circles. Just as I found the appropriate key, a male figure darted from the store doorway.

Hopping back, I nearly tripped over the

poor woman shadowing me as my hand flew to my mouth and I stifled a scream. I lashed out with the key ring.

Rob Landry dodged my swing and stood there, grinning goofily.

I shook my head, disgusted that he would think something so juvenile was cute, but relieved that I wasn't being robbed and I hadn't actually clocked him with the killer keys. I gave him the once-over.

Dressed in a starched white shirt, black tie, and sharp pressed black pants, he looked like the door-to-door recruiter for a cult. But it was that infernal briefcase. I stared at it. No doubt, it carried the paperwork that could signal my impending doom as a bookstore owner — if I chose to cooperate.

I tore my gaze from the briefcase and stabbed visual daggers through him. "Rob, one of these days you're going to give me a stroke. Then this building will be tied up in the litigation of my estate for the next twenty years."

I brushed past him and pushed the key into the lock.

"Mrs. Sloane Templeton, I have been authorized —"

"Dear Lord, save me!" I prayed and swung around to glare at him — his grin looking like the Joker from the Batman comics. "You've been authorized all right — authorized to drive me to distraction." Granted I didn't like being a bookseller, but I liked even less the idea of selling him the building I had grown up in.

I unlocked the front door to Beckham's Books & Brew and ushered the brunette woman past the still-grinning Landry. Swinging around to face him, I poked a finger in his direction. "And don't ever call me *Missus*. I divorced that lowlife six months ago." Let's not go into the fact that he kept trying to divorce me by way of Shady Grove cemetery, and the cheapskate would probably have buried me in a cardboard box rather than paying for pine.

I shooed him back and closed the door in his face. Why did men behaving badly always seem to gravitate to me like insects to grease? I needed to find cologne that worked as a roach repellant.

2

Rob Landry marched back down Fulton Street and crossed the road to the Coltrane Realty field office that had been set up for this project. His hand hesitated on the door handle. The store-front was all glass. Three men stared at him from desks on the inside. He lowered his head and opened the door.

"Yes, here's the man!" yelled Chuck Percy as he wiped the lens of his heavy black-rimmed glasses and put them back on. "Tell us that you scored."

Landry ignored him, walked past Dave Barker's desk, the first and largest in the room, and set his briefcase on his own desk further back and to the right.

Barker watched him walk by and swiveled in his chair to face him. "So? Did you seal the deal?"

"Nah, she's still not interested," said Landry as he slumped into his uncomfortable office chair and loosened his tie.

"Not interested is *not* an option, my man," said Barker.

Landry furrowed his brow. "What am I supposed to do if she refuses to sign the papers?"

"You are supposed to use your *creative* powers of persuasion," said Barker. "And by creative, of course, I mean dirty." He cocked an eyebrow and hitched a greasy smile. "Clock's ticking on this deal. Our bonuses for closing the deal have been tripled."

"He doesn't care. He's all googly-eyed for that old lady running the store," said Percy. He snorted a laugh and pushed his glasses back up on his nose. "He's getting his pay-day."

"You *wouldn't* want to be responsible for the rest of us not getting our bonuses, now would you?" asked Barker.

"Watch it. Don't you speak about her that way. She's a real nice lady, and we have a lot in common," said Landry. "Besides, she's not that much older than me."

"You've taken your eye off the prize, buddy," said the guy across from him.

"I'm beginning to think this is not the right job for me. I don't know how to go for the jugular like you guys." Landry slouched in his seat.

"You'd better shape up or you're going to be out on the street looking for another job. Your performance is being watched, you know," said Barker.

Landry smiled. "Yeah, right, by who?"

"That would be *by whom,* and the answer is *by the boss.* And believe me, I've heard stories about other deals and some of the extremes to get them done. If I didn't love the money, I'd be in a fast car out of town!"

Landry looked around the room. "What boss? I thought we were reporting to Corporate." He gestured to Barker. "You hired me. I thought you were the boss."

Barker leaned back in his seat. "Our boss. *Hello?* The owner."

Landry looked at him with a blank stare.

Barker's shoulders shook with laughter. "Are you telling me that you've been with this company all year and you don't know who owns Coltrane Realty?"

3

By the time I had turned off the alarms and turned on all the lights, I had expected the woman to be casually sitting at a table, but instead I found her by the counter gripping the laptop to her chest like a shield. I walked her across the sand-colored Italian quarry tile entrance and onto the hardwood floor of the bookstore.

I touched her shoulder. "What's your name, hon?"

She wheeled to face me, her eyes wide with fear. I jerked back my hand. Sheesh . . . I didn't think the gesture warranted her skittish response.

She backed into an overstuffed couch at the edge of the reading area. She steadied herself with one hand on the tapestry-covered arm and stared at the floor. "Barbara Nelson."

"Barbara, you look like you could use a strong cup of coffee."

The woman's shoulders relaxed. Her head rose and a timid smile flickered across her lips as her eagerness bubbled over. "I could make it for you. I know how. I watch you every day."

Whoa, instantaneous change. Let's not ask why the woman spends her time watching me. It's way too early in the morning to try to make sense of it. I gestured to the coffee bar at the back of the bookstore. "Okay then, have at it."

Barbara deposited her laptop on the closest table, sauntered behind the counter, and went about preparing the morning coffee. Well, that was weird. I thought she'd be clutching onto that laptop for dear life.

I did a tit for tat and now I watched her. She had on a rumpled sleeveless pink cotton blouse and equally wrinkled burgundy slacks. Her hair and clip seemed familiar. Yes, now I remember. Pencils usually stuck out of that clip, which presented a conundrum of an image since she worked at a laptop computer rather than with paper and pencil. And come to think of it, I never saw her so much as even gnaw on one of those pencils. Maybe she was using them as hair decorations . . . or weapons.

I lost interest in her appearance and moved behind the counter to the left of the front door, depositing the .38 Special in the drawer beneath the register. I paused, staring at the dark metal. What was I thinking carrying a gun? It was an act of providence the stupid thing hadn't gone off when I dropped it. I could have shot myself. Mom had been the sharpshooter type, while I was more like a disaster waiting to happen.

Resigned to my ineptness with a deadly weapon, I plopped onto my black leather chair, and spied the bag of white cheddar cheese puffs. Hey, they're made with real cheese. It's a food group. I'm hungry and it's better than eating a slice of Red Velvet cake at this hour of the morning, right? I removed the chip clip and dug in as I swiveled around to face the room. *Crunch.* I could pretend that this was a throne, and I was surveying my kingdom.

Truth be known, this four-story brownstone was the only home I'd known for most of my thirty-five years of life, other than when I was at school or during my short stint at being married. And therein lay my latest problem . . . neighborhood gentrification and urban renewal.

The silver bell above the door jingled.

Verlene Buford swept into the store like a Kansas City tornado on its way to Illinois. Verlene, at forty-nine, was the youngest of my mom's six sisters, and the only one living in New York. The smell of barbeque followed in her wake as she slid her oversized, wraparound sunglasses onto her head where her bun acted as a glasses stop. "Hi, Sloane honey. I need your help."

I love her dearly, but usually her need for help meant me tasting one of her new culinary creations that, in turn, had caused me to need help for heartburn or indigestion. She fancied herself as an Iron Chef. In reality, *you* needed a cast-iron stomach to partake of her disasters.

"Hey, Verlene. What's up?" The words stuck in my throat, or maybe it was a cheese puff. I sneezed, and the cheese puff flew out with the words. My hand flew up to cover my mouth, but it was too late.

Verlene pulled back and curled up her lip. "Are you getting sick?"

"Nah, just my sinuses. 'Tis the season."

Verlene moved to the counter and reached over to touch the stray locks of hair that had escaped my side barrette. "Child, I should be helping you. When's the last time you were at Bebe's to get your do done?"

I pulled my fingers through the hair framing both sides of my face and pushed the strays behind both ears. "I haven't had time to go. Besides, I found this new light golden brown from Textures and Tones, and I did it myself. I think I look pretty good." At least, I had until she started acting like she smelled something bad. Now I wasn't so sure.

"Child, Bebe's got a new stylist." She reached up and ran a hand along the smoothness of her hairdo. "I think he does excellent work."

"He?"

"Honey, hush. He's a Hungarian boy who thinks he's Mick Jagger."

"Hungarian? Mick Jagger? At Bebe's?" You have to understand the scope of multi-ethnicity at Bebe's consisted of Japanese and Brazilian hair straightening along with perms and braids, but men were not included as part of the process. "He must have a righteous game."

"Yeah, I can't even explain it. You gotta experience him."

"I'm thinking skinny, flashy, and loud."

She threw her hands up and laughed out loud. "He's all that and a bag o' chips!" She shook her head and put her hand up to smooth the side of her hair. "But he does rockin' do's."

Chips. I could use some of them too, but that was why I was wearing drawstring pants and loose tops this week. My jeans wouldn't button. I wanted to grimace at myself and grin at Verlene, all at the same time. Her hair was pulled back so slick it looked like it was spray painted on her head. I imagined if the glasses had not been intercepted by the bun, they would have slid around the back of her head and fallen to the floor.

"Verlene, that hairdo looks like it hurts. Your hair's got your face pulled up so tight, I swear I saw your belt buckle move when you raised your eyebrows."

She waved a hand. "This is how all chefs should style their hair. Neat and contained. But never you mind about my hair. I need you to ride home with me and help unload my groceries. And I've got a huge secret to share with you."

I cringed. *Chef* was the only word I heard. "Verlene, I can't leave the bookstore. I just opened."

Granted, business usually didn't start for another hour, but going to her house was always just weird. She was a wannabe chef with a penchant for buying every piece of equipment the kitchen connoisseurs recommended. Her kitchen looked like a torture chamber for runaway cooks. It creeped me right out.

"Child, I just came from Costco down on Third Avenue. My favorite new place! Love,

love, *love* that store. I made friends with a new chef who got me in early with the rest of the professionals, before regular store hours, and I got a ton of food fixin's that need to get refrigerated before they spoil."

I almost said, "With your cooking that might be an improvement," but I bit down on my wayward tongue and slapped on a sweet smile worthy of Dora the Explorer. "I would love to help you, but I have no one to mind the store."

Talk about a saving grace. At this very moment, I loved the store like no other. I sniffed the air. The barbeque smell was stronger. I knew it wasn't coming from the Ethiopian restaurant across the street, but it sure was making me hungry for ribs.

"Well, what about her watching it?" Verlene did a hand flick in the direction of Barbara, who was standing behind the coffee counter.

"She doesn't work here." I set down the bag of cheese puffs, lifted myself from the comfortable chair, and moved to the opening in the counter, all set to give Auntie a hug and send her back to her double-parked car, which I could see through the front windows was about to get a ticket.

Red! All I saw was red. Spread across the floor, dripping off the bottom of Verlene's

30

flower-print blouse, running down her moss green pant leg, all over her white Reebok sneakers. Red!

My heart jumped to my throat. I gagged a cry. "Verlene, oh dear goodness. You're bleeding! Honey, where are you hurt?"

She looked at me as if I were a cow with two heads. "Child, have you lost what little sense the good Lord gave you? What on earth are you caterwaulin' about?"

I pointed.

Verlene looked down at herself and started hopping around screaming and waving her arms. "Oh lawdy, I've been shot. I've been shot! I knew this neighborhood would be the death of me. They done kilt me. They done kilt me!"

I rushed to her side, slipped in the red mess, and with arms flailing, slid onto the tile entrance way. I managed to grab onto the counter and regain my balance.

The strange aroma. I leaned down and touched the red on her pants, rubbing the liquid between my fingers. Thick. Chunky even. I put the substance to my nose. The sharp vinegar and cayenne pepper smell assaulted my nose. Ugh! Barbeque sauce. "Verlene, you're covered in barbeque sauce! What happened?" I grimaced as I looked at the mess tracking from the front door to where she stood. "Barbara!" I yelled over my shoulder. "I need a roll of paper towels and a wet rag, please."

Verlene looked down at herself like it was the first time she had noticed she was basted and ready for the grill. "Don't that beat all. I knew I was smellin' it. It had to of been when I reached over to stop that big stick of pepperoni from sliding off the backseat. I leaned real hard on the plastic jug of Sugah's Special Sauce. I musta' popped the top."

Barbara scurried around the coffee counter with the towels and we proceeded to field strip Verlene of her tasty tenderizer. I glanced up from scrubbing the gooey mess from my oak floor as Felicia Tyler sauntered in.

With her unruly red hair bobbin' and groovin' to the tunes on her iPod headset, she looked like a Lucille Ball clone. Even though her head was all I could see from my position on the floor, I knew what she was wearing before she came around the counter. Her standard uniform was spiked high heels, a loud multicolored top, even louder-colored stretch Capri pants, and an arm full of gaudy bangles to match the large dangling earrings that pulled at the tiny openings in her ears. With my preferring baggy linen pants and tops, or jeans, espadrilles, and no jewelry, we were as opposite as ice cream and collard greens.

But books kept me and Fifi in the same orbit. Not that I loved books. I didn't hate them. I read for fun. But they were not my idea of business. My mom, Camille Beckham, had been a well-known figure for twenty years in the New York book trade and international antiquarian circles. Now that she was gone, the mantle of owning the bookstore had passed to me, whether I liked it or not, and Fifi had been Mom's store manager, so I inherited her with the store.

She planted her feet and slid her fists to her hips. "Good gravy, grandma! What happened here? It smells like a barbeque is fixin' to break out."

I jumped at the obvious chance. "Felicia, before you start work I thought you could drive over to the house with Aunt Verlene and help her unload her groceries."

"Well, bless your lil' pea-pickin' heart for thinking of me." Fifi glared at me.

I knew that look. She was going to pray things on me that Ajax wouldn't take off.

"But I got a bit of a problem this morning." She shifted her weight from one hip to the other. "By the way — y'all *know* I hate the name Felicia."

You'd never expect a Southern drawl from someone who looked so New York, but Fifi was a fifty-five-year-old Suwanee, Georgia, transplant who had been my mom's best friend and business manager for about thirty years.

"I'm sorry. I only say it to get your goat." Well, Sloane, you dummy, if you want her to spare you the torture chamber today, you'd better straighten up and fly right. I put on my sweetest butter-wouldn't-melt-in-my-mouth voice. "I'm so sorry, Fifi. Can you please help me out?"

Fifi leaned closer. The noisy bangles slid down her arm tinkling like broken glass. "I would, sugah, but I seem to have an intestinal dilemma today that's . . . how should I say it . . . workin' like grease through a goose."

"Grease through a . . . ohhhh. Ack! TMI." Too much information. I squeezed my eyes shut on the picture swirling through my head. The memory of her lack of intestinal fortitude would be with me for the rest of the day. That greasy goose trumped my torture chamber. I sighed. I was going to Verlene's.

Fifi strolled behind the counter sporting a smug expression. I don't know what irked me more . . . that I had to go, or that Fifi, who was much older, had outsmarted me with a faster excuse. I took one last swipe at the last bit of sauce and stood up.

"Oh . . . here sugah. This was in the store's mail at the post office." Fifi rummaged through the stack and handed me a manila envelope.

I studied the envelope. It was addressed to me from a law office in Manhattan. I pulled open the seal and removed the document. My hands gripped the papers. "Now I've heard everything!" My blood pressure pounded in my ears.

Fifi stared at me.

"The ex-Mr. Templeton wants half of Mom's estate saying that our divorce wasn't final until after she died. They want me to come into this lawyer's office to discuss a settlement before they decide to instigate legal action." My teeth gritted together and I envisioned planting him on an anthill. "How dare he? Has he lost the last brain cell that the good Lord gave him? No, no, no . . . not in this lifetime, buddy." I threw the papers on the floor.

"Sugah, just call your attorney. They're probably bluffing about suing you and are fishing around to see if you will take the bait and settle ahead of time. Besides . . . these papers aren't even a legal document.

They sent them to the store's PO box. You could pretend that you didn't even get them." Fifi whacked at the computer keyboard. "Ugh! Stupid computer."

My spirits brightened. I couldn't leave now. I hurried behind the counter. "What's the matter? Something I can help with?" Computers were *my* thing. No . . . that was a lie. I *wanted* computers to be my thing. I was great at the investigation part, but frankly I was barely passable at the *science*. I think I felt more relief than fear when escaping from my ex-husband had required leaving a dream job on the cyber-forensics team of a covert government project at NYU. Most of the time, I had felt like I was in over my head. Luckily, I had good and willing mentors around me to help.

"No, just nonsense spam mail. I deleted it."

My spirits sank. I envisioned having my clothes caught in Verlene's pasta maker. It reminded me of a paper shredder.

Fifi banged on the keys again and then redirected her ire to bang on the blinking message button on the answering machine. What was she upset about? I was the one who had to help Verlene. Messages started to play, and Fifi jotted phone numbers for book buyers.

"What's the matter?" If I hadn't known better, I would have thought I saw tears pooling in her eyes.

Fifi stopped writing and rolled a look up at the ceiling. "I was informed by certified mail yesterday that my apartment building is going co-op, and I either have to buy my apartment or move out. You know I don't have the kind of money it takes to buy a place." She replayed the last message and scratched the number on her pad.

I instantly felt guilty. Mom's apartment was sitting empty upstairs since her passing, but I couldn't bear to touch it yet. My glance darted from Fifi to the floor as my heart started to thump against my ribs.

She caught on. "Oh, sugah! No, no, I didn't mean . . . I wasn't hinting . . ." She patted my hand. "It will be all right. I'll find something. I'd never ask for Camille's apartment."

I let out the breath I had unconsciously grabbed. My mouth opened, but nothing came out. What was I going to say? That it was okay? "Sure, you can have it rather than be homeless." I didn't mean it. "Maybe you could ask Aunt Verlene to rent you a room. She's all alone —"

"Don't you even go there." She peered across the counter at Verlene who was still cleaning up sauce, then lowered her voice. "I'd rather live in a cardboard box than have to eat her food."

Fifi had a point. It did make cardboard look inviting, as either a shelter or a meal.

The third message caught both our attention. Dr. Carlton Mabry wanted to buy a book called *Histoire de la Magie*. And he was going to be here tomorrow to discuss it.

"I guess you have an appointment tomorrow." Fifi held up a finger with the sticky note attached.

"Me?" I took the note and looked at the title. "I don't know anything about books. That's your job." Before the words rolled off my tongue and were forever caught in the air, I knew I had sealed my fate. Fifi would remind me of this declaration whenever I tried to get her to take my place with Verlene. Yep! There it was.

Fifi flashed a Mona Lisa smile. She glanced over her shoulder. "By the way . . . who's that behind the coffee bar?"

"Barbara Nelson. She was sleeping in her car in our parking lot all night. I felt sorry for her, so I let her make coffee and gave her something to eat. Don't yell."

Fifi shook her head. "You pick up strays like you do pennies."

I winked. "Pennies make dollars." There I

go channeling Grandma again.

"Hey, I hate to interrupt you two, but I've got frozen food thawing in my trunk here, people. Can we shake a leg?" Verlene clapped her hands together.

Fifi raised an eyebrow at me. "Shake a lil' ol' leg, sugah."

The urge to reach out and touch her crossed my mind, but I reined it in. Reconciled with my fate, I joined Verlene at the front door. Scrubbing her had not dissipated the smell. She reeked of barbeque. The smell still made me hungry. Maybe this was how she lured victims into her web — where she stuffed them full of strange and supposedly edible items. She was like the black widow spider of food.

Actually, she was a widow. Her husband, Burt, had died last year of food poisoning. The coroner was careful to point out that it wasn't Verlene's food that had offed him. But I wasn't convinced. As often as possible, I took a food taster with me to her house, preferably someone I wasn't too happy with at the moment. Her cooking logic centered on the idea that if foods tasted good separately, they must taste good together.

Verlene pulled open the front door and there stood Rob Landry.

Ugh! Him again. The mood I was trying to cultivate dissipated as quickly as the onset of one of Fifi's hot flashes. Hey! Maybe I could take him to Verlene's as my food taster. Nah! Bad idea. He'd probably live long enough to add a lawsuit to my list of annoyances.

He slid through the doorway with another fake grin plastered on his face.

I almost prayed out loud but decided to keep it in my head because if he made a snide comment I might go rabid and bite him. Why me, Lord? I'm not a bad person. What did I do to deserve this man? My arm waved in desperation. "Can't I get rid of you? Are you going to be the bane of my existence today? Or can we pretend this is Burger King?"

"Burger King?"

"Yeah, you know . . . have it my way."

He returned a blank stare. Fifi and Verlene snickered.

"Never mind."

"Miss Templeton, I'm sure you can appreciate my position —"

Overwhelming exasperation narrowed my eyes to slits. I glared, deciding whether I wanted to rethink the rabid path. "The only thing I'd appreciate is you leaving me alone. I do not want to sell my building today, tomorrow, or even next year. *Comprende?*"

I bolted for the door. If Fifi could leave me with Verlene, I could leave her with Landry. "You are getting on my last nerve. My mom was against this, and so am I."

Landry nodded. "Sorry for your loss, but —"

"I did not lose my mom." We were toe to toe. "I know right where she is. Thank you, Jesus." My dear mom, God rest her soul, decided there was more pressing business with Jesus, and deserted me for a glorious Homegoing. I was left to deal with the lunatic fringe that had become her life.

I almost think I saw Landry blush.

"Miss Templeton, let's not get off point."

"The point is, you may have suckered a few of these old people into signing, but it will be a cold day in Bermuda before I sign away this beautiful facade to the wrecking ball. And you can't do it without *all* of us selling out." I was smug in my understanding that there would be no eminent domain issues. "Your high-rise project is *not* going to ravage this block of Fulton Street, unless it's over my dead body."

"Your mother didn't understand the concentration of businesses that could occupy this block when this project is completed. Coltrane Realty is willing to offer —"

41

"Yes, I know . . . three times what the building is worth, which is insane in itself."

"We could make you a very wealthy woman."

"Do you really think money is the only thing that makes people rich? Then you must not know the Lord." Verlene *amen*-ed me.

"I don't want to get into a religion debate with you —"

I bristled. "The Lord isn't about religion." I pointed at the door. "Now get out of my store."

Landry gripped his briefcase with both hands, not moving.

"Get out. Before I have a carnal snap." Pastor Dann always used that phrase to describe our missteps in our before-Christ lives. And at this moment I really wanted to revert to type and poke him right in the nose. For a split second the thought moved from downright violence to inviting him to Verlene's to sample her latest gastrointestinal fiasco, but my head cleared of the sugarplum thoughts. "I said, get out of my store." I moved back toward the counter and reached for the phone. "Do I need to call the police?"

His smile faded. Landry clamped his lips together, then raised a hand. "That's not necessary. I'll leave. The boss will probably take over from here. But this isn't the end. You should have taken my offer."

Was that fear or defiance in his eyes?

"Is that a threat?"

He didn't answer; he just stared at me.

I brushed past him and traipsed out the door. Old, recognizable fear gripped at my chest, making me light-headed.

4

I opened the passenger door to Verlene's '92 Oldsmobile, half expecting to see a river of sauce across the seat, providing me a perfect excuse for not having to go. The bucket seat was clear except for her over-sized leather purse where she had left it while she was in the bookstore. Good grief, the woman was just asking to get robbed! Her white Cutlass with the black vinyl roof was a very sought after vehicle in muscle car circles.

I dropped the purse to the floor and slid into the seat, acutely aware of the barbeque smell.

Fleeing from the scene of an impending disaster had forced back a repressed memory. Landry didn't answer my question. I ran away before he could. It had to be because of the flashback.

My hands trembled. The tone of his voice reminded me of my ex-husband. I shook my head and tamped the thought down, but it clawed its way back up. The incident happened a year ago, but was just as fresh in my mind as if it were yesterday.

I shifted on the seat and pulled my legs up tight, trying to draw them close to my chest. A shiver. A flash of recall. I often fought against going to that dark recess.

Smack!

I flinched. The movie in my brain rerolled the incident from a year ago . . .

"Is that a threat?"

The words had barely left my lip when Alan Templeton answered my question with the back of his hand crashing across my face. I tasted blood.

I reeled backward, tripping over the coffee table. I remember thinking, *I'm going to fall on it.* My body slammed into the center of the glass circle, shattering it and leaving a four-inch-long shard protruding from my left thigh and a mile-long scar on my psyche. . . .

A cold shudder spider-walked across my shoulders, propelling me back to the present and the aroma of barbeque sauce.

I raised my eyes to the ceiling, clenched them shut, and released a heavy sigh. Even though a year had passed, the pain hurt like it had just happened a minute ago. It took quite a while to get over being mad at God about that one. I still don't understand why He didn't protect me . . . sheesh — or at least give a girl a warning. When I left the hospital that morning with a two-inch line of sutures, the only option had been to hop on the train out of Manhattan and head home to Brooklyn. Fort Greene meant safety.

Shake it off. Those days are long gone. I will not be a victim again. It happened so many times in the past. I need to stop making excuses for the men in my life. But why did I keep picking men who needed excusing? Did I really have that much resolve or would it all melt like ice on a blistering hot day?

Verlene snatched a parking ticket from under the windshield wiper. She plopped onto the driver's seat and flicked her wrist over her shoulder, throwing the ticket into the backseat. Glad for the distraction, I swiveled around and watched as it floated into a large glop of "special sauce" covering the left floor mat, and join what looked to be about a dozen more tickets. At least the red sauce was color coordinated with the burgundy leather seats and carpeting. It all went together in a sort of bizarre Salvador

Dalí-esque kind of way.

"Are these all tickets?" My glance moved upward from the pile of colored papers and across the abundance of groceries overflowing the backseat. There had to be enough stuff here to feed a small country, and enough vegetable oil to fuel Mickey D's for the next month.

"Yeah." Verlene put the car in gear, drove down two blocks, then hooked a left onto Greene. "I haven't been over to the 88th all week. When I get over there, I'll get 'em taken care of." Two blocks over, she made a left onto Carlton Avenue, her street.

I sat up straight and turned to look at her. "Verlene, you can't just decide when you want to go pay a ticket. Good grief, woman! The po-po will be knocking at your door."

The 88th was the precinct for both Fort Greene and Clinton Hill, and it was only eight blocks away from her house in a straight line down DeKalb. With sirens turned on, they could be there to arrest her in less than a minute if they needed the money to balance their donut budget for the week.

Hold the phone! "You don't pay tickets at the 88th. Brooklyn Criminal Court over on Schermerhorn, between Adams and Smith is where you pay tickets." I stared. She

47

looked like she was avoiding me.

"If you must know, I have a fella that's sweet on me over at the 88th, and he takes care of my tickets."

I stifled a smile. Check this out. Verlene has a sweetie pie. "Honey, the days of 'fixing' a ticket are long gone. This guy must be actually paying your tickets. And with your lack of skills that could be quite expensive for him. Sounds kind of serious to me. When were you going to mention this development?"

"A girl's gotta have her secrets." Verlene winked at me. I'll be. Sheesh, I guess she must not have fed him yet.

I looked back at the tickets again. "And now you've basted them in barbeque sauce. That is not the way to win friends and influence people." Before Mom's passing I hadn't spent much time with Auntie, basically because I was avoiding her food. But now, I was beginning to wonder if she was splashing around the shallow end of the family gene pool. Wait a minute . . . was I missing something? "Why did you have to go to the precinct before? How many more parking tickets have you gotten?"

"That was to get my sweetie to take care of the citation. Maybe the next time those nice firemen come over, I can get one of them —"

"Citation? Firemen? What firemen? Why are firemen coming to your house?"

Verlene stopped at the corner of DeKalb. I could see Fort Greene Park in the next block. It encompassed an eight-block area of beautifully peaceful park. But therein lay the conundrum. During the day it was peaceful and at night it was full of pieces. It bothered me that Verlene lived so close to all that nighttime violence. But every time I thought about convincing her to move closer to me, I gagged . . . literally.

"Verlene? You didn't answer me."

She bit down on her lower lip, calmly crossed DeKalb, and pulled up in front of her neat brownstone in the middle of the block. "I wanted you to see that the house was all right before you exploded. You're just like your ma, always going off half-cocked when I make a little mistake. Don't you think I can take care of myself?"

"Verlene!"

"All right. So I had a couple small fires."

My chest contracted. I tried to get the words out calmly, rather than screaming like the homicidal banshee I felt coming on. "Why did you have a couple small fires?"

Verlene angled out of the car, and moved around to the trunk. "Nobody told me that

I needed to drain the fruit cocktail first."
She shrugged her shoulders, unlocked the
trunk, and grabbed an armload of groceries.

I snatched a couple of bags from the
mound in the backseat, and several stacked
cases of cat food came into view. It caught
me off guard. Verlene didn't have any cats
that I knew of. I hurried behind her. "You're
trying to avoid me by talking in single
sentences. I'm not going to stop until I get
the full story, so you might as well man up
and spit it out."

Verlene jostled to hold the packages and
get the key in the lock without dropping
anything or talking to me. The door swung
open.

Pop!

What is that sound?

We were greeted by impeccably polished
hardwood floors and the wonderful coolness of her central air, and an odd hot smell
that I couldn't quite put my finger on.

"I was learning how to make Fruit Noodle
Pudding, and I used fruit cocktail instead
of mandarin oranges, cherries, and wal-
nuts," she said, as we walked past the gleam-
ing mahogany staircase and down the hall
to the kitchen. "I didn't drain the fruit
cocktail and it bubbled over and set the

oven heating element on fire."

Pop!

I started looking for the source of the noise.

The hallway opened into the large airy kitchen that Burt had enlarged several years before he passed. He pushed out the back wall across the whole twenty-five-foot width of the brownstone and did a fabulous job of creating a huge gourmet kitchen. With the walls painted creamy white, the wide expanse of windows, and the triple French doors, it was almost as bright inside as it was outside.

"Okay, so that doesn't seem so bad. You had me worried that there was more than one fire."

Pop!

A sharp sound whacked the stove hood and a small object shot across the room in my direction. I ducked. The white minibomb smacked the kitchen cupboard and plopped to the counter. It looked like a scorched egg. "What the . . . ?"

"Oh no!" Verlene dropped her packages on the butcher-block countertop in the center of the room, and hurried toward the stove. *Another pop.* She recoiled.

Pop!

A blackened egg hit the inside top of the

hood and sizzled back onto the cooktop.

Pop!

With a hand in front of her face, she reached around the enameled Dutch oven and shut off the cooktop.

Pop!

Another egg missile hurled from the scorched pot and whacked the wall, bouncing off the edge of the counter and onto the floor.

I looked for empty counter space to drop the packages.

Pop!

I flinched. Everywhere I turned there were appliances — tall appliances that looked like guillotines, silver appliances that looked like drill presses, wide appliances that looked like they could eat a hand. I shivered, set the bags on the floor, and turned to face the exploding stove.

The two walls at the west end of the kitchen were dotted with small dark spots. There were even a couple of marks on the ceiling. It looked like the kitchen had caught the chicken pox. Eggshell carnage littered the floor.

"What's going on?" Another pop sounded. I grabbed up a quilted potholder and in the style of A-Rod, snatched a flying egg out of the air like a New York Yankee infielder.

Verlene wrung her hands. "I didn't know I'd be gone so long. It's Mrs. Stattler's fault. She made me try all the products on her sample table at Costco."

Pop!

Another egg ricocheted off the stove hood and directly at my leg. I hopped and made a backhanded catch into my oven mitt.

Another pop!

A prickling sensation ran up my nose. I put the back of my mitt-covered hand to my nose. I sneezed. A burned egg whacked me in the forehead. I stumbled back, blinking.

Verlene hurried to turn off the stove.

"Look at this pot. I'll never get it clean." Verlene slipped on a pair of potholders and scurried to the sink with the scorched Dutch oven. She reached for the cold-water handle.

"No!" I lurched forward but it was too late. That cold water hit the heat-blackened pot and eggs and steam blew up in all directions. I snatched Verlene away from the sink as the rest of the eggs exploded like popcorn. "Verlene, please tell me you didn't go out of this house and leave eggs boiling on the stove."

I eased over to the sink and shut off the water. A few remaining blackened eggshells swirled in the dark water.

Verlene touched one of the spots on the wall across from the stove. "Shoot! I just had this wall painted —"

"Verlene!" Count, Sloane. Count to ten. Augh! Count to fifty! Verlene's face scrunched up into a pucker. I felt bad for yelling but this could have been serious instead of just an egg-tastrophy. I threw her a dirty look. It wasn't as if she was actually going to listen to me or anyone who even remotely resembled family. It had been hard enough getting her to listen to Mom, and with me, well, she had purses older than me. I was like a gnat flying in front of her face. I got no respect.

"How did this happen?"

Verline grimaced. "I just told you. I went —"

"No . . . I mean the eggs. They don't normally turn into missiles like that. How did this happen?"

"I don't know. I even had one of these eggs shoot out of the microwave when I opened the door after heating it too long. One of the ladies at cooking class said that might happen if the eggs are too old. They get gas, or air spaces, or something like that."

I stared at the shells all over the floor.

"Then why didn't you throw them away?"

"Girl! That was a full tray of eggs!"

"Tray? Verline, how many eggs were there?"

"Well, I'm not sure. At least three dozen."

I could feel my eyes widening to where they could've fallen out of their sockets. "What in the world were you going to do with *that* many eggs?"

Verline shrugged. "I don't know, but they were on sale. I couldn't resist the price."

My mind whirled. "No wonder they were cheap. They were probably going rotten."

She looked around the kitchen with obvious disgust. "There were a couple dozen eggs in that pot. What a waste. I guess I don't have the hang of setting this new timer. It was supposed to turn off the burner after twenty minutes."

She completely ignored the obvious. I shut my eyes and prayed. Lord, give me strength so I don't choke her. "I think you should start by buying fresher eggs and practice using the timer. But stay at home so you can monitor the carnage."

She stifled a smirk and pushed open the French doors, fanning the air with her hand. "Let's get the rest of the bags before the frozens start to drip."

See? I was being totally ignored.

"Can I get clarification on the bubbling fruit cocktail thing?" I tromped behind her, glad to inhale fresh air that didn't smell like burned eggs.

"I was *trying* to tell you before we were interrupted. After the fruit cocktail debacle I had to have the element replaced in the oven, and the second element didn't exactly want to communicate with the thermostat, so it torched a chocolate cake." She put her hands on her hips. "Now *that* was a fire! It looked like a Roman candle."

Okay, maybe this was a reasonable fire excuse. But then again, with her stories, the absence of details was usually what created the facade of normalcy with Verlene. She plucked more bags from the trunk and a jug of oil from the backseat. I lifted the two cases of tuna cat food.

"And the fire marshall gave you a citation for the stove malfunction?" We walked back into the chicken pox–covered kitchen. I looked around for evidence of a cat.

She lowered her head and made busy with the bag in front of her. Uh oh . . . I knew that move. Here comes the real story. I moved to the kitchen table and pulled out a chair to have a seat.

Her fingers twisted her cloth grocery bag into a knot before she set about putting things in the freezer. "I sorta panicked when I opened the oven. It was full of flames. I tossed the cup of liquid I had in my hand at the flames and it turned the oven into a flamethrower."

Verlene screwed up her face like she was sucking on one of the burned eggs, and lifted her hand to her forehead. "I lost my eyebrows in that, but the good part was I didn't have to torture myself plucking them for quite a while."

I tipped my head to the side trying not to notice that her eyebrows hadn't completely filled back in yet. "What was in the cup?"

Verlene huffed out a sigh as she jammed the last of the icy bags in the freezer and shut the door. "Booker's Bourbon."

"Aunt Verlene! You don't drink. What would your ladies' group at church say?"

"I wasn't drinking it, you silly. I was practicing the Cooking Channel's Bourbon Shrimp Flambé."

"But why did you have a cupful? I've never heard of a recipe that calls for that much liquor."

"I poured too much and was trying to get some of it back in the bottle."

"But why didn't you just pour it from the bottle?"

"The instructions said never pour liquor

from a bottle into a pan near an open flame because the flame can follow the alcohol back up to the bottle and cause it to explode."

"So why'd you throw it into the oven? What? You thought the *bottle* was flammable, then, and not the bourbon? So much for that bit of safety. Why did they give you a citation? It sounds like you just had an accident."

Verlene sucked in her bottom lip, and for a split second, she looked like a petulant child . . . but then the Bride of Chucky reappeared. "How was I to know that using 129-proof bourbon was a fire hazard!" She walked to the stove.

"Oh, good googa-mooga! It's a wonder you didn't burn the house down!" She could have done less damage using gasoline.

"That's what the fireman said when he wrote out the citation. Ya know . . . one of them was really cute. I'm going to set you up on a date when I see them again."

"Don't you dare!" Cute to someone Verlene's age meant he had two eyes and walked upright. I wasn't about to broach the subject of Andreas-my-boyfriend with her. Not for all the tea in China . . . or coffee in Brooklyn for that matter.

Verlene smiled. My right cheek under my

eye started to twitch. I didn't like that Cheshire cat smile. It always meant trouble for me. I could smell her brain burning — on second thought it was probably the eggs. Either way, something was rotten.

She moved to the stove and rubbed her fingertips on the ceramic glass cooking surface. "I must admit the fire really did a number on that old stove."

I just noticed that I was not looking at her original implement of destruction. This stove was a brand-new brushed stainless steel model that, if I actually liked to cook, might have made me drool. But in Verlene's hands, it had the potential of scaring me more than her counter appliances. "That looks really expensive."

She bent over, rested her head on the cooktop, and wrapped her arms as far around the stove as she could. I recoiled, hoping that surface wasn't still hot. How would I explain that I stood here and let her cook her own face? Thankfully, the glass top apparently had an insta-cool feature and I wasn't facing a Southern-fried Verlene.

"I saw this on one of my cooking shows and fell in love. It has two ovens, is self-cleaning —"

"I don't want to hear about it unless I can just throw groceries in, and cooked meals pop out."

Verlene straightened up and stared at me like I had two heads. "It's just not that easy to be an accomplished chef."

"Yeah, I know, but you still keep trying . . . don't you?"

She made a face at me, and turned to go back to the car for more groceries.

I followed dutifully and we lugged in the last of the cooking oil and the leaking special sauce.

"You see this?" Verlene held the jug of Sugah's Special Sauce. "I'm going to be rich and famous."

Oh, bless the saints! She was on a roll with another new recipe. Let me out of here. "Auh breeze, look at the time." I snapped my fingers and pointed to my watch. "I need to get back to the store."

"But Sloane, honey, I need to show you my secret."

I headed for the door as fast as my feet would carry me. "Tell me about it on the way." I pulled her by the arm.

"No, I need to show you. Half the fun is seeing it."

Please let me make it to the car before anything semi-edible appears. Please let me make it to the car before anything semi-edible appears. Please let me make it to the car before anything semi-edible appears . . .

"Then you'll have to save this huge surprise and show me later."

5

I sulked back into the bookstore wondering why was I such a wuss when it came to my aunt. Verlene had conned me into helping her carry casseroles to the Seniors Center later on this afternoon. She was all hyped up about showing me her secret. Somehow, I knew I would get sucked into tasting something. I envisioned her holding my nose and trying to shovel food in my mouth like Mom had done with that stupid castor oil when I was little.

The delicious aroma of my favorite hazelnut coffee drifted by, beckoning with its promise to soothe my jangled nerves. I moved behind the counter to grab my oversized Beckham's Books & Brew mug. The computer monitor caught my attention. The inbox had a new e-mail with *READ NOW!* as the subject line. I clicked the envelope icon. The From box said it was *from* me. Ugh! Spam with address masking.

The message simply said, *"It's too bad you can't see reason."* Great! Good marketing ploy. What was next? *"You need to buy our used cars?"*

I hit the delete button and strolled to the coffee bar. "That smells great. I sure could use some." I looked around the store. "Where's Fifi?"

"She said she'd be in the storeroom if any customers came in. I brewed your favorite first, then the regular, and I just finished the decaf." Barbara looked pleased as she filled my triple B mug and reached into the under-counter cooler for the cream.

For a split second I marveled. How could she have picked up so much attention to detail when I had barely noticed her in the store? "You've been a big help. Thank you. Why don't you help yourself to coffee and a pastry? It's on me."

Barbara pulled the clip from her head and ran a hand through her disheveled hair. "Thank you. That is very kind. Could I use your bathroom to freshen up first?"

"Sure, help yourself."

Barbara scurried around the counter and into the corridor leading to the bathrooms.

I closed my eyes, raising the fragrant brew to my lips. Peace at last. And the feeling lasted for about ten seconds. The doorbell sounded. Sometimes I felt like taking a hammer to that little silver thing and making it flat enough to slide *under* the door. I looked up.

In traipsed a couple members of the Granny Oakleys book club. The name was a misnomer. They weren't just grannies; there were a few grandpas too. I don't know how that happened, but with old people I've learned not to ask. They get real crotchety when you question their reasoning. The first one up the aisle headed toward me was Kyoko Takahashi.

This sweet woman at the age of sixty-nine had vision so bad that it looked like she was wearing a pair of magnifying glasses. Looking through her frames made her eyes look like an anime character's. I doubted that she could see her own hand let alone the pages of a book without the glasses. She wore the most magnificently detailed Yukata kimonos, and always had her hair flawlessly coiffed in a bun held by dangerously long hair ornaments that looked like she was ready to create shish kebabs at the slightest hint of hunger.

I smiled. She smiled, then bowed at the waist, and scurried to her seat with tiny measured steps.

Next in, though preceded by her aroma of

food, was Greta Feinstein in her Marilyn Monroe blond wig and bright-red lipstick. Her black orthopedic shoes sounded like they were peeling away from the floor every time she took a step. As per her standard MO, she toted a quilted bag. It was filled with food and had a plastic-pocketed front showcasing pictures of her grandbabies. The food she carried, she insisted, was necessary because of her low blood sugar. I'd never seen the woman exhibit any ill effects of low blood sugar, but I sure have fought the ant colony effects that her trails of food crumbs have wrought. Sigh. I'll get the DustBuster out after she leaves. We can't have ants snacking on the books.

I turned back to my coffee, leaned my elbows on the counter, and savored several more sips. They'd all be here within the next few minutes, but I didn't have to worry. Fifi sat in on their group. I really admired her patience with them.

"Hello, my lady."

My eyes opened slowly. That deep, throaty tone sent delicious shivers rolling up my spine. I smiled. A pair of strong, male hands gently massaged my shoulders, thumbs pressing in, loosening the muscle knot invading my neck. I rolled my head into the massaging fingers, glancing up at him before letting my eyes slide shut again.

"Good morning to you too. One of these days I'm going to figure out how you sneak up on me without ringing that bell." I relaxed into his fingers. "I thought you had an early appointment at the clinic." The tall Greek with his charcoal-colored Armani suit covering an inordinate amount of hard muscle always pushed me to my limit of "dangerous man quotient." His slicked-back hair and swagger could pass for a mafia boss rather than a psychiatrist. I just grew goose bumps everywhere thinking of his gorgeous self.

His lips brushed by my ear leaving a trail of warm breath as he spoke. "I do, but can't I stop by to get a coffee from my favorite lady?"

I turned and looked into the adoring eyes of Dr. Andreas Comino. My skin prickled at the way he said "lady." "Of course you can, but I don't want you to be late."

But I didn't want him to stop rubbing my neck either. I extricated myself from his grasp and hurried around the counter to pour him a coffee to go. Yikes! He needs to go or I'll never get any work done today.

He chuckled. "BMC is only a stroll down the street." Andreas worked at the Brooklyn Medical Center in the next block and lived in a gorgeous brownstone a block in the other direction, over on South Oxford, putting Beckham's Books & Brew in the center of his world.

I loaded the coffee with cream and sugar then snapped a plastic lid on it. "You need to go to work. I'll see you for dinner." *Gag reflex.* I had to go with Verlene. "Make it after seven, okay? I have to help my aunt."

Andreas nodded. I placed the cup in his outstretched hand and shooed him toward the door, blowing him a kiss goodbye. He needed to leave before I became distracted.

A prickling sensation ran up my nose. I sneezed.

Andreas turned to look at me. "Are you getting sick?"

I sniffled. "No, it's just my sinuses. Pollen count must be high this week."

"Do you want a prescription for something?

"No. I hate pills. This, too, shall pass." I blew him another kiss.

Stavros Andropolis shuffled into the store with his head down. The old man must have an angel following him around, as often as he walked out into traffic without looking. He nearly plowed into Andreas's back as he stood making nice with me from a distance.

Andreas artfully sidestepped the man's frail carcass.

Stavros crossed to the group's table, removed his gray fedora, and tried his trick of rolling the hat down his arm and catching it. As usual, it plopped into the middle of the table. He sat down and pulled the hat over in front of him.

Andreas appeared amused as he watched the old man. He gave me an exaggerated wink, then pursed his lips, blew me a kiss, and left.

Two months of dates, and I was hooked. I couldn't resist him. He was like chocolate, without the resulting blemishes on my complexion or the extra weight on my behind.

We met at a Neighborhood Concerned Citizen meeting over at the Seniors Center, which was called to discuss Coltrane Realty's efforts to buy up the block for another high-rise office tower.

To the complete ticked-off dismay of my ex-boyfriend, Trey Alexander, Andreas and I had become an instant item. Could I have actually kissed enough frogs to have found a prince? Andreas felt like the answer to a long-suffering prayer. Even if Mom had voiced her ever-present opinion that he was wrong for me. I'm almost sure Mom was talking about his color.

But I could never understand what made her act like that given I wasn't even the right color for my own color growing up. I've got a honey color that caused me to be called "high yellow" more often than I care to remember. So, okay, kids can be rude and hurtful, but my fair coloring was the result of our mixed African American and Sicilian ancestry. There wasn't anything I could do about it. Andreas was full-blooded Greek, which pulled in the Mediterranean part, but he had no AA lineage.

Big deal. It wasn't going to stop me. I loved him.

All I ever wanted was a good man. I'm not hard to look at. Or at least I've never caused men to run away screaming.

Let me qualify that . . . I've never caused men to run away screaming from my face. Maybe that needs slightly more qualifying because I can most certainly look right mean and evil at times when my hackles are up, but my head doesn't spin around, split open, or spew pea soup in the same vein as the *Exorcist*. So I guess I should get big, fat, double-chocolate brownie points for that. The closest I've ever come to a physical transformation is having hazel eyes that turn brown when I'm angry.

I have a lot to offer a man. The right man. Not another bozo who wants my money or to imitate a caveman by dragging me down the hall by my hair or who wants to slap me around. That ship has sailed. And at my age, I wasn't booking passage on the boat.

Mom told me that I attracted *those* kinds of men by being needy. It hurt my feelings then. It still hurts now. I never figured out what *needy* meant because, unfortunately, Mom died of a heart attack the next day.

Maybe Andreas and I have a chance at happily ever after. I couldn't think of anything better than having a good man — correction, let's make that a gorgeous hunk o' man with more muscle than any single man should ever have. With Mom gone, *alone* was a very sad song in the sound track of my future.

Barbara walked up behind me. "You're very pretty."

I turned to face her. "Thank you for being so kind. But age is catching up with me." Mom used to have a saying that "black don't crack" to explain why in her late fifties she still didn't have any wrinkles or laugh lines. I hope I'll be able to use that same quip when I reach that age.

Barbara averted her eyes and gnawed on her bottom lip. "If I was prettier my husband might not have left me for another woman."

At first, I didn't know what to say. I barely knew this woman and she's pouring her heart out to me like we were home girls. Very strange. Something in her eyes reached me, and compassion flooded my heart. "I'm so sorry." I touched Barbara's hand.

Barbara turned away, and walked toward the coffee counter. "He said it was my fault. I was ugly and bored him."

She looked at me as if I should understand her position.

I winced. Those particular words were not unfamiliar. But I had overcome. Maybe I could help this poor soul. I had always been a sucker for a sob story. "Don't you dare believe him! The Bible says we are fearfully and wonderfully made. Men are . . . *some* men are just *not* worth the effort we expend on them."

I had an instant thought that I'd like to meet this rude dude and slap a knot on his head the size of Manhattan.

Barbara retrieved her coffee and pastry from the counter and walked to the table where she had deposited her laptop. "I should have been a better wife."

"Well, he should have been a better husband." I gritted my teeth. I had once blamed myself with those exact same sentiments.

But when I got my act together, the worm turned and my response was no longer self-recrimination, but self-preservation.

She slid onto the chair, and slipped the laptop from the sleeve. Her slender fingers opened the lid. Abruptly she dropped her head into her hands and began to sob.

Oh, Lord, help me with this one. I moved to touch the woman's shoulder but stopped short, pulling back my hand. I didn't want to scare her again. Then, a second thought, if I got too involved, I'd wind up sitting here with her all day. Change the subject. "So you said you wanted to get into here so that you could write. Are you a writer?"

Barbara perked up. A slight smile crossed her lips. "Yes. I write suspense novels for women."

She brushed the moisture from her eyes then pushed the button to turn on her laptop.

"Do you have anything published?"

"No, not yet. But I've got a couple of publishers that have asked for proposals."

"Good. You keep at it. Maybe it will be your novel I'm unpacking someday."

Using that as an exit cue, I marched back to the dull life of a bookseller. How much did I hate thee, let me count the ways. I could have had more fun poking myself in the eye with a sharp stick. This was Mom's gig, not mine.

I gently traced the worn spot on the counter where Mom rested her arms when she greeted customers. I gulped back the lump forming in my throat and lifted my face, rolling the tears to the outside corners of my eyes.

"Why, Lord?" I whispered so Barbara wouldn't hear me. I didn't want to be comforted.

There was always some trial in my life to overcome. I escape my ex-husband, only to fall in love with Trey, who turned out to be another nightmare. I broke free of him. Then nightmare three descended with Mom's sudden death. I still struggled with nightmare four: being stuck with a bookstore when I really wanted to be back working in computer forensics.

The old song came to mind, "If it weren't for bad luck, I'd have no luck at all. Gloom, despair, and agony on me." At least it felt that bad, anyway. My saving grace? Andreas.

The only thing nagging me was his job. He was a psychiatrist for women. Only women. All needy women. Did he see me as a true love, or as a patient whom he needed to heal? I shook my head to get rid of the thought. He loves me. Really loves me. I can tell. Thinking about him made me long for his arms to hold me and make me feel safe. What was he doing right now?

I'm thinking of him.

Is he thinking of me?

6

Andreas Comino stared at the framed picture of him and Sloane sitting on the corner of his desk, as he opened a container and popped a Tic Tac in his mouth to get rid of the onion breath from lunch. He rose from his desk and moved into the hall. Lifting the chart from the holder outside the examination room, he tucked it under his arm, then opened the door.

"Hello, how are you today?"

The woman slouched on the chair, one arm slung over the back, legs splayed, acting disinterested. She cocked her head to look out through disheveled hair, then scowled. "What's it to you?"

Andreas sat opposite the unkempt woman. "Because I care how you feel. What's your name?"

The woman jumped to her feet knocking her chair over backward. "Whad'ya need to know my name for?" She jabbed both index fingers at him. "I know who you are. The government sent you. You want to spy on me."

Andreas remained calm, writing notes on the chart in front of him. "What is your name?"

Suddenly she began to march around the room with the exaggerated high-step of a toy soldier. "What is your name? What is your name? Tammy Lane, and if you ask me again I'll tell you the same."

Andreas ignored the antics and the rhyme.

She stopped, thrust her chin in the air, and rocked her hips like a bobble hula doll. Then she turned away. Her voice turned singsongy.

"I am drifting in an azure sea that is floating toward the stars." Her fingers flickered as though she was creating wings.

Andreas noted on his chart that her pupils were enlarged.

She suddenly backed into the corner and clutched at the wall. A whimper escaped her lips.

Andreas slid a jigsaw puzzle from the drawer on his side of the table.

"Come, Tammy. Help me put this back in order." He said as he spread the dozen simple child-crafted pieces on the surface.

Tammy timidly approached the table. A

smile creased her lips and she set about restoring the puzzle to its picture frame.

"So, tell me Tammy, why are you here today?"

"Because I —" She swatted at the air to her right. "Stop that!" She backed up a step, pointing a finger in the same direction. "I'm telling him if you don't be nice to me." She swung back around, frowned, then drew her eyebrows together.

"Tammy," Andreas said evenly. "Have you brought a friend with you today?"

The woman cocked her head to the right. "Of course! He always comes with me." She planted her hands on her hips again. "But Zippy 22 wants to bite you today. He's being a bad rat."

Andreas's facial expression remained neutral as he scribbled notes on her chart. "Why is he a bad rat today?"

Tammy huffed, then grabbed the chair. She pulled it to the table then plopped onto the seat and leaned across the table. "Because he's eating me out of house and home. He's fat, fat, fat and he's trying to make me fat, fat, fat." She slammed her fist on the table and stared at Dr. Comino.

Andreas displayed calm indifference. On the chart, he wrote dissociative identity disorder. Reaching into the lower pocket of his lab coat, he retrieved a vial. He smiled softly through closed lips as he glanced over the top of his reading glasses. "Tammy, we've got some new medication that will keep you from getting fat like your rat. Will that make you happy?"

Tammy twitched her eyes while chewing on a twirl of her hair. "I don't know. I don't know." Her eyes darted to each corner of the room. "Rat might get mad."

Andreas held out the amber vial. "One pill a day will keep the rat far away."

Tammy grinned broadly, then released the soaked tendril of hair. "I like that." She nodded her head in long exaggerated sweeps. Her hand reached for the bottle. She turned it sideways and stared at it. "There's only three pills."

"That's right." Andreas jotted several lines of notes. "You come back in three days. We'll see if you need more. Remember . . . only one pill a day. Now let's discuss your schedule."

7

I spent most of the afternoon shelving new books and amusing myself by watching the Granny Oakleys. Now, I was back to drinking coffee and eating cheese puffs, and my waist was thanking me for the drawstring pants. I needed to stop eating snacks with all this salt or I was going to retain enough water to be considered a self-contained beached whale.

Fifi sashayed through the curtains of the stockroom.

"Hey, Sloane, honey, I meant to tell you this morning when you came back. Your new computer system keeps giving me fits."

I set my empty mug on the counter. Nine cups worked out to way more than enough coffee for one day. I looked around at the table terminals. Everything seemed in order. "What's the problem?"

"There were wacky messages in the terminals when I booted them up."

I walked over to my desk and opened the interface for the in-house system. Fifi followed behind me. She was a total disaster with computers — just like Mom. "What did it do?" I peered at the screen, scrolling through logs. Still, nothing looked out of place.

"A stupid skull and crossbones laughed at me in a strange voice." She looked aghast.

"Maybe it's some kids getting an early start on Halloween." I ducked my head down fast. I couldn't hold a straight face at her reaction to the obvious prank. I just knew she'd whack me in the head for laughing. "Where did you see it?"

"On the store's WiFi home page. It came up in the middle of the screen."

I logged into our website and looked around. Again, nothing seemed out of place. We had numerous advertising widgets on the page, but they were all reputable sites that had contracted with Beckham's. "Are you sure it wasn't just a pop-up? I told you about surfing the net. Are you scoping out hinky places again?"

Fifi lowered her head. I think her cheeks were about the color of her hair. "I didn't go to any place bad. What's a pop-up?"

"A box that opens in the middle of the screen."

She was doing the hand-wringing thing. Always a good sign that Fifi had actually done just the very opposite of what she was saying. I decided to let it go. I would run the antivirus software later to catch anything she may have picked up. I logged out of the website and closed the browser. Windows Mail downloaded several incoming messages. Another *READ NOW!!!* message.

I put my mouse on top of the message in the incoming box. It opened a preview in the parallel pane. *You really need to stop ignoring the obvious.* I pushed the mouse up to the delete red-X icon, but my finger paused above the button. Who was sending this stuff? The header said it was from "Concerned Friend." Like that was helpful. I clicked the File tab and opened the properties, then the details. It came from a dot-com site with numbers and digits as an address, all in no logical order. Spam! I clicked Delete.

"I don't have a good feeling about that stuff." Fifi looked at me and tipped her head.

"It's just junk. Don't let it bother you."

Fifi just stared. So what's the problem? Was something caught in my teeth? She reached out and touched the straggling hair that had escaped my barrette again. "Honey lamb, you need to do *something* with your hair."

"What is this, a conspiracy between you and Verlene?" *Okay, just dig at me today.* I ran my fingers through the sides of my hair to pull it all back and grabbed a rubber band from the desk drawer. "There. how's that?" The rubber caught some stray hairs and yanked them from my scalp. I winced. Probably Mom's spirit pulling my hair for being a smart mouth.

"Well, all *right,* child, there's no need to get your lil' knickers all in a bunch. I was just sayin'." She raised her hands in surrender and walked away to talk to the customer who approached the counter.

I sat there, watching her. Verlene had said essentially the same thing. Maybe they were right. It'd been a while since I'd had style of *any* kind. I had even succumbed to drawstring pants and loose tops to accommodate the fact that my jeans wouldn't button, and when they did, it was as though I would die of suffocation. But it was too hot and humid to look cute. Maybe I could get micro-braids and some extensions to my shoulder-length hair.

My elbow rested on the desk and my chin was propped in my upturned palm as I contemplated flowing lion locks. I envisioned myself as a darker version of Bo Derek in *10,* frolicking down the beach, beaded braids flowing in the wind. Who was I kidding? I wasn't even born that thin. I probably had a thigh the size of her waist. I mean get a grip. I had legs by Steinway. I glanced at the cheese puffs and pushed the bag to the back of the desk.

The incoming mail dinged to announce new messages in my Inbox. Without thinking, I clicked on the first message. "YOU NEED TO LISTEN!" popped up. I sat back and stared at the screen. Something inside of me tightened. What's going on? Listen to what? If this was an advertising prank, it was riding my last nerve. It was no longer cute . . . or catchy.

The phone rang. I reached for it while still staring at the message.

"Hello, Beckham's Books and Brew. Sloane speaking. How may I help you?"

"Hello, this is Dr. Lucius Barlow of the Beviard Institute. I would like to purchase a book that you presently own."

"And what book would that be, Doctor?"

"*Histoire de la Magie.* I am willing to pay —"

"Excuse me, sir, but I must advise you that someone has already inquired about that book. You will have to come in and submit to the bidding process."

"You need to listen —"

My head swiveled to the computer monitor. My concentration on his voice drifted. I stared at the same message on the screen. The pit of my stomach had become a vat of churning, bubbling acid.

"Are you listening to me?"

I snapped back to the one-sided conversation. "Um, I'm sorry. I was just checking the process for the book." Okay, so I'd lied, but I was trying to wrap my mind around this coincidence. Or was it?

". . . day after tomorrow." The phone disconnected.

My head snapped up straight. "Excuse me?" I gritted my teeth. Auh breeze. I hadn't been paying attention. What did he say? What was happening the day after tomorrow? I needed to check out this book everybody's so excited about. "Fifi, where do we keep this book the two doctors want to buy?"

Fifi finished ringing up a customer's purchases and handed her the bag. "That book is in the vault down at the bank. They have proper temperatures and secure storage."

Hello! She had my full attention now. "Doesn't that cost us a chunk o' change?"

"Yeah, I guess so. I never questioned your ma's book decisions. She was the expert."

"Umm . . . shouldn't we find out what it's worth? I just thought it was some old musty volume, sitting on one of the back shelves. I didn't expect it was being secured like the Hope Diamond."

"All right, I'll get on it first thing in the morning. It can't be too much or I'd have known about it." Fifi looked at her watch. "Umm, uh, Sloane honey lamb . . . I was sorta thinkin' that you . . ."

Uh oh . . . she won't look at me. This is bad. The only time she ever gets that expression on her face like she needs to expel gas is when she hooks me up with a blind date. Help me saints. The last one had so much hair growing out of his ears, he needed a weed whacker.

I lowered my head, raised my eyes, and put on my best Darth Vader voice. "What have you done?"

She nervously glanced at her watch again. The front door opened, she looked up and disappeared like Godiva chocolates in the hands of a menopausal woman. She darted through the curtains to the storeroom and I turned to face the man coming in the door. He was dressed in a dark suit and tie, and my first impression screamed *accountant.*

Yikes! Oh please, mother of Mary and all that is holy! Let him not be for me. Let him not be for me.

"Hello I'm looking for Sloane Templeton. My name is Harold Lammato." He held out his hand.

Ack . . . he was for me. Oh no, she didn't. *Fifi, you shall die shortly but slowly.* The man's head looked like the pointy end of an egg, bald as a cue ball and with baseball mitt ears.

"What can I do for you?" I scrunched my eyes shut for a moment. A tic had developed in the top of my cheek below my right eye. I hope he didn't think I was winking at him. I reached out to take his hand.

He pulled his hand back, sneezed into it, and nonchalantly held it back out for me to shake. "Sorry, I have allergies this time of the year."

Gag. I lowered my hand, not wanting to entertain the germ culture he had just populated. "I completely understand. I have them too."

"Miss Tyler said you might . . ." He stopped midsentence and opened his mouth as though he was going to sneeze again.

I felt the urge to dive for cover. He pulled a white, stained handkerchief from his back pocket and sneezed into it. Then he blew his nose into it and shoved it back in his pocket.

"Excuse me. Miss Tyler said you might be available for lunch someday."

Fifi would die even more slowly than before. Water boarding and ripping out fingernails did not seem inappropriate at the moment.

Not wanting to seem ungrateful, or hurt his feelings, I racked my brain. I know! "I'm very busy for the next few years . . . uh weeks, but how about if we step to the coffee bar and have a donut and a cup of coffee together. That's the best I can manage for this late in the afternoon."

Come on five o'clock. I had to go help Verlene. For the second time today, I loved her.

He pulled round-rimmed glasses from his shirt pocket and slid them onto his Jimmy Durante–like nose. Saints preserve us. The glasses changed him from egghead to Mr. Potato Head without the mustache! Good googa-mooga.

I guided him to the coffee bar, scooted behind the counter to pour us each a cup of coffee, and then lifted the lid on the donut tray. "Help yourself."

He reached for a powdered sugar donut, placed it on the napkin that he pulled from the holder. And then he pulled out his handkerchief and wiped his hands.

Gag. I'm going to hurl right on Fifi for this one. I gulped down the hot coffee, scalded the inside of my mouth and throat, and looked up at the wall clock. "Gosh, look at the time! Listen, I'm sorry Mr. Potato, er, uh, Lammato. I really can't sit and chat. I promised to help my aunt take casseroles to the Seniors Center and she will be here any minute."

I hurried away before he attempted to shake my hand again. I moved behind the front counter and pretended to be busy at my desk.

Suddenly, it occurred to me that Fifi didn't think Andreas and I were having a serious relationship. Hadn't I made myself clear or was she just not feeling it?

8

I glanced at my watch. Come on, Verlene. It's almost five o'clock. I just know he's going to come over here and try to start a conversation again. I dropped my head to the desk. "Why me, Lord?"

"What did you say?"

I lurched up straight. Verlene stood on the other side of the counter. Hallelujah! I grabbed my cell phone, yelled to Fifi that I was leaving, and followed Verlene outside.

She had double-parked in front again. One of these days, it wouldn't surprise me to come out and find her car gone. I swung open the passenger-side door. A wall of steam and that heavy pasta aroma hit me in the face.

"Whew, girl, we need to roll these windows down or my hair's going to kink up right before I faint from the heat." For July and late afternoon in the concrete city, it was actually hotter inside the car than it was outside.

"I didn't want to leave them down while I came inside. You never know when some miscreant is going to be enticed by the smell of my delicious cuisine and decide stealing it could be worth the jail time."

That'd be one time where the crime became the punishment.

Verlene pushed the button on the door console and rolled down the windows as she put the car in gear, and merged into eastbound traffic. "And for glory's sake, go get your hair done. That nothing-do will never get you a man."

"Yeah, yeah, I'll go in the morning. Does she take walk-ins?"

"Child, I will call her right now and get you slid in." She attempted to wrestle her cell phone from her purse, meanwhile weaving into oncoming traffic.

My heart lurched. "No, not now! Do it later when you have *both* hands free."

"I'll call when we get to the center. I just know you can get in, and I'll even get you set up with Gabi Fabian. He does fabulous braids. I just may come in for a manicure."

Oh joy. The Hungarian Mick Jagger is going to braid my hair.

I looked in the back at our cargo.

Verlene had organized thin boards between the layers of steaming casseroles lined up on the backseat. There had to be least a dozen of the triple-sized pans back there. I sure hoped the seniors at this dinner were praying people.

It only took a couple minutes to drive down the road to the Seniors Center in the nine hundred block of Fulton between Grand and Saint James. As soon as we carried the first trays inside, we were swamped with help. Stavros Andropolis, my favorite little shuffling Granny Oakley, hurried out to help us.

I stared at him, ready to declare some Jesus-induced healing. "Mr. Andropolis! You can walk. Is this a miracle or what?"

"Ugh, you crazy kids. You'll learn when you get my age." He grabbed two trays of casserole and balanced one across the width of the other.

I grabbed one pan and followed him back in. "You mean, you aren't really decrepit?" This reminded me of how my grandfather used to pretend he was too weak to wait on himself, and literally worked Grandma into the grave, and then after her passing all you ever saw was him dressing up to go out on the town. He had the same old-man swagger.

He stifled a smirk as he put the trays on

91

the Sterno warmers. "No, I can walk just fine . . . when I want to."

"But that seems dishonest."

"No more *anéntimos* than that *kleftis* that you are associating yourself with."

"Excuse me?"

"*Anéntimos* is Greek for dishonest. *Kleftis* means thief."

I could smell my brain matter burning, or maybe it was the Sterno. What conversation had I walked into? "Who are you calling dishonest and a thief?"

I felt like snorting with laughter. He must mean Trey.

"That Comino kid. I never did like him. He was always as much of a *listi* as his father."

My face formed a question mark again.

The old man looked like he was losing patience with me. "*Listi,* plunderer. The apple doesn't fall far from the tree."

My chest contracted in on itself. "Andreas is a wonderful man. I'm sure you are mistaking him for someone else."

Stavros shook his head. "I am eighty-two years old and there's snow on my roof, but there's a fire in my furnace and I'm sharp as a tack. I know that boy's family from the old country. Him and his *áplistos* father. Speaking of greedy, I need to get in line for the baklava before all these *áplistoi ánthropoi* scarf it up."

I was trying to decide if he was slick or just senile. I watched him walk away. "Wait! Mr. Andropolis, I need you to explain." I moved to touch his arm.

Verlene intervened. "Girl, that old man is a toy short of a Happy Meal. He doesn't know what he's talking about most of the time, and he's not the best at keeping these dinners on schedule." She snatched me by my shirt and pulled me toward the door and more trays of food. "I'm sure sorry that Enzo Mastronardi died. God rest his soul, even with his broken English, he was still the best organizer we ever had for these affairs."

"What happened?" I grabbed two more trays from the car.

"He died the day after we had the last dinner, the week before your ma died."

I stopped in mid-stride. "How?"

"Heart attack, poor old guy. I guess that's to be expected when you get up there in your seventies. But he was so full of life. He still worked every day and managed all his own properties."

I remembered him now. It was the talk of the neighborhood when he died because his wife sold one of their properties to Coltrane and left on an extended vacation. We dropped off the last of the trays and headed for the car.

That wasn't so bad. The people at the Seniors Center were actually very helpful getting all the trays inside without incident.

The real adventure was yet to come. Verlene was dragging me back to her house to sample something. I just knew it. I was trapped in her car, like a rat on a sinking ship. The water was rising —

"Are you coming?"

I snapped from my thoughts and looked around. We were parked in front of Verlene's brownstone. It never ceased to amaze me how she always grabbed a spot out front. Probably with all the fire trucks' regular visits, people were afraid of parking in front of her house and getting a hose run through their vehicle to put out her fires.

I accepted my fate as her sole New York relative, and trudged behind her to my doom, er, her kitchen. It smelled pretty good in here. And to my total surprise her kitchen had gained a whole new sense of order. All of her implements of cooking destruction were stored away, the egg pox had been cleaned, and even the cat food was gone.

"Sit down, sweetness. Let me give you a taste of my casserole." She snatched up a plate and shoveled steaming food from an aluminum casserole pan setting on the stove.

I knew better than to protest. I'd learned to just smoosh it around on the plate when she wasn't looking and let her see the empty fork leaving my mouth. I'm sorry, Lord, for the deception, but this is self-preservation.

"You're not going to believe my luck. I need you to help me." Verlene placed a plate, fork, and folded paper napkin in front of me and rushed down the hall. She passed the first set of mahogany pocket doors to her right that opened to the living room, and continued to the second set to the right of the front door, which led to her library. It held her computer and an impressive collection of first editions that she and Burt had collected over the years.

I stared down the hall and then at the plate of food. The aroma made me salivate. Could Verlene have actually learned how to cook something right? I picked up the fork and explored the savory concoction with a golden crumb topping. Noodles, cream sauce, peas, tuna.

Verlene rushed back in the room, and slid a dark brown leathery-type cloth-wrapped package on the table. "Check it out. I got it for a song." Oh jeepers, the only thing she did worse than cook was sing.

I laid the fork on the side of the plate and picked up the package. The brown cloth covered a leather-bound book that looked to be rather old. I leafed through the pages. Where Mom would have probably been oohing and ahhing, I was a well of disinterest. "What's special about it?"

I laid the book back on the table, and picked up my fork.

Verlene's face lit up with a broad smile. "Check out page seventy-one." She used two fingers to flick through the pages. She looked as pleased as I felt bored.

I inhaled again. "This smells delicious." For once, I was impressed. Maybe her luck in the kitchen had reached a new high. A prickle ran up my nose, and I turned my face into my elbow and sneezed.

Verlene grimaced. "Maybe you should get some allergy tablets."

"As soon as the pollen count goes down, I'll be fine. What is this?" I shoveled the creamy food onto the fork and lifted it into my open mouth.

"Tuna noodle casserole," she continued, carefully turning pages.

I stopped. My mouth closed. My mouth opened. I stared at the empty fork in front of my face. I stared at the spot on the floor where I had placed the two cases of tuna cat food. "Uhm . . . where's the cat food you bought this morning?" I pointed at the spot on the floor. Oh no, she would not!

Verlene followed my hand. "Ya know, that's a really expensive brand. It was on sale for practically nothing. They advertise on TV that it's good enough for people to eat."

I jerked the napkin to my mouth and disgorged the contents into the folded paper.

She slowly turned more pages.

My brain whirled like a fan. Would she actually feed people cat food? Better still . . . would she feed me cat food? I thought of rummaging through her garbage in search of cans. I hurried the napkin to the can in the corner and lifted the lid. It was empty.

I heard the whirr of the garbage truck motor outside. They must have been running late today to be doing pickup this late in the evening. If there was evidence, it just left the neighborhood.

"What?" Verlene stared at me as I returned to my seat and stared at the plate. "What's the problem?"

"Where is the cat food?"

"I gave some of it to my neighbor for her cat."

My brain vapor locked and I pushed the plate to the center of the table.

"What's the matter?" Verlene stared at me.

"I'm . . . I'm just not feeling well." Okay, so that was a lie, but thinking about putting maybe-cat food in my mouth would certainly make me ill. So I was just stating the obvious after the fact. I wasn't ready to abandon the source of the tuna just yet.

"What did you do with the rest of it?"

Verlene held up the book. "Quit worrying about the cat food. This is what I wanted to show you."

Willing to interrupt another of her culinary catastrophes with emphasis on "cat," I turned my attention to the book.

She pointed to a list of ingredients. "Do you have any idea what this is?"

I looked at her with a blank expression.

She opened her mouth and squinted her eyes. "Don't you get it?"

I shook my head.

She tapped her finger on the page. "Look! This is Frederick Hines's diary."

I gave another blank stare. I was getting good at the expression.

Verlene stomped her foot. "Honey! This is Sugah's original journal. This is his recipe for his secret sauce!"

I picked up the book and examined the

98

page. It was old, and definitely original. I flipped to the front. Hines's name and the address of his old house were in the front end-sheet "property of" page. That block has been razed twenty years ago for a high-rise, and Frederick aka Sugah had been dead for about fifteen years. But his secret sauce was an empire that was unequaled in the barbeque market. No matter how many people tried, no one had ever captured the same flavor. How ironic that the coveted recipe was now in the hands of the ptomaine queen. Okay, to be fair, not all ptomaines are poisonous, but I'm sure in Verlene's capable hands they could be. I wouldn't put anything past her bizarre abilities.

"What are you going to do with this?"

"I don't know. I think it would sell for a lot of money. What do you think about selling it for me?"

"But you don't need money. Burt left you very well taken care of. How would I sell it? I don't know anything about books."

"You own the bookstore."

For a split second, Verlene was smarter than me. "I have a dinner date this evening and a full day of appointments tomorrow. I'll get Fifi on it right away. But if this is as important as you say, then you need to keep this quiet until we get it taken care of."

"I know. For now I'm just keeping it hidden away, and not telling anyone . . . except my BFF Delores."

It sounded kind of cute to hear someone Verlene's age use Internet-speak for her best friend forever. But it concerned me. Loose lips sink ships. "Don't be talking about the book. It could draw unwanted attention before we get to find out what it's actually worth."

Verlene looked pensive. "Then I'll just keep quiet and not show anyone else."

I agreed that that was the best course of action. And I also internally swore that I'd never bring up the topic of tuna noodle casserole again, because I'd never find out the truth.

On second thought, I didn't want to find out the truth. I had to get back to the store before Andreas showed up, so I'd rather happily think that the cat next door was living the high life on expensive food.

9

The bell jingled as the door swept open.

"Sloane!" The angry tenor reverberated off the walls of the bookstore as the door handle slammed into the counter, prompting the front store window to rattle. "Come out here! I want to talk to you. Sloane! I'm lookin' for you!"

I parted the curtains to the stock room and held each brocade panel against the sides of the opening. Feet planted firmly. Lips clamped tight. Eyes glaring. And I prayed that my posture telegraphed my intentions, regardless of my shaking knees. His tirades no longer elicited that rabid fear. And to that end I could finally think of myself as his *former* girlfriend.

"What do you want, Trey?" I focused on breathing evenly. "What have I told you about coming into my place of business acting like a Neanderthal?"

Trey Alexander's six-foot-two muscular

frame filled out his white T-shirt and the open doorway. He stood before me snorting, as though he could breathe streams of fire at any second. His face screwed into a scowl as he clenched and unclenched his fists, making the tattoo on his right forearm undulate. That *Bad As I Wanna Be* slogan had at one time excited me. What a difference a couple beatings can make. The bad-boy attitude had been appealing, until he started acting bad with me.

I stared at those huge hands. My breath hitched, remembering the power of being belted with one of those pile drivers. I willed myself to ignore the tightness in my chest and glanced around the store. Good. Closing time had emptied the place. My knees continued to quiver, but I needed to move without falling down and wetting myself. I could do this. I let the curtains drop and moved from the safety of the opening.

I glared and shook my head. "Grow up." Great. Smooth move. That was just so profound. Sigh. Don't let him see you sweat. I willed my forehead dry. "And shut the door. Did your mother raise you in a barn?"

He stabbed a menacing finger toward me. "Don't you diss my moms."

My heart pounded, pushing against my

ribs like a caged bird fleeing from a cat. Remain calm. Get behind the counter. I strolled toward Trey. "Don't give me that. You know I love your mother. It's you going all gangsta on me that I can't stand."

I locked my knees to keep from quivering and reached for the gun drawer. My hands rested just inches from it. Pressing the heels of my palms to the counter calmed the shaking in my wrists.

"How do you expect me to act?" His eyes flashed wild with rage, and spittle formed white-foam droplets in the outer corners of his mouth. "Don't you think everybody in this neighborhood is laughing at me?"

I flattened my moist palms on the counter and pressed down hard to stop the tremors, but my hands turned into suction cups. Great! This was not the time to be imitating a refrigerator note holder.

"Laughing at you?" I shifted my hand to break the hold. "What on God's green earth are you talking about?"

Trey paced in front of the counter. His sneakers squeaked on the tile floor as he pivoted.

"You!" He stabbed a finger in my direction.

I flinched. Bad move. Never let him see you sweat. And of all days not to be using my Dry Idea antiperspirant. I'm sure he wouldn't see the humor in it. Frankly, I wasn't seeing the humor in it, but my nerves were getting the better of me. I hoped that I didn't burst out laughing or something as equally inappropriate for the occasion.

The whites showed around his dark eyes. "You goin' out with that white guy. Don't you think that makes me look bad?"

"He's not white, he's Greek. That's Mediterranean, not Anglo-Saxon." Go ahead. That's it. Wave red in front of a bull. Preservation set in. My own blood would probably wind up being the red. I stifled a nervous giggle, knowing full well it might push him over the edge.

Trey bared his teeth. "Whatever, same difference."

I rolled my eyes, but quickly returned my stare to him because I could feel his willingness to slap me while my eyes were scouring the inside of my eyelids. "My breaking up with you had nothing to do with Andreas. It had to do with you whippin' on me and always trying to control me."

"That's because you're too uppity and headstrong. I'm the man in this relationship." He stabbed his thumb into his chest. "Just because you make more money than me doesn't mean you can walk around with a bad attitude all the time."

"Bad attitude —" I balked. "You spent every penny you could get your hands on for getting high or entertaining *your* boys. I never got jack from you." I glanced at the diamond stud in his right ear. He had at one time declared that he only bought bling for himself, and not for women. I rested my hands on my hips. "You leave me to fend for myself, and yeah buddy, you're gonna' get attitude!"

"You just tryin' to be the man in our relationship. You ruined it for me."

"Excuse me, so this all boils down to *you* and your status as a virile black man." I was beginning to feel confident. My face stiffened. "Get over yourself, and we won't have to discuss you beating me."

His face softened. "Baby, you know I said I was sorry. I was having a bad time of it. That was the day I lost my job."

His typical make up response. I'd heard it a million times. With this, a million and one. It didn't cut any ice with me. "Oh . . . yeah, and that was a reason to beat me? Let's not forget you pushing me down the back stairs."

"I told you, that was an accident."

His look could have easily been mistaken for repentance but I wasn't fooled. I'd seen it more often than I cared to remember, and fallen for it just as many times.

My face radiated warmth. Don't get too angry. Don't push him. Just get him out of the store. Keep the lips zipped.

"Like the accident when you threw the pot of boiling water on me while I was lying on the couch." So much for zipping it, but I couldn't resist that slap. Deflecting the pan toward my legs had saved my face, but still resulted in second-degree burns. Lucky for me, I'd been wearing jeans.

Trey appeared contrite. "I said I was sorry. You made me crazy. I thought you were stepping out on me." He looked down at the floor and shoved his hands in the pockets of his baggy-legged painter's jeans, pulling them down a tad lower on his hips and exposing the waistband of his underwear.

Remembering the pain and the week in the hospital making up stories to hide the truth straightened my spine. "I can't be around you anymore." My voice softened to align with his posture. "I'm afraid of you."

That wasn't necessarily true, but any port in a storm. I just wanted him to go away.

The old, soft and sweet Trey shone through the belligerent facade. "Is there anything I can do to show you how much I love you?"

My heart hitched. His handsome bad boy face was sucking me in like a black hole. My mouth opened, then snapped shut. I almost succumbed. I shook my head. "No, and I'm closing now, so I'd like to lock up."

I did it! My resolve had just sustained a major assault and I emerged unscathed.

At first, he didn't move.

My heart rate ticked up a few beats. Was this going to be a war of wills?

He glared at me.

Sweetness evaporated. I couldn't read his posture. My heart pounded faster, making my eyes feel like they were pulsing in their sockets.

He turned toward the door.

Relief washed over me. I let loose the breath I'd captured in my chest and waited for him to move before I came out from behind the safety of the counter.

For once, he didn't look back. He walked out and slammed the door.

Exhilaration. I rushed to the door and flipped the dead bolt. It locked with a re-assuring thud. I paused to feel the safety of the cool, metal lever. Leaning against the door frame, my heart pounded like a war drum. My cheeks puffed out and my lips parted as I exhaled.

Then the exhilaration evaporated like a

snowflake in a rainstorm.

He gave up awful easy.

What's coming next?

An old wives' tale said that a girl always found a man just like her father. Trey sure fit that bill. Mom had tried to warn me. But as hardheaded as I am, I just didn't listen. I knew so much better. Yeah, right. Grandma always said a hard head made for a soft behind. I still haven't understood the logic of that, but whatever. Mom always seemed to feel that no man was good enough for me. She even said that Andreas was no good.

I sighed and looked heavenward. "If only you had a chance to know Andreas, Mom. You'd have loved him."

Tap! Tap!

My stomach clenched. Him again. I bolted away from the door and whirled to face the glass. I could feel my eyes stretched open wide, pulling at my cheeks.

With his hand raised to knock again, Andreas stood on the other side of the window, grinning sheepishly. A muffled, "Hey lady, let me in," permeated the heavy door.

Nervous relief mixed with laugher. I unlocked the door. "Speak of the devil."

Andreas stopped in the doorway and

frowned. "What does that mean?"

I giggled and fanned the air with my hand. "Never mind, silly. Just an old saying. You scared the daylights outta me."

Andreas strolled into the store, lifted my chin with a gentle hand, and planted a soft kiss on my cheek. His cologne, a gentle blend of spice and moss and mystery enveloped me. I shut my eyes and inhaled the Marc Jacobs scent, drinking in a feeling diametrically opposed to the last ten minutes. A prickle ran up my nose. I directed my face into the crook of my arm and sneezed.

Andreas looked concerned. "Are you sure this is just sinuses?"

"Sure." Shaking off the euphoria, I leaned out the doorway and glanced up and down the street. Trey wasn't in sight. Silently I mouthed *thank you* to the Lord.

"Are you all right?" Andreas touched his forefinger to my chin and lifted my face again. "You're looking pale."

He couldn't find out. There was no telling how he'd react. I played with our private joke about my honey complexion.

"How can you tell?" I winked. A little shiver graced my neck. I shouldn't be lying to Andreas. But it wasn't a lie, just an avoidance.

Grinning with a wry expression, he lowered his glance while still waiting for an answer.

I feigned exhaustion. "Nah, just a tiring day."

Another lie. If I told him about Trey, his temper might get the better of him, and I didn't need a war on my hands. They were both large and powerful men.

"I've made us a reservation at Cristos, so we have to get going." Andreas tapped his watch as he checked the time. "We have fifteen minutes before we are tardy."

The tension melted.

I grinned at his choice of words. "Cristos is only on the next block. We'll make it, Mr. Fussbudget. Besides, I'll need the fast pace to get a head start burning off the calories from the slice of Red Velvet cake I'm going to have for dessert."

Andreas tilted his head back. "What are you grinning about?"

My heart squeezed. "You. You make me happy."

I could relax again, but it nagged at my good mood. How did I tell the man I was dating that an ex-boyfriend is jealous of my being with someone new? And that, unfortunately, this ex headed a street gang, suspected in two neighborhood killings and a disappearance. In my estimation, those facts alone came together to create a perfect storm and a deal breaker. Andreas would run for the hills.

I grabbed my keys from the tray on my desk, and playfully pushed him out the open door. "Let's go before they give away our table."

We stepped into the sultry summer evening. The essence of freshly baked bread drifted from Domino's Bakery next door. I inhaled deeply. Mom always said just smelling the delicious carbohydrates made her gain weight. A carb coma was the ultimate happiness.

Peace enveloped me. Andreas was close by. I felt normal again and safe.

The sun crawled behind the horizon of the brick-and-stone cityscape. Crimson and orange arrows of color streaked the fading day-blue sky. *Red sky in the morning, sailor take warning. Red sky at night, sailor's delight.* Mom's old sayings had been rolling into my mind on a regular basis during the last few weeks.

"So what do you think?"

Jerked from my thoughts, I turned to look at Andreas. "Excuse me. What?"

He playfully poked out his bottom lip. I could tell he was only pretending to be hurt. Andreas wrapped his hand around the back of my neck, pressing with the tips of his fingers as he rubbed. "Lady, you haven't been paying attention to a single word I said."

"I'm sorry, love." I lowered my head to take advantage of his pleasing fingertips. I slowly rolled my head from side to side. "I was thinking of Mom."

"I understand." Andreas slid his arm around my shoulder, pulling me to his side as we walked down the busy street. "Have you made any decisions about renting her apartment yet?"

Sadness stabbed at my peace. I pressed my shoulder closer to Andreas. Even on a sultry evening such as this, feeling his warmth joining with mine, it was a small consolation for my lonely heart. "I can't even bear to go down the front stairs, let alone go into her place. Passing her summer decorations reminds me that it's the last seasonal celebration I'll ever see on her door." I shook my head. "I can't." A lump welled up in my throat. "I've been purposely using the back stairs to avoid it."

Andreas leaned over and planted his lips on the top of my forehead. "When you're ready, I'll go into the apartment with you. You shouldn't have to face that alone."

I looked up at him, the sadness washed

away by his love. "Thanks for the support."

"That support works both ways. I feel like I could conquer the world with you at my side."

"Yeah, I'm sure you could be just fine without me." I scuffed my feet, as though kicking away the thought that had just rolled from my lips.

Andreas stopped short, and turned to face me. "You have no idea how I feel about you, do you? I need you to make my life feel complete. You are literally the key to my happiness."

I could feel my face flush, guilty at being self-absorbed. I breathed a nervous laugh. Such heady declarations were more than I expected. "You're being so sweet when I wasn't even paying attention to you."

"I was asking what you thought about going away with me this weekend. We could go to the Hamptons, lie on the beach, and see the sights. You could use the break. Some distance from here would do you a world of good."

I groaned. "This weekend? I don't think I have time. I'd need to clear it with Fifi to watch the store. And I've still got that whole file of paperwork to finish for mom's estate. I've been procrastinating for too long. The lawyer is getting antsy."

A hint of displeasure crossed Andreas's face.

Oh, no. I didn't want him to think I didn't care about him or his feelings. "How about if we go next weekend?"

He recovered quickly. "That sounds fine."

"Are you going to be a gentleman and get us separate rooms?"

Andreas slid to a stop. He bent from the waist in an exaggerated bow. "Yes, ma'am. Thy wish is my command."

I burst into laughter, threw my arms around his neck, and drew myself up to his face. I planted a quick kiss on his soft lips and snuggled close to his hulking frame as we continued down the sidewalk.

We strolled past the outdoor café and crossed to the other side of the street. Its colorful green awning complemented the Mediterranean music, and the ambiance created by the aroma of the fresh-ground coffee. It reminded me that, on the way back, I needed to stop in for another bag of hazelnut grind. I usually bought it on the next block over at the Coffee Bean gourmet coffee shop, but the café had a new blend I was dying to try.

A group of young men congregated in front of the outdoor market on the corner. Several of them leaned against the angular setup of fruit box displays and two were resting against the railing going down to the subway.

My body tensed. The blue FUBU hoody. The guy leaning against the subway railing chewing on a white, plastic soda straw. Those were Trey's boys. I scanned both sides of the street. Chantel's beauty shop. The Bistro. Charlie's Barbershop. Then I spotted him.

Trey sat on the flagstone stoop of the café brownstone next to the grocery on South Portland. His elbows rested on his splayed knees, hands clasped together, as he stared at me.

A wave of panic washed up my spine, gripping at my throat, cutting off my air. My steps faltered.

"What's the matter?"

I glanced at Andreas. Concern marred his handsome face. I feigned a half smile. "It's all right." Sigh. I lied, again. Lord, please don't strike me with lightning. "I was just wondering if I left the lights on."

My eyes darted between watching the boys while trying to perceive any signals to them from Trey.

"I thought they were all off when we left."

"They probably were." I absently answered as I stared across South Portland, fixing my eyes on Trey. My thoughts were running a mile a minute in four directions.

Trey made an exaggerated wink, pointed his two fingers at his eyes, and then pointed his index finger at me. *I'm watching you.*

My knees wobbled. Darts of adrenaline shot down my arms making my hands shake. What were his boys about to do?

Andreas, with his arm still around my shoulders, led me through the crowd of noisy young men.

Nothing happened. I was too afraid to glance back. The sheer act of turning might set them off like rabid dogs. Thank you, Father, for your grace and mercy and legion of protective angels.

I heaved a sigh. I hoped the boys would be gone by the time dinner ended. Why did it feel like eyes were staring a hole in the back of my head? Trey must be watching.

Andreas kissed the top of my head again. I disengaged myself from his arm.

We stopped.

He frowned. "What's the matter?"

"Nothing. But your arm is tugging on my hair. I don't want to be bald by the time we get to the restaurant." I playfully fist-bumped the offending arm.

Andreas slid his arm around my waist and with a slow, easy movement, pulled me to his chest. The earthiness of his cologne filled my nostrils. I gazed into his eyes. Soft inviting lips brushed across mine. I closed my eyes and drank in the moment. Cologne. Lingering warmth trailing across my mouth. His arms held me protectively. The moment faded.

Andreas released my waist and continued walking.

The sounds of the street invaded my space.

Despite misgivings, I stole a glance back.

Trey wasn't on the stoop. My eyes darted in the direction of the grocery. The group congregating in front of the market had also disappeared.

My smile went slack.

I slid my hand into Andreas's grasp. My steps resounded with the tremble in my knees. Trey wouldn't dare try anything out here on a public street. Would he? Just a dozen more steps. We'd be inside the restaurant.

My heartbeat counted the footfalls. *Please, Lord, let us get inside. Trey, don't be stupid in public.*

Andreas opened the door to Cristos. "Enter, *s'il vous plaît,* m'lady." He did another exaggerated bow from the waist.

I burst into laughter, or maybe it was an

expenditure of relief. "Okay, a Greek speaking French has *got* to be an oxymoron."

I entered the bustling establishment. The immediate gratification of being safe momentarily, mixed with the pungent sauce and grilling meat aromas, created a heady deliciousness that I wanted to savor. My stomach growled in protest.

Andreas smiled. "Great, now you're calling me a moron."

I elbowed him playfully. "Tsk, tsk, you silly man."

I stole one last glance through the glass doors behind us. Was it all in my head or was I actually hearing the theme music from *Jaws*?

10

I perched on the edge of my bed fingering the thick cream-colored patchwork quilt that Mom made for me last Christmas. The morning sun streamed through the wall of glass, warming my fourth-floor bedroom and causing visible heat ripples to rise from the polished wood floor. Regardless of the ninety-degree summer heat, I kept the quilt on my bed as a security blanket.

My hand moved across the stitches, tracing the patterns as I stared at the polished oak-trimmed circular staircase on the other side of the wide room, twirling down through the floor into the rest of my apartment on the third floor. I felt stupid. I half expected Mom to poke her head up to announce that the coffee was on.

It was our own mother-daughter ritual. She would come up from her second-floor apartment every morning using the circular stairway connecting our living rooms. My apartment consisted of the third and fourth floors of our building. She'd put on the coffee and use the other circular stairway in my kitchen to stick her head up here and wake me up. It was the sweetest alarm clock I'd ever had.

The stairs. A stark reminder of what was lost. I didn't want to look, but it was the focal point from this position on the bed. The only other thing to see on this floor was the blank wall with a singular door in it, beyond my walk-in closet and bathroom. A storage area from years gone by. My chest tightened. I needed something . . . anything to cover the stairs.

My glance trailed to the oak dresser. I hopped off the bed and hurried to the five-foot-tall dresser against the wall near the bathroom. All the furniture had been fitted with wheels at Mom's insistence, so as not to mar the floors when moving them for cleaning. I rolled the dresser in front of the stairs then hurried back to my perch on the bed.

My lip quivered. The view was changed. But I didn't want the view to change. It had served me well for a long time. Why hadn't I come home sooner? I'd have had more time with her. A tear slid down my cheek. I swallowed the lump forming in my throat as my eyes glanced heavenward. "Mom, I need you. You were my rock. You always tried to keep me straight."

I brushed away the tear with the back of my hand as I expelled a huge breath of air. This is my new fate, so get used to it, chickypoo.

A voice inside my head said, "Put on your big girl panties and get on with life." Sigh. I hear you, Mom. I slid off the bed again.

You'd like my new man, Mom. I done good this time. Unfortunately, Mom and Andreas had only met a couple of times and Mom wasn't especially enthused with him. *He's a wonderful, sweet, loving man. He'll be my protector.* Yeah, my wonderful protector is going to be MIA today. He's swamped with work.

I trudged down the circular stairs to the kitchen. My fingers wrapped around the handle of the coffeemaker carafe before I caught myself. I snatched my hand back. Morning coffee was a ritual I'd always enjoyed with Mom. I was better. For a few weeks I couldn't even stand to stay in the kitchen. But I still couldn't bring myself to make coffee alone.

I turned my back to the counter and glanced down at my watch. Seven a.m. Fifi wouldn't have the store open yet. The coffee wouldn't be on until about nine, especially if that lonely woman comes in again today to help. I had to go down the street to Bebe's to get my hair done so I didn't have to take any more fashionista abuse from Fifi or Verlene, and braids were going to take quite a few hours. Maybe I could get coffee at Bebe's.

I grabbed my cell phone from the charger in the TV bookcase and the green folder of estate paperwork off the coffee table. The stupid paperwork. I kept hemming and hawing with Mom's lawyer and I hadn't finished going through it all yet. Maybe today. I could drop it off at the store before I went down the street. My hand automatically reached for the front doorknob. A shiver zipped up my spine. My fingers held onto the cool metal knob as though welded. My heart pounded against my ribcage. It felt like it was beating hard enough to break a rib.

I chomped down on my lip so hard I expected to taste blood. Unable to move, my knees wobbled. My fingers willed themselves loose of the burnished metal doorknob. My hand fell to my side. I still couldn't do it. I couldn't go down those front steps past Mom's apartment door. I could barely stand to look at the staircase on the other wall that circled down into her apartment. We used to joke that we could hole up in the building for months without needing to go outside our apartments to see each other.

How strange that the last time I'd seen her was in the hallway. Correction . . . the last time I had seen Mom's body was on a gurney, in one of those black plastic bags. It felt so wrong, like they were just carrying away a trash bag. I squeezed my eyes shut at the thought.

She was already dead when I found her. Died of a heart attack. But Mom was young by today's standards. Fifty-five was not old. That didn't matter now. She was gone. I still couldn't face those stairs. I'm not that strong . . . yet.

I set my jaw and turned in the other direction.

Walking through the apartment to the back door in the kitchen, I checked my pockets. Keys were there. The gun. I'd left it downstairs when I went to dinner last night with Andreas. Just thinking of him kept me grounded to the present. The euphoria was like a teenage experience. The giddiness. Don't be silly. I pulled the door shut behind me and floated down the stairs on a cloud. Ugh! To be that young and innocent again.

The light-blue car was next to the Dumpster again.

I glanced inside as I passed. Today it was
empty.

11

Bebe's Beauty Shop sat six doors up on the same side of the street as the bookstore. It took all of five minutes to walk there, so it was not enough time for me to have a logical change of heart about letting a Hungarian kid who thought he was the epitome of the Rolling Stones crank on my head.

I opened the frosted-glass door to the shop. I had not expected instant musical assault at seven in the morning. Inside was the same crew, just a different day. A bunch of twenty-somethings who thought they had the world all figured out.

I nodded at Marley Howard and Janelle Wilson sitting in the waiting area. Both had on microminis, loud sparkly tops, and heels that came out of one of those sleazy catalogs and had the ability to stab you clear through to the heart. These were the night people on their way home, but at the moment they were reading magazines and waiting their turns. That thought caused me to take note that all of the *ladies* here now, and I use that term loosely, were of the nightly persuasion. I made a mental note to make my next appointment later in the afternoon when more of my normal friends were scheduled.

The *O* magazine and *Essence* were about as dog-eared as they could get. People made appointments just to get in here and read them for free. I had been known to do it a time or two my own self, since there were specific articles I cared to check every month.

Aretha Franklin's diva voice was rippin' about R-E-S-P-E-C-T from Bebe's station, the first one past the waiting area and appointment desk. Hah! I needed to play that tune for Trey.

Bebe Harrington was swingin' to the jam. She was full-figured and fifty. Not only didn't she appreciate the youthful singers of the day, but she didn't like their skinny bodies either. Said they needed more weight behind their vocal cords to get her attention. She applied a dollop of moisturizing cream to her client's head and worked a comb and flat iron, from the woman's scalp down the strand of hair. Bebe was the queen of intricately laced hairstyles of human hair lacquered stiff. She always sported her own creations, but all of hers were wigs that she could work on at home and take off and on at will.

The next station was quiet. Tiny Tina Trabocchi was home with her newborns. Poor girl hadn't been tiny in nine months, carrying those triplets. But her workstation proclaimed loud and clear, along with the posters of sculptured fingernail designs, that she loved her some Lady Gaga. But personally Gaga made me gag gag. Ugh!

I stared down the long black-and-white checkered floor trying to get a good look at the new guy, but the person sitting in the booth chair at the end had his back to me. Posters of a young Mick Jagger covered the area. I knew I had the right station.

"Hi, Sloane. Verlene dialed in a 9-1-1 on you. Said you needed emergency help." Ellie Pembrook, the receptionist and manicurist, giggled behind her fist and went back to buffing her client's nails. The client looked like she was one of the night owls getting repaired before she went home and slept for the rest of the day.

I could feel my face getting red. "Verlene's chronic like that." I whispered past the back of my hand. "Is this Gabi guy really good?"

"Gir-lll, he can micro-braid his butt off! His fingers are like greased lightning. Just ignore the strangeness." She raised her eyebrows a couple of times and flipped her thumb toward the back booth.

The scents of shampoo, straightening chemicals, and women's cologne grew stronger as I walked toward the last chair. Was I doing the right thing? After all, Verlene recommended him.

"Hey, Gabi, you're up!" Shari yelled down the row.

This young guy in skintight, black leather pants and a sparkly royal blue tank top hopped from the station chair and swiveled it around to me. "Welcome! I am going to make you fabulous today." He grinned broadly through full lips that actually did remind me of Mick Jagger.

I turned back to the front. What was I about to do? The ladies all raised thumbs up. Sigh. I sucked in my attitude and plopped into the seat. He spun me around in the chair to face the mirror. I grabbed onto the armrests. He was holding up a large tri-fold of head shots. "Which would you like, my love?" He flicked his head back, knocking his shoulder-length hair back from his face.

My love? This kid called me "my love." I'll reach . . . ohh, I liked the style on the right. Her extensions, much lighter in color than her own hair, created a neat patchwork, plaiting the two colors together. My defiance melted. I could imagine myself with that do. Like a lioness, I pointed. "That one please."

"Let's rock and roll." Since his booth was the last in the line, he bordered the shampoo stations. I didn't even need to get into another seat for the washing. He stepped on a pedal, lowered the back of the chair to a reclining position, and spun me around to the shampoo sink. I grabbed onto the armrests again. My stomach lurched as my eyes tried to catch up. He was going to have me barfing if he didn't take it easy.

"My new shampoo formula has an aromatherapy component. Enjoy!" Gabi jabbed the button on his CD player and made a wide air guitar move as strains of "Jumpin' Jack Flash" drowned out my sighs. It took all of fifteen minutes to wash and dry my hair and I must admit that the shampoo he used had a delicious fragrance of honeysuckle and mint that made my head tingle. By the time he started braiding I was thoroughly relaxed, but a familiar voice cut through the peaceful aura.

"Sloane, honey, I'm glad you got here."

I opened my eyes to Verlene waving at me from the front of the salon. Help me, saints!

Talk about my being a captive audience.

"Hi, Verlene, what are you doing here?" If I'd known, I'd have picked another day.

"Well, honeybun, I had to see if you'd really come in. Besides I'm still telling my girls about my good fortune."

I tensed. She would *not* dare.

"Tell them, Sloane. I'm going to be rich. Tell them. Yes, sir, I done found the secret." She did an exaggerated neck roll with her head.

I bolted upright. "Yeeow!" Gabi's hands were still attached to my head. "Verlene! What did we discuss?"

I crooked my finger in a "come hither" movement. Verlene sauntered down the aisle looking like an old runway model. "Honey, these are my home girls. The secret is safe with them."

I glanced at each of the women in turn. The two magazine readers were furiously texting. Unfortunately, I knew I couldn't swing a cat in the room without hitting one of them who hadn't been involved with some form of larceny, even if it was only a five-finger discount. I didn't trust any of these early-morning beauty shop babes as far as I could throw them.

I snatched Verlene by her arm and pulled her down as I spoke through clenched teeth.

"Stop talking about the book in front of these people, until we get it safely locked up."

I knew I should have taken the book with me. Why didn't I? Because I was too worried about her trying to poison me with food. Sheesh, Sloane, you're a grown woman. You don't have to open your mouth for food if you don't want to. It brought back the memory of Mom and the ole airplane-in-the-hangar spoon trick. I guess I was still a pushover.

But I really thought Verlene would have listened to me and kept it quiet. Now I didn't know how many people she had blindly trusted, or who these women would be telling about her good fortune as soon as her back was turned. I had to get that book into the store for safekeeping.

"I want you to go home, get that book, and bring it back to the store. Now!"

Verlene looked at her watch. "Honey babe, I've got a doctor's appointment in an hour. Then I have to be at a dress fitting. You know how seamstresses are if you cancel their appointments. It's not a pretty sight. But I'll be in as soon as I can get there." She started back forward.

I weighed how much I should argue with her in front of these women. The more important I made it sound, the more danger she might be in. I opted for praying as I felt my head tighten up from the braiding. Gabi pulled up on my forehead. A prickle ran up my nose, and I sneezed into the crook of my arm.

Gabi looked at me. "Are you getting sick?"

I shook my head. "Just sinuses."

Gabi swung me around to the other side and the CD player clicked to another track. "Under My Thumb" bounced from the speakers. Sheesh, if I could only keep Verlene sequestered under my thumb.

12

I opened the front door to the bookstore. Rhythmic calypso music slapped me right in my freshly braided head. Ugh! Enough with the music already. "Fifi, just give me a few hours to hear myself think." I marched to the stereo wall unit, dialed it to a soft jazz station, then on second thought turned it off. I just needed a break from the Rolling Stones ringing in my head. But it had been worth it. I loved my new stylin' do. Gabi was a genius . . . weird, but still a genius, and amazingly fast. He had braided my whole head in less than five hours.

Behind the counter, a dancing Fifi raised one hand, put the other one across her middle, and did a few steps of the cha-cha. "You weren't here, sugah. I thought I'd get my blood moving."

"Drink coffee, it's just as stimulating but much less noisy."

She raised an eyebrow at me. "Love the

hairstyle."

"Thanks. It is kinda righteous, isn't it?" I felt on top of the world. The new do was about six inches longer than my own shoulder-length hair and the micro braids flowed softly around my shoulders. They were a little tighter than I liked, so it felt like I had had a facelift. But what the hey. At thirty-five a little face-lift was a good thing.

I grabbed my mug and headed for the coffee bar. Fifi's steps tapped behind me. I didn't even have to look back to know what she was wearing: stretch Capris and spiked-high heels.

It tickled me that we were total fashion polar opposites.

"Have you called your lawyer about that ex-husband lawsuit thing?" Fifi slid onto a stool at the coffee bar. She fingered the small banana comb holding back the long, tightly curled tendrils of hair. Her wrist full of bangles tinkled like broken glass as she raised then lowered her arm.

"What is it with you? No, I haven't had time to call the lawyer. I'll get to it. I don't feel like dealing with that problem right now."

"Well, sugah, you also had another visit from Coltrane Realty this morning."

She had to say that name. My face warmed. I grimaced, filled my mug, and added cream before I turned to her. "I told Rob Landry to get lost yesterday."

I glanced over her shoulder. Barbara sat on the far right of the store, hard at work on her laptop. A stately looking gentleman with a bowtie and wire-rimmed glasses sat at a table close by reading the store's acquisition brochure.

Fifi ignored my obvious irritation and fiddled with repositioning the comb on the other side of her head. The bangles slid in the other direction. "It wasn't Robby this time. I've never seen this guy before."

"Robby, is it? Does *someone* have an interest in the bloodsuckers who are trying to take mom's building?" I couldn't picture those two together. It was probably the age thing that tripped my trigger.

Fifi blushed. Her cheeks turned pink. "Robby isn't like that. It's only a job to him."

"Hmm, you seem to know a lot about *Robby*." I blew across the surface of the steaming coffee, venturing a few sips, as I watched the expression on Fifi's face with amusement. "Are *we* dating?"

The crimson in Fifi's face darkened to match her hair. "I don't know about you, but me and Robby are. It's only been a couple of dates, but he loves books as much as I do!"

"Isn't he kind of young for you?"

Fifi did a comical chicken neck movement with her head. "He's stirrin' ma' grits! Age is only a number, sugah." She winked. "It's not like I'm robbin' the cradle — he's thirty-five. And besides, he's trying to hook me up with a new apartment."

Great on the apartment! But yuck on him being my age. "Just tell him to stay away from me. I'll let him live to date you another day." I glanced around the store again. "Who's that professor-looking guy reading an acq brochure?"

"He's been waiting for you. One of those doctor guys who want to talk about your ma's prized acquisition." Fifi shook her head. "Y'know, Camille was right. I always thought she was nuts for going all the way to Europe last year to buy that book, but she swore one day it would be worth its weight in gold."

Fifi had worked with Mom from the very first day that Mom took over the store. The antiquarian cloak had passed to Mom when Grandpa decided to retire before he took off to travel the world.

"You know more about the book than I

do. Why didn't you talk to him?"

Fifi flicked up her pinky finger, pretending to act haughty. "For one, I've taken an instant dislike to him and, second, because he wanted to speak to the 'owner of the establishment.' "

I smirked and held my hands up in surrender. "Okay, so your feelings are hurt because you and Mom are . . . were . . . the book people, and I'm supposed to be the computer person. Don't take it to heart."

"I still don't like him." Fifi screwed up her top lip in a fake snarl.

I strode off toward the old man's table.

The gray-haired gentleman looked over the top of his wire-rimmed glasses as I approached. He rose, extending his hand. "Miss Beckham, I presume."

I extended my hand, smiling in amusement at his choice of vocabulary. "I'm Sloane Templeton. My ma was the Beckham. And you would be?"

"Dr. Carlton Mabry." He looked around the store. "You said 'was.' I don't understand. Where is Camille, er, uh . . . Mrs. Beckham?"

Something about his tone rang of familiarity with my ma. "Mom passed away a few months ago. Did you know her?"

His cheeks flushed as he groped for words.

"Yes . . . I mean no . . . I knew her . . . because of her fine choices in books." He lowered his head. "I'm sorry for your loss."

I smiled softly. That wouldn't have been possible even a few short weeks ago, but now I was beginning the healing process. "I haven't lost her, Doctor. I know right where she is."

His chin pulled back and he glanced over his glasses. "How so?"

I raised my index finger.

"Yes, Cam— er, Mrs. Beckham was a good Christian woman."

I felt a lump in my throat working its way up and wanted to change the subject before I acted sappy. "Dr. Mabry, I see you are looking over our acquisitions brochure." I knew which book but I didn't want to seem overeager. "Are you still interested in the book we discussed yesterday?"

Mabry motioned me closer. He smelled like pepperment and a distinctive cherry-blend tobacco that reminded me of being eight years old and playing with Grandpa's pipe stand.

I seated myself across the table from him but did not lean in to mimic his manner. Something told me he was not the grandfatherly type, and I should beware. Recently I had started paying attention to those lead-ings.

"I need to purchase this book." He pointed a strong, straight finger at the line in the brochure that read Christian, P. *Histoire de la Magie* (Paris, 1876).

I leaned back in the chair. "You are not the only one this week inquiring about that book." My curiosity level ratcheted up a notch. Bizarre book choice. Two strange characters.

The doctor's facial muscles contracted into a scowl. His sunny grandpa disposition morphed into that of menacing man. "Are you saying that you no longer have this book?"

I tried to lean further back but the chair remained rigid. "That's not what I'm saying at all. The sudden activity with that particular volume has piqued my interest. Naturally it will affect the asking price of the book."

Mabry ignored my statement but appeared flustered. "Who is asking about the book?" He waved a hand absently. "Never mind . . . I know who it is. He is not going to beat me to this treasure —"

"Whoa! Treasure? What treasure?" Now I sat forward. This would definitely be the makings for an immediate discussion with Fifi.

"I have said too much already." Mabry tossed the brochure onto the table. "How did he find you so quickly? There must be a leak in my office."

What office? Where did this man come from? I needed answers to make an intelligent decision. "With this much interest, I think I should announce a public auction —"

"No!" Mabry jumped from the seat. "Do not do that. Your life would literally be in *danger* if it were widely known that you have physical possession of the book."

I faced him head-on. The last thing I was going to stand for was a little old man trying to intimidate me. "Excuse me. Are you threatening me?"

"No, no, not me." Mabry raised his hands in mock surrender. "There was an Egyptology consortium in Amsterdam last week. The director of Giza Saqqara of the Egyptian Antiquities Organization almost came to blows with an American scholar group over their assertions that the Sphinx wasn't built by Egyptians but by an advanced civilization several thousand years before the Egyptians."

My eyes rolled. A casual grin worked its way across my face. "My ma told us that one day men would be fighting over this book." I chuckled and shook my head. "I must confess, we didn't believe her."

"This is no laughing matter." Mabry tapped the table. "These men will kill over this book."

I bristled. "But why? They can go online to Google Books and read the stupid thing."

"That only lets you read twenty percent of it, and they use low-resolution scanning."

"So you have already tried."

He frowned. "Yes, this is one of only a few surviving copies of a special edition of the original manuscript. It has subtle nuances that cannot be picked up with that inferior scan quality."

I started thinking treasure hunt. "Like what?"

Mabry set his jaw and swallowed hard enough to make his bow tie bounce with the movement of his Adam's apple.

I folded my arms and stared with no emotion. Possession of the book is nine-tenths of the law. If he didn't want to cooperate, there would be others who would.

He huffed, and leaned forward over the table. "This was an edition commissioned by an elite and secret organization. It is said that there are invisible writings on the pages."

I burst out laughing. "No way! This

sounds like a science fiction movie."

Mabry maintained his composure, his steel blue eyes drilling into my head. He leaned forward and spoke in a whisper. "The book holds the secret for opening the Sphinx to untold wealth and unimaginable power."

I fought to control myself. Laughing in the man's face would definitely appear rude. But talk about both oars out of the water. "All that in a book? Why has no one figured it out in all these years?"

"There was a cipher key discovered in an Egyptian dig last year that will unlock part of the coding in the book."

"Part?"

"Yes. Even as we speak there are teams racing to the area where the other cipher is said to be located."

I squinted at him. This had to be one of those hidden camera punk jobs. "So am I to assume that the other person interested in this book is also racing for this other cipher?"

"Yes. That would be Dr. Lucius Barlow."

My chest tightened. That was the name of the other person who called yesterday. "How can I get in touch with you? I'm going to have to think about this for a while."

Mabry pulled a business card from his

breast pocket and slid it across the table as he stood. "Please do not hesitate too long. Time is of the essence."

I reached for the card, and the old familiar prickle ran up my nose. I sneezed into the crook of my arm. So much for being in control.

"You should see a doctor for that cold." He turned and hurried from the store.

"It's . . . not . . . a cold." *Sigh.* I fingered the edge of the card. How would mom handle this? The other guy had asked to buy the book also, so technically both men were on an even playing field. Maybe they could just have a bidding war. But Mabry talked about there being danger surrounding the book.

Great. Just what I needed. More drama, danger, and apparently allergy tablets. Ugh . . . I hate pills.

13

I slid the business card into my shirt pocket and decided to look this guy up on the Internet for a better sense of his qualifications and status. I happened to glance around the room at the table terminals. None of the computers were booted.

Moving to the table to my left, I flicked the monitor switch. Nothing happened. "Fifi," I flicked it again. "There's nothing happening here."

Fifi looked up from the desk behind the counter. "Oops! Sorry kiddo." She reached beside the desk and flipped the switch. "I was engrossed in unpacking the new shipment and forgot to turn them on."

The dozen monitors all blinked on at the same time.

I'M WATCHING YOU!! flashed across the screens simultaneously in large white letters on a stark black background.

A shiver radiated down my arms and out

my fingers, but I shook it off and laughed out loud. "Cute, Fifi, and I'm watching you too."

"What?" Fifi turned with a stack of books in her hand.

"The monitors. . . . Cute."

Fifi peered out into the room. The expression on her face turned from amusement to concern. "Umm . . . I didn't do that."

"I thought you had one of these college kids spoof me."

"I wouldn't even know what to tell them to do."

She plopped the books on the counter and turned to the main computer on my desk.

"Hold up. Let me look at it before you change anything." I slid onto the leather chair. I tapped several commands as screens flipped.

"I set it so Chat Central opens first." To Mom's chagrin, books were not in my blood. But I had used my limited computer skills to bring Beckham's into the twenty-first century with an ever-expanding online bookstore.

"So are you saying someone sent that message from here?"

Other than teaching her to use Twitter once in a while, I couldn't get the woman to understand the Internet, so Fifi's attention amused me.

"Yes . . ." I typed in a few more codes. ". . . and no. It looks like someone hacked into the system to put that up there."

Fifi's forehead wrinkled. "Why would anyone do that?"

A twinge of adrenaline stabbed my chest. The same question crossed my mind. I shook it off. Trey came to mind but his computer skills didn't rise to comprehending the use of a Wii.

"It could be one of the college kids who come in here, trying to be smart." I tapped the keys a few more times, changing screens again. "But I think I'm at least better than they are." I smiled and wagged my head back and forth like a bobblehead. "And that route of entry has just closed."

I whacked the enter key, and the monitors in the room rebooted to the colorful and tastefully decorated *Welcome to Beckham's Books & Brew* screen.

"So we're good?" Fifi looked around the room at the screens. "I don't understand all this computer stuff, but are we safe? I mean the online bookstore and all?

"Yes. I had just never set up a password because I didn't think we needed it. But now people who want to use our system will have to create an account and log in with a

146

username and password."

Fifi squinted.

"That's why you're the boss, sugah." Fifi crossed her eyes in mock confusion. "Listen, while you're sitting there, Goober or whatever you do to find out what you can about that professor guy."

I bit down on my lip. "Fifi, the word is *Google*."

"Well, that too." She tapped a finger on the desk. Her armful of bangles created a racket. "I'm curious about him and the other guy who came lookin' for the same book."

I fished the business card out of my pocket and set it on the keyboard. "How much information do you want?"

"Whatever you can get. We should know what kind of money range these guys are working in before we set an asking price."

I knitted my brow.

"Child, don't look at me like that." Fifi tapped me on the arm with the back of her hand. "I spent a lot of years learning from your ma how this rare book business works."

"So did you and Mom ever have any discussions about this book?"

Fifi shook her head. "No, unfortunately I was goofing on her about the trip to Europe, so we didn't have a real conversation about it. The only note I found in her records indicated twenty thousand dollars. I guess that's what she calculated as a selling price at the time."

"You can just make the price anything you want?"

"If there's going to be an auction. We set a base price and let them haggle from there. It might get up to thirty thousand with vigorous bidding." Fifi rubbed her hands together.

The more I rolled the idea around in my head, the more I wanted to know if this guy had enough sanity to know what "danger" could mean. I opened one of my own search programs, set the parameters, and put in the two men's names. This personal data program would even show any public interactions between the two subjects.

The program started its search. I glanced up as Barbara Nelson entered the store and scurried back to her regular seat. I hadn't even noticed her leaving.

"This could take a couple minutes. Watch the screen for me." I turned from Fifi and walked toward the woman.

"Hello, Barbara. How are you feeling today?" I approached the table slowly in case the woman was still jittery like yesterday.

Barbara looked up as she opened the laptop and smiled broadly. "Hi, Sloane. I'm fabulous. And you should just call me T . . ." Her eyes glazed over for a second. She shook her head. "Barbara, just call me Barbara."

I frowned but quickly recovered. "Okay . . . uh, er, Barbara. I'm glad you're feeling better today."

The familiar prickle ran up my nose. I turned my face into the crook of my arm and sneezed. "Excuse me . . . sinuses."

Barbara looked at me like I'd said I had bubonic plague. "Seriously, it's just sinuses. They'll last as long as the pollen count is up, and then they'll subside."

Barbara beamed from ear to ear. "When life hands you lemons, make lemonade."

"Uh, okay . . . I guess." What a difference a minute makes.

"Have I told you about my latest writing project? I'm writing suspense for women's fiction. And I have an editor waiting to see my proposal, but I can't stop actually writing the story to do the proposal. I'm already halfway done." She gestured at her laptop screen.

I tried not to grin. This was a 180-degree turn from her mood yesterday. "I'm glad it's coming along so well." I sidestepped to keep moving back to the front of the store. "Good for you."

I made a face after I passed the table. Whoa! That woman needs to lay off the high-test and go to decaf!

"Hey, sugah!" Fifi motioned me to the front with a stage whisper. "Wait till you see this!"

I scooted around the counter. "What?"

Fifi held up the business card. "This guy is world class. He's not only wildly rich, but he's a premiere archaeologist in the *Who's Who in Science.*"

"Ah, that kind of doctor." I stared at the records on the screen.

The bell tinkled as the front door opened. Fifi vacated her seat to greet the customer. I slid into her place to get a closer look at the doctor's list of accomplishments.

I whistled under my breath. He was the leading United States expert in Egyptology. "Uh-oh . . ." At the bottom of the academic biography it gave a list of his prior associations. Dr. Lucius Barlow had been his archaeological partner for fifteen years. A hotlink to one of what looked to be numerous conspiracy sites said that the two of them had come to actual blows over an archaeological dig in the Sinai desert last summer. And several worker deaths at the dig had not been explained to the government's satisfaction.

I shook my head as I clicked a couple more of the news links. "Maybe that idea of danger isn't so far-fetched."

Fifi turned away from the counter as her customer navigated his way across the store to the fiction section. "What? What danger? Are you talking about those two professors?"

I put my elbow on the desk and my chin in my upturned palm. The other hand continued to click through the news sites. "Those two guys are learned professionals, and by all accounts, have a propensity to act like a pair of Trey's street thugs."

Fifi chuckled. "But he looked like a sweet little professor . . . *not.*"

A scream pierced the air.

Startled, Fifi and I spun to face the store.

"Help me! No . . . this can't happen!" Barbara pounded on the keyboard of her laptop.

Fifi and I scrambled from behind the counter and hurried across the room, approaching Barbara's table just as one of the keys flew off her keyboard and bounced across the table and onto the floor.

"No, no . . . let me in!"

"What's the matter, Barbara?" I surveyed the situation and waved off Fifi, who shrugged and returned to the counter.

Tears rolled down Barbara's cheeks. "I can't get onto the Internet. I'm locked out. I was on it last night, and now I can't get in. I'm locked out. I need to check my e-mail!"

I looked at the screen. "Barbara, it's okay. See . . . we just put up a log-in screen." I fingered the mouse pad on the laptop, and clicked the Enter link. "Just make a user name and password, and it will be okay." Sheesh. How important could her e-mail be?

I slid onto the seat opposite Barbara and watched her type. Barbara's fingers trembled, uncontrolled. She clenched and unclenched her fists and then wrung her hands together before continuing to type.

I reached out and touched her hand. "Honey, what's the problem?"

Barbara looked up and burst out crying again. An uncontrolled stream of glistening tears trailed down her cheeks and onto her keyboard. "I can't take it anymore. My husband locked me out of our house." Her hands flew up to cover her face, as her shoulders heaved with sobs. "He threw me out, so he could move his girlfriend into our home."

This was not what I expected. Saying "I'm

sorry" seemed hollow. A thought stabbed me. The pit of my stomach hollowed out. I tipped my head to the side and studied Barbara's face. "Barbara, . . ." I slid my hand onto the woman's shoulder, "Is that why I found you in your car? Have you been sleeping out there?"

Barbara looked up through tear-filled eyes and nodded.

I had an immediate rush of fear and loathing for a man who would treat his wife like this. My heart absorbed the pain wracking Barbara's spirit. But for the grace of God, there go I. Tears welled in my eyes. How could a man be so cruel? That was a stupid question.

I wrapped my arm around Barbara's shoulder. I had also been the subject of a man's venom more times than I cared to remember.

I had to do something to help.

14

"Sloane! Can I see you, please?"

I slid my arm from Barbara's shoulder and turned to Fifi. "Hang on. I'll be there in a minute."

"Uh, now, sugah. . . . Can I please see you *now?*" Fifi displayed a pasted-on smile, and a pair of wide eyes.

I shifted my position so that Barbara couldn't see my face and mouthed to Fifi, "Knock it off."

Fifi grinned even wider. "I need you, *now.*" Her smile, coupled with the wide-eyed stare, struck me as slightly maniacal. Mom often had that look and it always meant I had trouble coming, right on the other side of the horizon. I wasn't sure I wanted to go over there.

"Go. I'll be all right," sobbed Barbara as she wiped at her tear-streaked cheeks with the back of her hands. She sucked in and exhaled a big breath, appearing to regain control.

I huffed out air, and looked back and forth between them. I laid my hand gently on Barbara's shoulder. "Okay . . . but we need to have a talk." I offered her a sympathetic smile.

Barbara nodded and I hurried toward the counter.

"What is your problem?" I hissed between clenched teeth, as I came around the counter.

"You are my problem. Your ma told me to keep an eye on you, and there you go again." She motioned toward Barbara. "Picking up another stray? Child, when are you going to learn?"

Fifi put her hands on her hips.

I snickered. I knew Fifi's posture was feigned indignation. "She's in trouble and needs my help. Her husband threw her out."

Fifi wagged a finger. "That's why they have the Department of Social Services."

"But she . . ." I extended an arm in Barbara's direction. What? I swiveled around searching the store. Again, Barbara was gone and this time, so was her laptop. My shoulders slumped. Barbara must have assumed that I didn't care.

"She hightailed it out of here as soon as your back was turned." Fifi grinned. "She'll be back. *They* always come back." She pointed a finger with a flick of her wrist. "This is what I wanted to talk to you about." She held up Mom's .38 from the drawer. "What in the world are you doing with your ma's gun?"

My mouth flew open then twisted into a grimace. With a careful touch, I extricated the gun from Fifi's fingers, and placed it back in the drawer like fragile crystal. "Sheesh. Don't be waving that thing around in here."

"I repeat. What are you doing with your momma's gun?"

"You know I've got a permit." Actually, I think I'm keeping it because it was Mom's and she handled it. I feel like I am holding her hand when I grip it, despite the fact that I don't like guns.

"Yes, you have a permit, but you hate guns. So what are you doing with it in your immediate area? Here's a new-style nylon pocket holster for it. You shouldn't be just laying it around unprotected." She held out the small, black sleeve.

"For protection." It was the only reasonable thing I could think of to say, but in reality I had a nagging feeling about my safety around Trey.

Fifi reared back. "Protection? Protection

from what? Or should I say who?" Her expression bordered on fierce. "If that no-account Trey is —"

"No, no, Trey isn't bothering me." Okay, so I just lied, but I didn't need her going ballistic. "I just felt the need to have it. But after yesterday morning, I'm not so sure."

Fifi crossed her arms, and set her jaw. "What else happened yesterday? You didn't mention a single word about anything with a gun."

"I almost shot myself." I remembered with all too much clarity how I had nearly ended my own life by being careless. I would never learn to like guns, but, at the moment, it looked like a necessary evil. Lord, help me.

Fifi uncrossed her arms and grabbed me by the arm. "Oh, sugah, are ya all right?"

My face warmed with the glow of embarrassment. "Yes, I'm fine. It caught on my pocket and I dropped it. The Lord must have been watching over me that it didn't go off."

Fifi covered her mouth to stifle a giggle that sounded in harmony with the tinkling of the bangles slipping down her arm. "Is that all? It wouldn't have gone off."

I trained my gaze on Fifi. "And how would you know that?"

"Because, my dear child . . ." She reached

into her cavernous red leather purse. "I own the sister to that little beauty."

Fifi grinned as she held up a hot pink–handled gun that looked almost identical to Mom's.

I recoiled. "What is wrong with you people? I thought my mom was the only nut job around here."

Fifi puffed up with obvious pride as she rattled off the statistics. "Six-hot, breech-loading, swing-out cylinder with a hand-actuated extractor for easy loading."

"Like I said . . . what is wrong with you people?"

"There's nothing wrong with us, honey. Your mama and I are . . . *were* . . . card-carrying members of the Fort Greene Rod and Gun Club. Besides," Fifi directed her stare at me, "you went and got a permit to carry your momma's gun. So I know she had to take you to the gun club and register you. Should I ask you what's wrong with you?"

I bristled. "You're just like my mom, answering a question with a question. I only joined that smelly club because it was necessary to get the permit, and Mom made me shoot with her a couple times."

"Okay, so maybe we should have told you."

"Told me what?"

Fifi shrugged and looked at the floor, mumbling under her breath.

I turned my right ear in Fifi's direction. "Come again? I didn't hear you."

"I said . . . it was because we were robbed twice last year."

My mouth flew open. "What? Why didn't I know this? Did mom call the police?"

"Please, child! In this neighborhood?" Fifi waved the hand still holding the gun. "The cops were the ones who told us to get weapons."

I wrinkled up my forehead and plopped onto the leather swivel chair at the desk. "So you and mom are members of a shooting club?" I shook my head. "Now, I've heard everything."

"Sheesh. Where've you been, girl! A whole lot of us shop owners are packin'."

"Yeah, right. These little old people around here can barely walk let alone shoot guns."

"Sugah, do you actually think the Granny Oakleys are a book club?"

I stared at her. My brain vapor locked. Please tell me I'm not hearing this. "Are you saying that those oldsters are all packin' heat?"

"That would be exactly what I'm saying."

"But this is New York. They need permits. Who would give permits to someone wearing Coke bottle glasses?" I tried to imagine Kyoko Takahashi sighting anything smaller than the Chrysler Building.

"Someone who deals with pillars of the community who are continually being robbed and has been paid a lot of money." Fifi crossed her arms.

"Is that legal?" Just what I needed. Octogenarian Bad News Bandits.

"Oh yeah. Carrying concealed in New York is legal if you have 'carry business' permits. We all have them. I know that's what your ma registered you for. Didn't you pay attention to what you were signing?"

I stared at her. How did I get to this point? My life seems to have an agenda of its own. Lord, is this you? "Mom just kept harping at me like a fishwife. I really wasn't interested at the time. They explained a ton of stuff. Made me sign all kinds of stuff, and then there was that ink from the fingerprints. Ugh!"

"Don't you worry your little head about details. I'll get you right as rain on the shooting part." She winked. "We go to the range once a week. Tonight's the night. Would you like to come with us? I'm a certified instructor, you know." Her chest puffed up in pride.

I stared again. This was becoming my signature position as my brain melted. Actually, the tic in the muscle below my right eye was becoming more predominant too. "Uhm, yeah, okay." This I had to see, if only for the surreal visual of a bunch of geriatric gunslingers.

I glanced at Fifi's gun. "Hey . . . where's the hammer pullback thingy?"

Fifi grinned. "This is a hammerless model. It won't get caught on my pocket and flip out of my hand." She snorted with laughter.

I leaned back in the chair and held up both hands. "All right. I give up. . . . but I still could have shot myself."

Fifi leaned forward. "No. actually you couldn't have. Your mom's is a model 64. It's double action. That means the hammer has to be pulled back and the trigger squeezed for it to fire, or the trigger has to be squeezed and held . . . ergo, no misfires."

I rubbed my forehead with my fingertips. "This is way more than I wanted to know about any gun." And way more than I wanted to know about a bunch of old people running around with lethal weapons. Just the thought gave me shivers.

At exactly fifteen minutes to five, the first couple of the Granny Oakleys filed in the

161

bookstore. I watched with amusement and a slight amount of fear. The group name had a whole new meaning now that I knew that each of these seniors was packin' heat. And I didn't mean Bengay. It was probably too much information but I was dying to know where they were concealing the weapons.

Fifi had told me to put on closed-toe shoes and a long-sleeved, tight-necked shirt. I sat at my desk feeling all bundled up from head to toe. It felt like I was going to suffocate in the heat, or maybe it was my angst at being around so many guns at one time. I rolled up my sleeves and opened the neck of my linen blouse so I could breathe.

"By the time we close they should all be here." Fifi and her noisy bangles breezed by the counter on her way to greet her comrades in firearms.

Angelica Scarpetti, the longtime family owner of the Italian bakery next door, strutted to the group's table with her fanny pack slapping against her broad backside. Now her I could picture shooting somebody. When I was a kid, I watched her chase her husband, Guido, down Fulton Street, brandishing a long-barreled gun. That was one memorable, hot summer night. She screamed at the top of her lungs that she was going to geld him. It took a lot of youthful years for me to understand that this was not a glowing testament of his moral aptitude. I waved. She waved back.

Next came Kyoko Takahashi. She owned the sushi restaurant down by South Oxford. Her family didn't have kids my age so I never really knew them. Since eating raw fish was low on my priority list, we kids never patronized her place as an after-school haunt.

I turned back toward my desk as the bell tinkled, and made eye contact with Augustyn Grabowski. He was "Gus" to all his friends including us kids when we were young. Gus was my favorite person in the whole neighborhood. We thought it was just the coolest thing that an adult would let us call him by his first name, and it didn't hurt his currency none that his son Marc, by his first wife, Sophia, was my first crush. Ha cha. Marc was the captain of our high school football team and every girl's dream date. I even had a shot at him a couple of times before he married the same night we graduated, and then again, after he divorced. I gave up after his marriage-divorce sequence repeated too many times for my comfort. Either the women had figured out something about him that I hadn't or he had lousy taste in women. Neither choice appealed to me.

I pushed the invoices strewn on my desk into a pile of organized chaos and shoved them into one of the file trays stacked against the back wall. I smelled food. It had to be Mrs. Feinstein. The woman never met a stick of pepperoni she didn't like. She always carried that, a couple bagels, and who knows what else. I once saw her pull out a butter knife and dinner roll. She could probably create a four-course dinner out of that huge quilted bag. But it was always food. Sheesh, who cared about food? When I was hungry, I wanted chocolate, or at least a slice of Red Velvet.

And Stavros Andropolis. Hmm, what could I say about that geezer? A strange feeling tickled in my chest about him. He was out to lunch about Andreas. I mean really, look at how inept he was at staying out of traffic. I probably should just ask Andreas. But I didn't want him to think the rants of an old man, suffering from a case of mistaken identity, meant anything to me. Still . . . there was a niggling in my mind that I couldn't put my finger on.

I watched Fifi bend over the table and all heads went into a huddle. As they leaned back up, all those same heads turned toward me. What? At least I knew they weren't all looking at my hair. My do was stylin' now. But they still looked at me. Was I supposed to go over there, or join witness protection because I now knew they were packin' heat? On second thought, all the guns among the group should have made me head for the hills. But did I have the good sense the Lord gave me? No. Sigh.

Fifi motioned me over. "Sloane, sugah, come over here and meet our club."

I wrinkled my forehead and squinted. No escaping now. I pushed off from my comfortable perch and dragged myself toward the table as I pasted on a smile.

"Bring your gun, sugah."

I raised my hand to shush her. Who was I hiding it from? This was the geriatric cast of *Annie Get Your Gun.* I cringed when I thought about the firepower in this room right now and how one false move could wreak havoc. I mean, really. Most of these people weren't capable of driving a car, let alone shooting a gun. How do I get myself into these things? I turned back and slid the gun and nylon pocket holster Fifi had given me from the drawer and into my slacks pocket. The added weight pulled on the tied waist of my linen slacks. The padded metal slapped at my leg as I approached the table.

It felt like it was trying to remind me that it was my friend.

I stood there. "Hi" sounded stupid, but I couldn't think of anything else to say other than "Ready, Aim, Fire," and I didn't want them taking out the recently installed globular lights.

Fifi threw her arm around my shoulder, hugging me to her with several short jerks. "Well, folks, you all know our sweet Camille's child. She's going to join our merry little band."

Great! Now I'm part of the whistling gnomes or whatever they were, following behind Snow White, er . . . Snow Red.

"Can she shoot? You know her ma was the marksman of the group," Gus said.

"You're *meshugga,* old man," Greta said as she peeled an apple. She pointed the paring knife to her left. "Angelica hits the bull's-eye more."

"Angelica only hits things that she pastes Guido's face on," said Stavros.

Everyone snickered in agreement. Angelica crossed her arms across her ample chest. A smile played at the right corner of her lips.

Fifi raised her hands in surrender. "Okay, okay. No, Sloane can't shoot. Well, not well anyhow." She smiled at me as though I was the odd man out, which I was at this point.

"I'm a quick learner," I beamed. Ugh. What was I so eager to learn? How to make holes in people? Great.

Several nodded in agreement.

"That's a girl," said Fifi. "We need to get going."

The phone rang. I scooted around Fifi and grabbed the handset. "Beckham's Books and Brew. How can I help you?"

"Sloane, honey," said the soft voice, "I think I'm in trouble."

I pushed the receiver tighter to my ear. "Who is this?" The *honey* clicked. "Verlene, is that you?"

"Yes," she hissed. "I have a problem."

My heart felt the fear in her voice. "What's the matter?" I gripped the receiver tighter.

"I think someone's in the . . ." Scuffling sounds. "Get out of here!"

"Verlene! Talk to me." No answer. "Verlene!"

Fifi rushed to my side. "What's the matter?"

"I don't know. It's Verlene."

"What are you doing in here?" Verlene screamed.

Fifi jumped. She heard it too. "Let's go!" She charged for the front door. "You guys watch the store!" She yelled over her shoulder to the startled group at the table.

15

I tore out of the store behind Fifi, and around the building. She slowed to dig her keys out of her handbag and I ran past her. It occurred to me that I had never been in her car. I didn't know which one was hers. I stopped at the large sedan next to the Dumpster.

"What are you doing over there?" Fifi stood beside a hot red sports car with a hood scoop.

"I-I thought . . . ," I pointed.

"Let's go!" She hopped into the black leather bucket seat and I scrambled into the passenger side.

"Did you call 9-1-1?" Fifi turned the key and the engine growled to life. She pumped the gas several times as needles spiked on several meters. The dashboard looked the cockpit of a fighter jet.

"I am." I wrenched my cell from my pants pocket and attempted to dial as Fifi slammed the car into reverse. We peeled out of the parking lot in a hail of scattered gravel. I was grateful there were no cars behind us or she'd have been paying for damages. I dialed 9-1-1. The car's acceleration drove me back into the seat. I pulled the phone to my face and reported the incident, then shoved the cell back into my pants. Fifi shifted gears. The car seemed to crouch down and growl as Fifi pulled off a slick maneuver between two cars that left my heart back at the curb. We turned onto Fulton Street.

"Watch out!" I flinched as Fifi nearly sideswiped a woman opening her driver's-side door.

"People need to watch where I'm going."

Fifi zigzagged between cars that were going in both directions down Fulton. Horns blared. She swerved around another slow-moving car.

I grabbed at the dash and glared at her. "We're going to get killed going this fast. You're breaking about a dozen laws."

"Verlene needs us, sugah. No time to spare the horses." She jammed her palm down on the horn, dodged around an idling car, and shot through the red light.

"That was a red light!" I squeaked. "We're going to jail." I hung onto the armrest. My heart pounded in my throat, for both Verlene's and my own safety.

"Good, maybe it will pick up another RMP. We could use a Radio Motor Patrol to plow us a path to her house."

The car careened left onto Greene Avenue, throwing up a plume of tire smoke in our wake.

A blue car pulled out of a driveway in front of us. I squealed again. "We're going to get killed!"

"Stop front-seat driving." Fifi slammed on the brakes, whipped the wheel to the left, and did a skidding swerve around the back of the blue car.

I shut my eyes. This was the end. That "life flashing before your eyes" thing was gaining merit.

I clung to the center console as Fifi side-slid onto Carlton Avenue and floored it, throwing me back against the seat again. We rocketed through the Lafayette intersection and then DeKalb intersection amid blaring horns and burning rubber as other cars maneuvered heroically to avoid collisions with us.

Fifi skidded to a stop in front of Verlene's house. We bounced from the car and vaulted the stairs two at a time. The front door was open. Fifi drew her gun and looked down at my hand. "Where's your weapon?"

I threw up my hands. "Excuse me. I'm new at all of this." I fished the gun out of the holster in my pocket.

Fifi shook her head and motioned me behind her as we entered the doorway.

My hands quivered, relieved that she grabbed the lead.

The silver phone from Verlene's kitchen lay at the base of the stairs.

"Verlene!" I screamed, overcome with dread and panting for air. "Verlene, answer me! We're here!" Please, Lord, let her be safe. I couldn't bear to lose her too. Not so soon after Mom.

"I'm here." A small voice answered.

I glanced around, scouring several directions looking for the source of the voice. I heard the deadbolt on the bedroom door upstairs disengage. I looked up. I'd forgotten about that safety feature Burt had created for Verlene for when he was traveling out of town. Their bedroom had a steel safety door. God bless Burt for being so smart.

Verlene, clinging hand over hand to the banister, scrambled down the stairs in her stocking feet. I pulled her into my arms and burst into tears. "I was so scared for you. Are you all right? We called the police." I checked her over for damage and rubbed the tears off my cheek with the back of the hand holding the gun.

Verlene pulled her head back and held me at arm's length. "What are you doing with a gun?"

I stuck the gun back in its holster in my pocket. What's wrong with me? This is twice in two days that I've pulled a gun. Did I really have enough nerve to pull the trigger? "It was Mom's. I decided I needed to learn to use it. We were on the way to the shooting range when you called."

"Your ma sure did love her gun." Verlene shook her head. "She said it made her feel secure. Ugh! That's what I have locks for."

My face flushed at the stupidity of brandishing a weapon that I probably had no intention of firing. The sad point was that I'd probably do it again.

Fifi walked through the first-floor rooms but quickly returned. "It's all clear." She hitched a thumb over her shoulder. "The French doors in the kitchen are open. They must have gone out that way as we were coming up the front. What happened?"

"I was in the kitchen when I heard the front door open." A pained expression crossed Verlene's face.

Fifi walked to the front door. "How did

they get in?" She ran her hand along the outside edge of the door.

Verlene lowered her eyes. "I didn't lock it. I just ran in from Tracie's and I was going back next door after I grabbed the cheese grater."

"How many were there?" This neighborhood is not safe. Could I convince her to move?

"Three. One of them had a gun. He was waving it around real nervous-like and they knew right where they wanted to go. They opened the doors to the library first thing."

I glanced at the intricate mahogany wainscoting running the length of the hall, only interrupted by the two doorways. The first led to the library, while the second, closer to the kitchen, opened to the living room and dining room area.

"Do you think it was just coincidence? They were the first set of doors inside the house?" I wrapped my arm around her shoulder.

"No. They knew. When the first guy looked in the library, he motioned the other two inside and basically ignored me."

"How did you get upstairs?" Again, I was blessing Burt's dearly departed soul for thinking of that panic door on the bedroom.

"I ran upstairs when they went inside the

library. One of them tried to grab me by the leg as I was going up the stairs, but I kicked him in the face and kept going."

"So that's why the phone is on the floor." Fifi holstered her weapon and bent over to pick up the phone. She handed it to Verlene.

At that moment, I could hear the police siren as the car turned onto Carlton from DeKalb.

Verlene pulled back from hugging me again. "How did you beat the police here?"

I grimaced and did a glance at Fifi. "I came by jet with Mrs. Andretti."

Fifi beamed at her obvious driving skills, and closed her jacket over her weapon.

I looked around. Nothing looked disturbed. "What did they look like?"

Verlene sat down on the steps and put her head in her hands. "It was three guys in black clothes and stupid ski masks. Can you imagine that in all this heat? Ski masks, of all things."

"What did they want? Money? Drugs?" I rubbed her shoulder again.

Verlene looked up and slapped her hands onto her knees. "The only drugs I have in this house are the Tylenol in the medicine chest. And I'm smart enough to keep my money in the bank. Your guess is as good as mine."

The three of us crowded into the doorway of the library. The disturbance around the desk was obvious.

Verlene ran toward the desk, searching around the jumble of papers, folders, and trays. "They took the book."

This had to be connected to her opening her mouth in the beauty salon this morning. I wanted to strangle and hug her all at the same time.

Two police officers — one tall and lanky like a basketball player, and the other average height with a barrel chest — hurried up the front stairs and entered the open doorway.

The officers stared at us congregating in the hallway. "Someone called about a break-in? Were there any injuries?"

I stepped forward. "This is my aunt, Verlene Buford. She's been robbed of a book that she recently purchased." I wrapped my arm around her shoulder for like the third time. "I think the only thing hurt at the moment is her pride."

The tall officer examined the door frame. "It doesn't look like there was a forced entry. Are there any other ways they could have gotten in?"

"No. They came in the front door. I saw them. It's my own fault," said Verlene. "I was going back next door to Tracie's. The door was unlocked. How stupid can I get?"

"It's all right, Verlene. We all make mistakes." I patted her arm and pulled her back close to me. "Just please don't do it again. My heart can't take it." Verlene nodded.

"You said they stole a book. What book and how did they know where it was? Show us where it was located," said the tall, lanky officer, as the barrel-chested one used his shoulder unit to call detectives to the scene.

"Unfortunately, Verlene has told numerous people about her recent purchase. It was a valuable cookbook." I raised my eyes to the ceiling. I was beginning to use mannerisms just like my mom. She used to do that eye roll every time she felt exasperated with me. Sigh. Another revelation. I have become my mom. I took Verlene by the hand and motioned toward the library.

We followed the tall officer into the library while the barrel-chested officer walked through the house. Verlene didn't need to tell him where she had kept the book. The drawer was ripped from its rails in the desk and the contents were strewn on the floor.

The officer turned 360 degrees while surveying the room. "They knew right where it was. There's nothing else disturbed in here."

I looked around. Everything in the room was in the perfect order that was Verlene's signature. She always said everything had a place, and everything should be in its place. I wanted to scream at her. I told her about those miscreants she called her friends. But she was safe, and she looked too rattled at the moment to take any more grief.

I heard voices behind us.

I turned as two men entered the house. One was a tall Denzel Washington clone with a mustache. The other was a short blond guy carrying a large black case and wearing dark-blue cargo pants with a white polo shirt and a royal blue windbreaker with "N.Y.C. Police Crime Scene Unit" stamped in white letters on the back of it.

The barrel-chested officer spoke to the detective and pointed in our direction. The detective in turn motioned the CSU investigator into the library and entered behind him.

Mr. Denzel clone approached us. He pulled a pen and notebook from the inside pocket of his dark-gray pin-striped suit as he spoke. "I'm Detective Griffen Justice. I've been advised that there has been a robbery."

His voice was as smooth as Godiva chocolate. Okay, so I clearly have a fetish for chocolate. Good chocolate. What woman doesn't? It also sometimes included men, but this one didn't have enough hard body muscles to grab my attention. He just looked really ordinary in his pale gray shirt and gray, black, and white diagonally striped tie. But I liked his voice.

I took Verlene by the arm. "This is my aunt, Verlene Buford, and three men violated her home and stole her property."

Justice looked at me intently, almost too intently for comfort. I wondered if there was a booger under my nose or something. I ran my hand nonchalantly across my face just in case.

He turned to Verlene and smiled. "Derby is interviewing an arson perp, so I told him I'd take the call."

Verlene smiled demurely. Demurely! I didn't know my aunt Verlene had a demure bone in her body. I let go of her arm and pulled back my chin at her. "Excuse me? Derby?"

I swore her face turned red for a split second.

"Derby Weller is my *friend,* and a great detective."

Aha, Derby Weller must be her friendly

ticket-paying officer of the court. At least he was a detective. Not that I was a social snob or anything, but Verlene was kinda financially solvent because of Burt. I had to watch out for her welfare. I felt better that it wasn't just *anybody* off the streets, considering all the kinds of people she hung out with.

Justice watched our exchange, the corners of his mouth ever so slightly raised. "Verlene, tell me what happened."

"I have a feeling that we know the group that these perps came from." I put a hand on my hip.

Justice smiled slowly.

"What?" Was he laughing at me? "Did I say that right? They are perps right?"

Justice nodded. He looked amused. I needed a mirror. I still thought I might have a booger.

I turned to Verlene. "Did you tell anybody outside of Bebe's Beauty Salon?"

"No," Verlene thought a second then shook her head and raised a hand. "I swear. No one else."

"What did you tell them about the book?" A germ of an idea began to grow.

Justice leaned back against the doorjamb and crossed his arms.

I noticed his relaxed posture. "I'm sorry.

Am I butting in?" I felt self-conscious that he was watching me.

He grinned wide. "No, go right ahead. I'll listen. I can tell you're related to Verlene."

Well, I'll be. He's enjoying this. Wait a minute. He's insinuating that I act like Verlene. Strike one, buddy. I turned back to Verlene. "You didn't answer the question."

"I was thinking. I didn't tell anybody about the recipe. I just said the book was going to make me a lot of money when I sold it."

I slapped my hand to my side. I could feel my gun. I pulled my hand away so Justice wouldn't see the bulge. "Okay, so they are going to try to sell the book. The only place they could do that is to a bookstore." I clapped my hands and looked at Justice. "If you alert all the local bookstores to be on the lookout for it, we can catch them red-handed."

Justice pursed his lips and nodded his head. "I may have to get you a job as an investigator. That's very good deductive reasoning."

I was feeling pretty proud. I glanced around to enjoy the approval. Verlene and Fifi were just staring at me. "What?"

Fifi laughed. "Nothing. I'm just enjoying the view." She raised an eyebrow in Justice's direction.

Verlene didn't say a word. She just smiled.

"But that's a good idea, right?" I turned back to Justice. "If these perps are from outside the neighborhood, they could theoretically even come into my store with the book."

The smile on Justice's face faded. "Do you own a bookstore in Fort Greene?"

"Yes, over in the six hundred block of Fulton, Beckham's Books and Brew."

He jotted in his book. "And your name would be?"

"Sloane Templeton, and this is Fifi Tyler, my store manager."

He reached in his breast pocket and handed both Fifi and me his card. "Be sure to call me if you get any leads. And I will get a BOLO out to the other local booksellers."

"Okay, I know a little police lingo, but I don't know that one. What's a bowlow?" asked Verlene.

"A BOLO is 'be on the lookout.' We use that when we are looking for people of interest."

"These aren't people of interest. They are thieves." I wagged a finger.

The corners of Justice's mouth turned up again ever so slightly. "They are people of interest until we are sure they are the actual thieves. They may pass the book off to someone else to sell."

Sure, but that wouldn't stop me from giving those Mata Haris at the beauty shop the once over.

Tracie Fellows, Verlene's friend from next door, came rushing in. "Verlene, I was down on the garden level when I heard the sirens. Are you all right?"

Verlene nodded and proceeded to try to talk to Detective Justice and Tracie at the same time. Ah, back to normal. Minus a book, but at least Verlene's not all shaking and pale.

Fifi looked at her watch. "We need to go if we're going to make our range time. We only get two hours."

I touched Verlene's arm. "Are you going to be all right if I leave?"

"Yes, honey, I'll be fine. Tracie's here with me."

"If you need me, you have my cell number. I want you to meet me at the store in the morning at nine sharp. We have some stuff to do."

"Miss Templeton, I hope you are not going to get actively involved in this case." Justice clicked his pen and returned it to his inside pocket.

"What would give you that idea, Detective?" My voice rose too high. I could see the look in his eyes. He's not buying my innocent act. Rats!

"Because you're related to Verlene." He raised an eyebrow.

There he went with the Verlene thing again. If he kept that up, I was going to take a dislike to his sorry self. I put on my best indignant face. "I fail to see the resemblance."

"That's because you're in there, and I'm out here. My view is very different."

Okay, exit stage left. This act is done. I smiled. I hugged Verlene, turned on my heels, motioned to Fifi, and left.

I'm sure it was not lost on him that I didn't ever really answer his question. But it was for the best. I would have had to figure out a whopper of a lie on the fly, and I wasn't good at deception.

16

We drove back to the bookstore. When Fifi and I walked in, we were met by a group of blank stares. We explained the robbery, and Fifi announced we needed to get to the range or risk losing our time.

I looked around at the crew. "How are we getting there?" I hadn't owned a car since I moved back to Brooklyn. The subways were all too convenient for me to spend the extra bucks for personal transportation when I didn't stray far from the neighborhood. And I was really hoping that I didn't have to ride with Fifi "Andretti" again anytime soon.

"Greta's son Levi always takes us in the Seniors Center van." Fifi turned toward the front window. "He's here now. Let's bust a bustle."

I didn't want to bust anything. Sigh. In for a penny, in for a pound.

We piled in and, I must admit, they were quite a merry bunch. I watched as we turned down South Portland, and made a right on Atlantic. I felt like a foreigner as they jabbered on about new holster designs and laser scopes. Truly frightening to think about one of them out at night with a gun. Not so much for their personal safety, as for that of their prey.

The van turned left onto Hoyt, then took a sharp right onto Pacific and pulled up in front of the two-story brownstone. I'm not sure what I was expecting — maybe something more commercial, a country club–type setting, or even a landscaped lawn. But there was none of that. Just an ordinary building with an equally plain black-and-gold lettered sign filling the arch above the wide center door.

We filed inside and the rest of the group immediately abandoned Fifi and me, heading through the glass door at the back. Fifi walked me to the scoring desk where a guy with a dark crewcut sucking on a toothpick popped his head up over the waist-high counter.

"Hey, Fifi, you know those crazy old people are not supposed to be left alone back there."

Fifi raised a hand. "I just wanted to stop and add Sloane Templeton here to our group. She was coming in with her mother,

Camille Beckham, a few months ago."

"Can I have your membership card, please?" He extended a hand toward me. I fished it out of my pocket as he nervously looked in the direction of the glass door.

"Yeah, well don't leave them alone too long. You're their certified instructor and you know how much trouble they can get into. Ya know, I can't even schedule other people for your group's range time. People are afraid of them." The guy scribbled quickly on his forms.

I glanced around while he added me to the roster. This was one of the last "outings" I had with Mom. We sat on the Naugahyde couch and she helped me fill out the paperwork. They took my picture, and my check for dues, and I was made a member in good standing of the Fort Greene Rod and Gun Club. Then we came back several times for my lessons. It never occurred to me that I would be coming here, and she'd be gone.

I slid the card into my pocket as Fifi unlocked a wall locker and pulled out a gym bag. "The stuff you were using before was rental stuff. I guess it would be fitting if you use your mama's gear, sugah. I couldn't bring myself to get rid of it. Now I'm glad I didn't."

187

I followed Fifi through the glass door to the firing range.

Rapid-firing shots filled my head with brain-rocking explosions. The smell reminded me of old fireworks. Large fans set into several wall vents stirred the ambient air back to breathable, but the acrid mustiness from decades of gunpowder lingered in the walls.

Fifi opened the gym bag and handed me two lime green foam plugs that looked like suppositories. I looked at them, and then at her.

"Squish them and put them in your ears," she yelled over the explosions. She rolled them in her fingers to demonstrate how to narrow the tubes to slide them into my ears. She thrust a headset that looked like earmuffs at me. "Then put these on."

I dutifully inserted the plugs, wincing from the loud sounds ringing in my head, and pulled the headset over my ears, hearing blessed silence. Well, not quite, but it did go a great length in muffling the noise. Fifi did the same.

She thrust safety goggles at me and pointed at my eyes. "Put 'em on."

Sheesh, this was just like when I was a little kid and Mom dressed me up in a snowsuit to go outside. By the time I was dressed, I usually had to go to the bathroom. This time I didn't have to go. Praise the Lord for that favor.

"Roll down those sleeves and close your shirt up to your neck." Fifi yelled again as she led me to a firing station. It looked like one long counter running across the length of the room but it was divided into six sections by walls. From there to the targets, it looked to be about 50 feet.

"It's too hot to be all bundled up." I stepped back, which put me between her and the edge of the wall of Stavros Andropolis's lane.

"Sloane! No!" Fifi reached out to snatch me back behind my side of the wall, but it was too late.

Stavros squeezed off several rounds in rapid succession and hot brass casings flew in all directions. One of the hot shells skipped off his wall, onto the upper sleeve on my arm and slid toward the opening in my blouse. My hand flew up to brush it away. "Ouch!" The heat stung my little finger.

Fifi pointed at me. "That's why I told you to close up that shirt. And for goodness sake, stay in your own lane. That's what the walls are for."

Stavros turned to me and lifted his ear

cover. "I'm sorry. You should be covered better."

I quickly saw the error of my ways and buttoned up my blouse before I wound up doing the hot-brass-in-the-bra dance.

Fifi yelled over the constant discharges. "You need something to hold your hair back. It's going to stink from the gases in here. Don't you have a hat?"

I felt my pockets. Nothing usable. I just had my hair done, and now I'm going to smell like a fireworks factory. A great eau de cologne for Andreas. He'll feel like he's hugging a gun. I'd never even broached the subject with him. He's so sophisticated. He might not like me playing around with weapons. I probably should bring it up before I scared him with the stupid gun. I was beginning to wonder if all this was worth it.

Greta Feinstein watched us from her lane, the second down on my left. She laid her gun on the shelf in front of her and found an elastic band in her huge quilted bag for me to tie my hair back. She handed it to me, then held her other hand to the button for the electric target carrier.

I slipped the colored elastic around my large wad of micro braids and watched the paper target zip toward Greta with tight groupings of holes in the head and chest. The range was marked off in ten-foot increments. She had plugged that target from fifty feet away. Man, oh man, remind me never to mess with her in a dark alley.

Before I could protest messing up my do, Fifi reached in her bag of tricks, pulled out a ball cap, and jammed it on my head. Maybe I would end up resembling that little kid in the snowsuit after all. I looked around. Our posse looked like professionals. Hats, headsets, goggles. I had stepped into an alternate universe where the oldsters were as capable as Dead-Eye Dick and Annie Oakley, and I epitomized Barney Fife.

"Let me see your shooting stance." Fifi moved away from me and stuck her hands in her back pockets.

I gawked at her. "What does that mean?" I did a smarty-pants Dirty Harry stance and wiggled my backside. Fifi cut her eyes at me. I wanted to laugh, but she looked dead serious. Sheesh, she has no sense of humor about this *certified instructor* stuff. I must remember to behave or risk getting clocked.

"Watch." Fifi positioned her legs and feet. "You need to have good balance to absorb shock. What you're shooting now will have almost no recoil, but you need to get in the habit until you're better versed with various weapons." She rocked back and forth.

For the love of the saints! All I wanted to do was learn how to handle this one itty-bitty gun, and now she's signing me up for an entire armory.

Fifi snapped her fingers to get my attention. She demonstrated how I should hold my arms and the weapon. Then she raised my arms and put them in the right positions. I felt awkward, but not out of place. I matched her step for step and arm for arm. She made me repeat the movements a dozen times until I could do them without thinking first.

She raised the weapon to demonstrate how to line up the sight on the target. "Never jerk on the trigger, just squeeze slowly." She completed the movement and the weapon discharged. I jumped back. Fifi turned to look at me. "Sugah, you need to get over being so skittish."

"It-t startled me." I guess I didn't expect it to be so loud for something so small. I put my finger across my nostrils. I could smell an acrid mix of gun oil and fireworks. "It smells like that gun oil you have with that kit in the stockroom at the store."

"Because I cleaned it for you this morning. You said you had dropped it. I didn't know if it picked up any grit. I'll show you how to clean it yourself this week." She pressed on the conveyor button and the target zipped toward us.

She pulled me into the stall and handed me the gun. "Come, show me what you've got, girlfriend." She clipped a fresh paper target to the line and zipped it down the range. Hmm, maybe I need glasses. It looked so small that far away. I squinted at it. It wasn't blurry, just small.

"Does it need to be that far away?"

"Yes," Fifi chuckled. "The better you get at shooting something really tiny, the easier it will be to shoot something big." She looked very proud of that statement. It gave me pause. What world was I in?

I hesitated but stepped up to the opening, spread my legs slightly, and took bead on the target. I unstanced. "Do I need to say 'fore' or something before I shoot?"

Fifi doubled over laughing. "No, sugah, just shoot the target."

I restanced, proud of the two new words I'd created for my vocabulary. "Hey, I created new words for these positions —"

"Just shoot the gun." Fifi looked impatient.

I guess I had stalled as long as I was going to get away with. I restanced, looked at the target, raised my gun, closed my eyes, and squeezed off a single round. A tiny jerk in my hand, and then the smell of fireworks and a bare hint of the oil.

"How's that?"

Fifi squinted at the target. "I have no idea how you did that with your eyes closed, but you actually clipped the edge of the target."

"I hit it?" A smile spread across my face. Hey maybe this wasn't so bad after all.

"Yeah, but you have to keep your eyes open, sugah." Fifi shook her head at me. "You can't hit something you can't see."

"It's instinct. I don't want to see what I'm shooting."

"Sloane! It's a piece of paper."

"But it could be a real person someday."

"Think of it as Trey." Fifi smirked.

I watched Gus Grabowski in the next lane. He popped off a few rounds, putting a tight grouping right in the center of his target's chest.

Watching the force that was expelled with each shot gave me pause. "I don't know that I dislike him enough to shoot him." Yes, he's a Brooklyn bad boy but he's oh so handsome and sweet . . . when he wasn't using me as a punching bag.

"Then how about your ex-husband, ol' mister —"

"Don't you dare even say his name."

Storm clouds hovered over my head. I bet I was attracting lightning.

Fifi threw her head back and laughed. "Okay, we won't invoke his name. But you need to understand the importance of keeping your eyes on the prize."

Fifi continued to act the part of a mother hen and stuck right beside, guiding me in gun safety and shooting techniques. After the first hour and about a hundred cartridges, I graduated to be a pretty fair shot. Deaf, perhaps, but a pretty good shot.

Fifi tapped me on the shoulder. "Take a break. I need to run to the little girls' room. Be right back." She hurried off.

I glanced down the row and then to my right. Stavros stepped out of his lane and nodded at me as he held his finger to the button to retrieve his target.

Angelica Scarpetti strolled over. With her bun tight up under her hat and the jean jacket and pants she had changed into from her locker, you would have thought she was a man, if not for her ample, old-Italian-lady chest. "Hey, watch what I can do."

Quick as a flash she slid her fanny pack from back to front, unzipped the pouch, slid her .45 Long Colt from its pocket holster, and peppered Stavros's approaching target.

Stavros jumped out of the way. "You old

195

bat! You scared the daylights outta me!" The target reached the end of the track and stopped. "Look what you did to my target."

Fifi swung open the glass door and stormed in. "Hey! I've told you about those kind of shenanigans, Angie! That's not safe!" She scowled with a look that could turn weaker women to stone.

Angie grinned. "Yeah, and we were running with scissors when we were kids and still lived to tell about it." She waved Fifi off. "I've been shooting guns since before you were even a glimmer in your mama's eye." She put her weapon away. "I'm practicing my new quick draw." Angie had practically decapitated the paper man.

Poke me with a fork, I'm done.

I turned to Fifi. "I could use a slice of Red Velvet."

17

What a difference a day makes. Yesterday, I woke with visions of getting my hair done and ended the day blowing away paper targets with a bunch of old people that I had a new respect for. Before my eyes, they had transformed from doddering misfits into Rambo and the Rambettes. It pained me to even think about it, but then again everything pained me at the moment.

Gabi had done my head up nice and tight. And then, having that hat jammed down on it before the braids had a chance to relax overnight had given me a huge headache. Some of that I could attribute to the cacophony at the shooting range. A good eleven hours later, and my ears were still ringing. I almost missed the alarm at eight because I accidentally flicked the switch from music to alarm and the mechanical sound matched the tinnitus.

I padded into the bathroom and turned

on the shower to let the hot water steam up the room. My head felt so tight that it hurt when I yawned. I grabbed up the Advil and a chug of water to wash down the pill and glanced in the mirror. I raised my eyebrows. Stabbing lasers of torture radiated from my forehead to the back of my skull. I had to admit the two-toned braids sure looked good, though. Now I knew why Bebe hired the Mick Jagger wannabe. His work was righteous. I looked smokin' good. I grinned. Pain ran up my face. A good hot shower would help.

I slid into the steamy stream and pulled the glass door shut. Hot water slid down over my head, soothing the sore nerve endings at the roots of my hair. I stood still and let the shower massager head pulsate its way into my aching brain.

Ten minutes later, I began to feel human again. The pain in my head subsided a bit. I was wrapped up in my fuzzy, terry cloth robe, which was great for drying off without effort, and strolled across the hall to my walk-in closet.

I opted for linen drawstring pants again, pale green and the matching gauzy shirt with a subtle geometric print and loose sleeves. It promised to be another 90-degree day, and few things irritated me more than tailor-fit clothes sweat-stuck to my body. My choice was a perfect outfit for comfort and for hiding the fact that I still couldn't get my jeans to button by about two inches. Sigh. I needed to lay off the Red Velvet cake.

I slipped into a pair of corded espadrilles. My stomach was growling. Ill-fitting jeans or not, I needed breakfast. I marched downstairs and pulled open the fridge for ingredients. I whipped up a two-egg omelet with sharp Cheddar cheese. Hey, I used an Egg Beaters egg for one of the eggs, so I was conserving cholesterol while staying low carb. Okay, so I was dying for cake. I microwaved three strips of bacon while the omelet was cooking, and seated myself at the counter to eat.

I stared at the coffeemaker. I still couldn't bring myself to use it alone in the morning. I looked down at my watch as I scarfed up the last of the bacon and eggs. Verlene was meeting me in about ten minutes.

I sat at my desk, sipping on my second tall cup of hazelnut and thinking I should call my lawyer about Templeton. I still couldn't bring myself to use his first name.

Verlene barged into the bookstore. The ex would have to wait.

"I'm sorry that I'm late, honey lamb, but

I had to go to Costco first thing." Verlene plopped her purse onto the counter and leaned against it.

Gulp. *Please, Lord, don't make me be a food taster again so soon. I'll be good today. . . . I promise.*

"I needed more chain locks for my doors." She looked proud of herself.

But I bit down on my tongue. Yes . . . I really bit my tongue. That was about the only physical exercise that kept my trap shut. I just rolled my eyes.

I motioned to Fifi that I was leaving, grabbed Verlene by the arm, and hustled her out the front door.

"Where are we going?" Verlene scurried to keep up with my long stride. Even with short legs, annoyance lengthened my determined stride to that of someone six feet tall.

"We're going to the beauty salon. One of them no-account working girls is the source of your theft. I'm sure of it." Thinking of those thugs scaring Verlene infuriated me all over again.

Verlene's sandals slapped against her heels as she tried to keep up. "But they all seemed so nice to me."

"Those kind of people are only nice when they want something you possess."

Her arms pumped air as she huffed behind

me. "What are *those* kind of people?"

"Users. Life-sucking leeches who will disrespect you as fast as they can speak." Okay, so at the moment I was thinking of Trey, probably not the greatest talking point. "You let me do the business when we get in there. We're looking for someone who acts guilty."

"What will guilty look like?" Verlene panted, looking ready to drop. It's a good thing the door was in front of us.

"I'll know it when I see it." I pushed through the front door of the beauty shop ready for bear.

Ellie Pembrook's head angled up from her book. "Hey, Sloane. Your do looks righteous. What's shakin'?"

I ignored the hair compliment. Both hands fisted on my hips. "My aunt Verlene was assaulted last night in her *own* home and her property was stolen."

Verlene touched my arm. "Honey, it wasn't that big a deal. I wasn't —"

"Yes you were! They robbed you at gunpoint." I snatched my arm from her grasp, and watched the faces around me for any indication of guilt.

"Verlene, I'm sorry," said Ellie. She looked genuinely concerned. "What did they steal?"

Verlene opened her mouth. I cut her off.

"The hoodlums jacked a valuable book." No face displayed instant guilt, which really messed with me. I expected it to be much easier to spot the miscreant.

"Valuable? How valuable?" Ellie put down her book.

"*Very* valuable. But only a bookstore would be able to pay that kind of money for it." Hopefully I was baiting a trap.

Marley Howard didn't acknowledge our presence, but Janelle Wilson looked up from her cell phone, smiled weakly, and shut the cover on the phone.

Marley glared at me, as though I had singled her out. She stood up. "Are you talking to me?" She jabbed a finger toward her chest.

"If the shoe fits . . ." I planted both feet.

Even in her five-inch spike heels, she reached my air space in less than three seconds flat. Standing nose to nose, I could smell the lingering scents of her indiscretions. She hadn't taken a shower yet this morning.

"Why you be gettin' all up in my grill about this old lady?" Her breath smelled like an ashtray.

I refused to give this kid the satisfaction of even blinking. But suddenly, a prickle ran up my nose. I turned my face into my

202

arm and sneezed. So much for looking tough. I put back on my game face.

"Let me give you an instant replay. I walked in the door and announced that my aunt was robbed. Exactly what part of that was directed at you?" I stared her down till she flinched. My hands were still planted on my hips.

Her expression remained defiant. My shock and awe was having the desired effect. She glanced around. Suddenly, it must have dawned on her that everyone was staring at her with their mouths open. Her face softened a touch. Gotcha Marley, m'girl!

"You just need to pump the brakes on all that negativity you bringin' up in here." She pointed a freshly lacquered nail in my direction.

I noticed out of the corner of my eye that Janelle Wilson had pulled her cell back out and began to text.

I shrugged and feigned innocence. "I just made a statement. You're the one who became all defensive about it. Besides, if you want to talk about anybody bringin' somethin' up in here, you need to back off your stank self. Funky fresh is not a cologne."

She lunged.

I backed out of her short reach in those heels.

The door burst open and two twenty-something thugs sauntered in. Both wore wife-beater t-shirts and homeboy low-slung jeans that showed the top of their boxers.

One, wearing a heavy, linked gold chain, slipped his arm around Marley's shoulder and whispered into her ear. She settled down. The one wearing a sideways ball cap with a blue panther on it faced off with me.

"Ain't you Trey Alexander's old lady?"

My shoulders straightened at the insult. "I'm *not* anybody's old lady."

He snickered as he looked me up and down, and rubbed his chin with three fingers.

Why, you disrespectful . . . Okay, that let me know that Marley is in on this too, because these two definitely knew what they were walking into.

Hold the phone! Duh, I just got whacked with my own clue stick! Even though Trey is a little hot with me right now . . . uhm let's say *a lot* hot . . . he would never allow anyone to harm or rob my aunt. These are not Fort Greene peeps. This is Trey's territory, and these two homeys aren't his.

"What are you doing over here? You're from Bed-Stuy." I figured I'd bait them to see if they're from Bedford-Stuyvesant. It's a straight shot from here if you travel up Fulton Street.

Mr. Mouth piped up. "You don't know —"

The homeboy hugging on Marley, shoved Mr. Mouth, and pointed his finger. "Keep your trap shut. Let's bounce." Gold chain jerked his head in the direction of the door, grabbed Janelle by the arm, and hauled her out of the shop. Marley reluctantly followed along, whining that she hadn't gotten her hair done yet, while the other two picked up their purses and scurried out behind.

I turned to Ellie. "Where are those girls living?"

Ellie avoided my gaze, replanting her nose into the novel she was holding.

"Ellie?"

"Don't get me involved with them, Sloane. Please. Those chicks followed Tiny Tina here from Bed-Stuy when Bebe hired her." She raised her head with a pained expression on her face. "All I can tell you is, those dudes are dangerous. They all got guns, and most of those little hoodlums aren't even old enough to drink."

"That's what I was hoping for. They're young and dumb. They'll slip up." I prayed that I had planted the right clue and that

the girls were too self-absorbed to know that
I owned the local bookstore.

18

Verlene followed behind me. "Sloane, I don't understand what you called the clue."

"I let them know that the book was no good to them unless they sold it to a bookstore."

"I see," said Verlene. She touched my arm as we approached Beckham's. "But I still don't get it. What good did it do to tell them where they could sell it?"

God love the woman. She's my relative, but I hope I don't get that clueless when I reach her age.

"Remember your friend said they would alert all the bookstores with a BOLO."

Verlene pulled back her chin. "My friend? You mean Griffen Justice." She laughed. "He's the partner of my friend, Derby Weller. You know, you could do worse in men. Griffen is a nice guy."

"Ugh." Saints, give me strength. "I'm not in the market for a date. I have one. I can't believe how easily you get sidetracked. Your book, concentrate on getting your book back." I pushed open the door. Fifi was ringing up a purchase.

I sauntered behind the counter and sat at the desk, a big grin plastered on my face. I felt pretty proud. I had planted a course of action, one that would be their downfall if they followed through on it.

The customer took her bag and left. Fifi looked at Verlene leaning on the counter, then she turned and looked at me. "Okay. Why do you two look like the cats that swallowed the canary?"

"Because I just baited the hoodlums who stole Verlene's book to take it to a bookstore to cash in on its value." I leaned back and put my hands behind my head.

Fifi cut her eyes at me. In her best Desi Arnaz voice, she crowed, "Lucy-y-yy."

I snorted with laugher. "Well, chickypoo, you're the only redhead up in here, so I must be Ethel!"

"Sloane Amanda Templeton . . ." Fifi put on her adult face.

Good grief! She sounded like my mom.

". . . didn't Griffen Justice tell you to stay out of police business?" Fifi turned to Verlene who shrugged, raised upturned palms, and grimaced. I knew that look. She was staying right out of this.

I sat forward. "Hey, I didn't go looking for them. They found me at the beauty salon."

Fifi lowered her gaze. "Sloane!"

"Okay! So I went to the salon, but . . ." Gulp. I ran out of excuses.

Fifi reached under the counter for her purse. "Then I guess we should be prepared." She pulled out her .38 and slid it into her pocket. "Where's your gun?"

I opened my eyes wide. "Gun? What are you doing?"

"When you mow the grass, the snakes show up. If they come in here with the book, and you call them on it, what do you think those little hoods will do? Just leave it and say 'Sorry, just kidding'? No, they're gonna pop a cap in your backside, sugah. Where's your gun?"

"Uh, in the drawer . . . I think." So maybe I hadn't thought this plan *all* the way through. Her assessment slapped me back to reality. I pulled my gun from the drawer and showed her.

"Stick it in your pocket, and keep it there until this robbery is solved." Fifi pointed a finger. "You started this, but I hope I get to finish it."

"But I don't want to walk around with a gun —"

"Stick it in your pocket!"

I huffed a sigh and stuck the cold metal into my linen pants.

"I guess I'll leave you two to play Deputy Dawg. I'm going home where there are no guns." Verlene waved over her head and sailed out the door.

I glanced at Fifi. She glared at me. How did I get myself into these things?

I glanced up at the clock. It was almost noon. I reached for a couple more Advil and washed them down with my favorite carbonated black cherry–flavored water. I rested my chin in my upturned hand. Did I have fun last night? No. "I don't like guns." There. I said it out loud.

"But it's something that may save your life." Fifi turned from the stack of books she was pricing at the counter and nodded in the direction of the door.

I looked up in time to see Trey entering. Fifi snatched up the books and walked away. She couldn't stand to be in the same universe as Trey, let alone the same breathing space.

"Sloane, I want to talk to you." His presence took up most of the doorway. At one time I had viewed his large muscular presence as commanding, virile, and breathtak-

210

ing . . . in a good way. Now the only emotion he elicited from me equated to fear and loathing.

I tensed. Trey had that high-as-a-kite, evil look on his face.

Fifi stepped back behind the counter. "Well, she doesn't want to talk to you. Get out."

Her intervention surprised me.

Trey moved toward the counter and curled his top lip, exposing his teeth. "You need to mind your own business, you frizzy-headed white —"

"Is there a problem here?" Andreas Comino entered the store and removed his sunglasses.

This was the first time I had seen the two men in close proximity of each other. Andreas actually towered over Trey by a good three inches. My heart fluttered. I was safe.

I smiled sweetly at Andreas. "No. He was just leaving." I glared at Trey. "Weren't you?"

With his back to Andreas, Trey bared his top teeth. "I'll see *you* later," he hissed at me through his clenched teeth. He turned and brushed by Andreas, leaving nothing behind except the musky smell of his aftershave.

I wanted to jump in Andreas's arms but it would give him a better understanding of the Trey situation and he might go hunting for the jerk. I wanted to avoid more trouble at all costs. The drama needed to end.

Andreas sauntered around the counter and slid his arm around my waist, pulling me toward him. "Are you all right, woman?"

I melted into his grasp, careful to keep his hand away from the gun in my pocket. "Of course, I'm fine." I raised my head to look at him and he planted a kiss on my forehead. Thank you, Jesus. "Now that you're here."

"Oh gag me. You two are too much." Fifi vacated the counter area with a wave of her bangled arm.

Andreas motioned in the direction of Trey's retreat. "What was that all about?"

"Nothing to worry about." Change the subject. "What are you doing here at this time of day?"

Andreas smiled. "How about a day trip with me into Manhattan?"

"Manhattan? Driving in daytime traffic is going to be a bear."

"Look." Andreas gestured toward the front door.

I moved toward the front of the store and glanced out the section of window behind the counter. A white stretch limo sat double-parked in front of the store.

My mouth dropped open. "A limo? You rented a limo to go on a day trip? Why are you going into the city during the week?"

He pushed back the front of his open suit jacket and shoved his hand in his slacks pockets. "I have a meeting with a psychiatric panel later on this afternoon, and I thought we could spend the time together having a picnic lunch in Central Park."

He looked so commanding and masculine. I melted. "A picnic lunch? You have lunch in there?"

He winked. "Fruit, cheese, crackers . . ." He raised and lowered his eyebrows a couple times. ". . . and some of your favorite dessert."

"Red Velvet? You bought Red Velvet cake?" I groaned. "I'm yours." Diet be gone. Okay, so real soon I was going to become a thick madame. At the moment, I didn't care.

The jingle of the phone interrupted the seduction. I raised a finger to Andreas and lifted the receiver.

"Beckham's Books and Brew. How can I help you?" My eyes wandered to the limo outside the window. I almost missed the point of the conversation. "Excuse me?"

The man clipped off the words. "I said this is Dr. Lucius Barlow of the Beviard

Institute and I want to speak to the owner."

My posture shot to attention. "That would be me."

"I will be there in two hours to discuss the *Histoire de la Magie* that you have for sale." The phone returned to a dial tone.

I stared at it for a second. Bossy dude. Who does he think he is? Thinking reminded me of the Google search. Beviard was a very high-brow organization, big bucks, but very hush-hush, almost like they didn't exist. Everything I could glean about them intimated that they were almost some kind of secret society.

My spirits sank. I would have to be here to meet with him. Replacing the phone in its cradle, I could almost taste the smooth creamy goodness of the cake I was about to miss.

"I'm afraid the slice of Red Velvet is going to have to wait. I have an important client coming to talk to me about an expensive book."

Andreas frowned.

I cringed. I didn't want Andreas to feel rejected. I didn't mean to intentionally slight his offer of lunch. He was trying to be so sweet, and I'd just crushed him. I'd make it up to him this weekend with something real nice for dinner.

19

I stared at the computer screen. This antiquarian book stuff stymied me. It made no appreciable sense why people would pay big bucks for a moldy book that would disintegrate within the next generation, considering you could find anything you needed on the Internet in digital format.

I researched everything I could find about this strange book. Great. It was written in French. My command of the language had lapsed with the learning of several less than desirable phrases at the end of high school, so I couldn't even examine what all the fuss was about. And yikes, the book had 666 pages. An involuntary shiver moved up my back and across my scalp from back to front. Was that biblical number a precursor of evil things to come?

"So when is Dr. Barlow supposed to get here?"

I flinched and sucked in a halted breath.

My finger pressed down on the left mouse arrow and scrolled the cursor down the page. "Fifi! You scared me. He said in two hours, and that was two and a half hours ago."

I puffed out the breath and lowered my eyes to slits as I glared at Fifi leaning over my shoulder.

Fifi snapped her chewing gum. "Are you going to start an auction for this book like I suggested?"

I backtracked the key strokes to get to where I had been. "I've read mom's notes on it, and it's all as much Greek to me as the book is French. Why is it worth multiple thousands of dollars?"

"To start with, it's a first edition with marble quarter-cloth . . ."

Yawn. I willed my expression to remain blank. Who cared?

Fifi stared at me wide-eyed. ". . . and even the gilt lettering on the spine is pristine."

Another blank expression. The only thing that could make me more excited would be winning the Metamucil grand prize at the Seniors Center's Saturday Bingo Bonanza.

Fifi spread her hands apart. "Huge bucks . . ." She jerked up an eyebrow and grinned, rubbing her palms together.

I smiled at her apparent delectable ideas

of a windfall.

"Ack!" Fifi recoiled from my monitor.

I whipped around to face the screen and a gasp escaped my lips. Superimposed on a screen of undulating dark waves of water sat a large, bright yellow skull and cross-bones with the words *I WILL GET YOU!!!* stretched across the screen. I could feel the flush in my cheeks. At that moment I might have had a "carnal snap" if the perpetrator had been in front of me.

On the other side of the room, laughter erupted from a table of college kids as they hovered around the monitor on their table-top.

Those little brats! A hot flash shot to my face. My chest constricted with anger. I pushed back, sending the rolling chair into Fifi's legs and then into the counter.

Fifi winced. "Sloane, they're just kids. It's a prank."

I stormed the table like a charging bull. "I've had enough of you kids. Which one of you did this?" Hands on hips, I stared at the laughing faces and shouted through clenched teeth. "Answer me!"

Fifi followed in hot pursuit.

The three young men glanced back and forth among themselves and then at me. The anger ripping across my face changed their expressions from amusement to fear.

The young man wearing the Pratt Institute basketball jersey held up his hands in surrender. "Hey, lady, we didn't do that."

"Dude, er, uh . . . Ma'am. That's a system-level hack. We're not even logged in." The boy wearing the backward baseball cap pointed at the screen.

"Yeah, see?" The third kid wearing a black t-shirt and baggy jeans whacked the escape key on the keyboard. The login screen popped up. "It's either malware or a root-kit."

I glared at them with my eyes in the same slits I had just used on Fifi. "I originally thought that too, but I scanned the system yesterday and the day before when it happened. There were no infections. I have top-level IT security, and I haven't opened any attachments today for it to get by the firewall. So you're wrong!"

Fifi raised her right hand. The bangles slid down her arm as she wiggled her fingers and grimaced. "Uh, I . . . there was an e-mail this morning, and I thought it was from the bank, and I opened —"

"You didn't!" I raised my head and closed my eyes. Dear saints, give me strength.

"Yes, I opened the attachment. I'm sorry." Fifi chewed on her lip, and put her index finger up to her mouth. Her red lacquered fingernail disappeared between her teeth.

I shook my head and looked back at the guys. "Sorry, guys." I motioned to the coffee bar. "Go get a coffee. It's on me."

"Dude, thanks."

"Don't mention it." The boys scrambled to the bar to order drinks.

I glanced around the room to see who else might have been exposed to the prank. The other three people sitting at tables weren't on the computers, and Barbara had left before lunch and had not come back this afternoon. Thank the good Lord, because that image would have triggered a meltdown. I frowned at Fifi and marched her back to the desk.

Fifi looked like a contrite schoolgirl. "I'm sorry. I'm sorry."

No sense staying mad at her. She just didn't get it. The same way I didn't get the rare book thing. "One of these days, you'll get the hang of this. Let me see if I can isolate this bugger."

I found the original e-mail and copied it onto a CD. I had a friend with more equipment and a better knowledge of forensics than I do and could tell me where it came from. The pranks were getting on my last nerve. This one I was determined to hunt down, even if I had to get the police involved.

The bell on the door jangled. We turned from the computer to face a rotund man with a white handlebar mustache.

Good grief. I stifled a smile. He looked exactly like the picture of him on the site for his Sinai archaeological dig last summer. On first impression, he was a funny cross between rich Uncle Pennybags from the Monopoly game and Indiana Jones. He wore a straw fedora pinched into a "V" at the front and perched back on his head, with the brim bent down over his forehead like the movie character.

He let the monocle drop from his right eye. "Excuse me." He tapped the ivory and crystal handle of his walking cane against the counter. "Who is in charge of this establishment?"

Great. More "establishment" talk. The man appeared cultured and not at all like the ruffian the Web articles portrayed. "That would be me." I smiled and stood as I extended my hand.

Fifi zipped from behind the counter, fingered an "OK" sign with her forefinger and thumb as she passed behind the doctor's back, and strolled to the coffee bar.

Dr. Barlow glanced at my hand and

seemed to stare through me. He did not return the gesture.

Rude dude. I pulled my hand back. The muscle in my cheek twitched as I raised the corner of my mouth in a nervous grin and wiped my palm down my pant leg. Why did I do that? My hand wasn't dirty. "I'm the owner, Sloane Templeton."

"I am Dr. Lucius Barlow and I would like to know why my original query of the *Histoire de la Magie* was not honored."

The terse comment matched his stern expression. Deep lines etched his weathered face, testifying to long exposure to harsh outdoor weather. Either that, or it was just his meanness coming out.

I rested my arms on the counter. "I'm sorry." I laced my fingers together loosely, trying to appear calm. "Your query was taken as just that . . . a query." His brash tone was unnerving. I needed to bite my top lip to keep it from trembling. I willed it still. "No discussion of a purchase price has been initiated. In fact, you merely asked to examine the book."

Barlow whacked his cane against the counter and swore.

I jumped back a step and blinked but regained my composure. I glared at this new aggressive male in my life. Is there something in the water?

"I assumed I would be buying the book *after* I examined it." Barlow grated his teeth, causing the handlebar mustache to rock up and down on each side.

The image relieved my tension. I did well to restrain myself from laughing at the seesaw movement. "Well, Doctor, I think we all know what *assume* does for you." I pulled back and cleared my throat.

"Indeed, young lady."

"I'm sorry that you did not communicate your desire sufficiently. There are, of course, other interested parties. You can't really believe you're the only person to ask to examine an item of such repute." I put on my best business face. I got good at playing that part with the Feds when I was in the Cyber Crimes Unit. One little old professor would be child's play.

"So what does this mean? Are you telling me that I can't purchase this book?"

"The book is set to be auctioned after the examination phase."

His voice grew menacing. "And when, pray tell, does this travesty begin?"

I grabbed a business card from the holder on my desk, jotted the times on it, and held it out to Barlow. "There will be a Brinks Security team here with the book for inspection on Monday morning at nine sharp. The auction will be conducted after the inspection."

Lord, I hoped it didn't show that I had just decided that on the spur of the moment. But I didn't know what else to do. He was making me nervous.

Barlow snatched it from my hand. I flinched. If he was a kid, I might have whacked him already.

His cheeks reddened in contrast to the snow-white mustache as he stared down at the business card. He bent his head and his eyes disappeared under the protruding brim of his straw hat.

I plastered on my calm businesslike smile and locked my knees to keep my legs from trembling. Don't let him see you sweat. Breathe. "Please make sure that all funds are certified."

Barlow looked up at me and shot another glance at the card, crumpled it in his balled fist, and flicked it back on the counter. Why you . . .

I made a grab for it and missed as it bounced across the counter and dropped to the floor. I refused to pick it up with him staring at me.

"This is an outrage!" His voice rose. "I saw the book first."

He moved forward.

I backed up a step and moved my arms out of his reach, thankful that the counter was between us.

At the sound of his raised voice, the door slammed open, whacking the counter and shaking the storefront windows. Two burly men stormed in. I hadn't even noticed them outside the store.

"Is everything all right, Dr. Barlow?"

The first man filled the doorway with his six-foot frame, squared-off jaw, and crew cut. He glanced around as though he expected to find an assailant. I could clearly see a bulge in the left side of his suit jacket that spread taut over his muscular arms. The man was carrying a gun. Barlow silenced him with a look.

I placed my fingers on the handle of the gun drawer. Why did I do that? The stupid gun was still in my pocket. Did I really think I could pull a gun on somebody standing in front of me?

Fifi sidled across the store. "What's all the fuss about over here?"

Her sweet smile masked the dogged determination I had frequently seen her exhibit with ornery customers. Usually it was directed at rowdy college students and not gun-toting thugs. She stepped behind the counter next to me and rested a bangled arm on the counter as though creating a safety line between me and the doctor.

My heartbeat notched back down. I faced Fifi, trying to ignore Barlow's steel gaze.

"Dr. Barlow was expressing his displeasure with our auction on Monday." I was decidedly braver with backup.

Barlow shook with rage. "That book was mine! This is sheer incompetence."

The phone jingled, and Fifi broke her fierce gaze from the doctor and turned to answer it.

The other bodyguard, an apparent technonerd guy, stepped to the doctor's side and opened the lid of his netbook. His combed-back hair and black glasses created an air of competence as he fingered the touch screen, moved a page into position, and opened it to cover the ten-inch screen. He held it up to Barlow, which unfortunately turned it away from my line of vision.

Fifi finished the call and turned to face off with the doctor again, gently nudging me out of the way so that she could stand eye-to-eye with him. "Sugah, you'd better calm down before you bust a blood vessel."

At this point, I didn't mind the help at all.

Barlow reached for the cord holding his Mr. Peanut monocle and slid the corrective lens back into position over his right eye. He peered at the netbook screen.

He didn't even give Fifi the courtesy of looking at her as he spoke. "And who would you be?"

"I would be the older, wiser manager of this store. And I would suggest that you check your attitude at the door, darlin', if you want to conduct business in this establishment."

I opened my mouth to protest but reconsidered. Fifi knew this business better than I did. It was times like this that I wanted to sell the store and go back to my computer life. But the memory of Mom wouldn't release me.

Barlow's head turned from the netbook. A tiny smirk crossed his lips from one side to the other and disappeared as his head rose to come in line with Fifi's gaze.

The monocle, tethered by a black cord, dropped to his chest like a hooked fish. "Do you know to whom you are talking? I am the foremost archaeolog—"

"Yeah, yeah," Fifi waved a hand. "We know who you are, and that don't excuse your bad behavior."

Barlow gritted his teeth and glared back and forth between us.

Fear clutched my chest as I backed away

from the counter. Prickles of pain radiated across my heart in tiny starbursts. The look on his face. Memories of that look flooded my mind. I had seen that same raw vengeance on other men's faces. The emotion overwhelmed me. I wanted to run but my feet were rooted to the floor and Fifi blocked my exit from behind the counter.

I couldn't make my feet move closer. "Dr. Barlow, I apologize —"

The half-closed front door opened and the regular UPS guy strolled in carrying a rectangular box. His summer uniform of short pants always made me smile. This was no exception. Or maybe it was just nervous relief to see a friendly face in the middle of this storm. Thankful for the tension reliever, I moved to the counter to sign for the box.

"How's it going today, Ralph?" I scribbled my name on the electronic tablet with the stylus.

"It's a hot one out there, Sloane. I'll tell ya', in this heat I need air freshener in my truck. Everything smells."

My nose sniffed the air in front of me. The hint of a noxious rotting smell touched my nostrils. "Whew . . . it's clinging to everything, even the boxes of books."

Barlow's henchman reached to open the front door.

I assumed it was to get rid of the stench, but as soon as the door opened, Barlow turned on his heels and left.

I raised my hand. "Mister, uh . . . Professor —"

"*Doctor* Barlow will return on Monday for the inspection and auction. He hopes all will be satisfactorily resolved at that time." The gun-toting thug sneered as if to dismiss me and then sauntered out the door like a Mafia good fella.

Ralph smiled sheepishly "Ugh, I'm sorry for the smell. It's just that my truck has been overwhelmed by the heat today." He shrugged and left, trailing a cloud of decaying odor behind him.

I put a hand to my face and wrinkled my nose at the stench. I grabbed a box cutter to open our latest acquisitions. I gripped the box and turned it so that the seam was in the right direction for my opening stroke.

With that box around, it suddenly occurred to me that everything smelled like death.

20

Dr. Carlton Mabry muttered to himself as he crossed the college courtyard to his office. He ambled along the sand-colored cement of the quadrant, weaving in and out of the pockets of heat where the cement was not shaded by the overhanging trees. Heat. Cool. Heat. Cool. Sweat dribbled down his temples. He tugged on the bow tie attached to his shirt collar.

"Professor Mabry!"

He continued walking, appearing deep in thought.

"Professor Mabry!"

Mabry's head flashed up as he turned to face the voice. Reggie Hatland, his research assistant, lumbered across the quadrant, all two hundred pounds of him. Mabry held up a hand. "Stop running in this heat. You're going to have a heart attack. I've told you before, boy, you need to lose some weight."

Reggie ignored the comment and huffed, puffing out his cheeks as he staggered to a halt. "Professor . . . you need to see . . ." He bent over and put his hands on his knees to steady his breathing.

"For heaven's sake, how do you think you're going to join me on a dig if you can't even navigate the width of this courtyard?"

"That's why I was trying to find you." He inhaled deeply and pushed out the long breath, steadying himself. "Your second team in Egypt just reported in. They found the reliquary."

Mabry grinned broadly. "Outstanding." He'd beaten his brother to the punch on finding the first key of the cipher. "Now all we need to do is gain control of the book."

Reggie pushed up the right side of his mouth in a smirk, then winked. "I think I've created a solid plan to do just that." His cell phone rang. He fumbled with the folders in his hand and reached in his pocket to retrieve the phone.

"Hello, Professor Mabry's office. . . . yes. . . . one moment." He pushed the mute button and turned to Mabry. "Lucius wants to talk to you."

Mabry waved a hand to dismiss him and continued walking toward the building.

Reggie trotted behind him through the

lobby doors. "Professor, please! What should I tell him?" He held out the phone.

Mabry pushed out a sigh, snatched the phone from Reggie's hand, and jammed it against his ear. "What do you want, Barlow?"

Lucius Barlow laughed into the phone. "I guess I know that you're having issues with me trying to buy the book."

"How can you tell?" Mabry spit out the words as he marched into his office, dropped his briefcase on the desk, and lowered himself into the swivel desk chair.

"You called me Barlow. You always fall back on the discrepancy in our patriarchal lineage when you're annoyed with me."

"Well even though our mother was not monogamous, I'm still older, and it will always be that way." Mabry leaned back in his chair.

"That can be remedied."

"What! Like the *accident* to my work crew in the Sinai last year?"

"You know good and well that I had nothing to do with those deaths. You're just angry about that young wife of yours. How is she, by the way?"

Mabry sat up poker straight. "I'm no longer with her. I bet that makes you exceedingly happy. I couldn't trust her any

231

more than I can trust you, *brother.*"

"Listen to me. Blood is thicker than water. We need to come together on this."

"Come together?" Mabry spit out the words. "You mercenary! You cheat at every turn, and now that I've reached the book first, *now* you want us to come together?"

"Face it, Carlton. We need to close ranks. I just came from the bookstore. They know the true value of the book. The woman said there would be an auction. This means other interested parties may be involved."

"She said the same to me." Mabry slapped his hand on his desk. "How dare she insist on an auction for the book? I should have mentioned our involvement with her mother."

"No, it isn't the time to tip our hand. Neither of us alone can afford the book. But together, we can do this."

"And how can I be sure that you won't cheat me out of it?"

"There is enough unrevealed information in our recent dealings that either of us could send the other to prison for many years if there is any double-cross."

21

I pinched my nose to block the odor. Man, oh man, it smelled horrific. After this box disgorged its contents, it was going to take a quick trip out back to the recycle pile. I hoped the books hadn't picked up that wretched stench.

The box cutter followed the grooved flap line on the corrugated top, splitting the tape. Brown cardboard flaps eased apart. A putrid smell radiated from the box and slapped me in the face. "Phew!" My stomach lurched.

I closed my eyes for a moment as the rising stink had begun to make them water. But I needed to see what I was doing so I turned my head away from the container and scooped a pile of Styrofoam peanuts from the box and into the garbage bin. I lifted the final layer of corrugated stock keeping the books in place, then bent over and shoved the slice of cardboard down into the side of the garbage can.

Straightening up, I pushed open the flaps.

My eyes stretched open wide as my heart jumped into my throat and erupted into a scream.

It was a large, rotting rat. A long gash in its side was held open by a three-inch pen knife buried to the hilt in a broiling mass of maggots, with a note that said "Sloane, now it's your turn."

I stumbled back from the counter and my hands flew to cover my face. Bile rose up in my throat. My hip banged into the nearby chair, propelling it into the desk, where it bounced off and into the aisle like a bank shot on a pool table.

"Oh, my God, my God!" I wailed into my hands. "Jesus, help me!"

Fifi scrambled from the coffee bar, grabbed me by the arms, and tried to remove my hands from my face.

"Honey, what's the matter? Did you cut —" Her hands flew to her nose. "What is that rank smell?"

I pressed into the corner beside the desk, lowered my arm, and pointed at the box.

"What?" Fifi looked back and forth between the box and me. She touched my arm. "You're not hurt, though?"

I shook my head violently and continued to sob.

Fifi approached the box.

I could hear myself wailing, but I couldn't stop. Tears blurred and doubled the images of Fifi and the box. I didn't want that evil box to be a double anything.

Fifi looked back at me and then carefully opened the flaps of the box.

An audible gasp blew from her lips as the contents came into view.

Fifi released the flaps and gagged. "Oh, my Lord, save us from this evil." She turned to me. "Who would do something like this?"

Braids slapped the sides of my tear-covered face as I shook my head. I bent over, holding my middle, and slid to the floor in the corner. My insides clenched and convulsed like I was going to hurl. I hadn't eaten lunch. My stomach muscles just continued to wretch without disgorging any contents.

"I don't know." My head shook from side to side. "I don't know."

Fifi grabbed me by the hand and raised me to my feet. "Think, child! Who would do this to you? We need to call the police."

I gulped in air. It was still putrid and my stomach wretched again. I gagged. "No one hates me that much. No one except . . ."

235

My eyes grew wide with fear.

"Who?" Fifi grabbed my arm. "Tell me!"

I winced under the tight grip. Tears rolled down my cheeks, splashing onto my gauze top and soaking in as though they were never there. "Trey is the only person I know that cruel."

Fifi pushed the errant chair from her path. "That's it! I've had enough." She grabbed the phone from its dock and punched the buttons.

"Who are you calling?" My stomach subsided. I wiped my hands across my face.

"The police!"

I raised my head heavenward and closed my eyes. "This is just going to get worse. But it really doesn't seem like Trey's style." My head swum with thoughts. "I should just stop going out with Andreas. Trey will calm down. I know he will. And it would let this be over."

"Not on my tintype! That hooligan is going to pay for this." Fifi pursed her lips and paced with her cell.

I felt panic. This was only going to get worse. "Who are you calling?" Like I didn't know.

"The detective unit at the 88th."

With flaps closed, I dared to look back at the box. There were no labels or identifying

236

marks on the box other than the UPS information. Why hadn't I noticed that before? Because I'd just *assumed* it was books. Ironic. I had just used that word against Dr. Barlow.

I would never again look at a shipment of books with excitement. The contents of this box were etched indelibly on my brain.

I closed my eyes again. My whole life careened from bad to worse. But after today, what could worse possibly look like?

I sat at the coffee bar resting my head on my arms. Fifi had made me sit with my back to the box, like a child in timeout.

A knock sounded at the front door.

I raised my head and turned, my glance sweeping across the offending box. I stopped as an involuntary spasm clamped my stomach. I inhaled sharply to quell the desire to upchuck.

"I'll get it, sugah. You just sit still." Fifi strolled to the door. She passed by the box with her hand held to her nose while the other fanned the air.

I wanted the box gone from the building. Actually, I would have preferred it be moved to the next county, but Detective Justice instructed us not to touch it.

Someone felt compelled to try to terrify me. I wanted to act big, bad, and bold, but it felt like slapping at the wind. Who was my tormentor? I was beginning to understand that all these threats were aimed at me. They weren't stupid pranks. This was about real death. I struggled to wrap my brain around the concept that someone wanted me dead, like now.

Fifi closed the shop early, sent everyone packing, and stuck to me like the skin on a banana. For that, I was grateful. Andreas's cell phone went to voicemail whenever I tried to call him. The meeting must have gone longer than planned. Normally, I could have run upstairs to Mom or down the street to him for comfort. Even with Fifi present, I had an odd sense of isolation.

Fifi unlocked the front door for Detective Griffen Justice, who stepped inside followed by a CSU investigator carrying a large, black case.

How ironic. A week ago, I would have been thrilled to meet a New York CSU. Those shows on TV were my favorites, but this was the second time in two days that I was actually part of an investigation. It sure left something to be desired. I tamped down my gag reflex as the CSU investigator put on gloves and pulled a large plastic bag from a compartment in his case.

He handed Justice a probe. Mister Denzel

clone used it to part the flaps and look inside the box. His head jerked back and he covered his nose with the back of his hand as the look of revulsion zipped across his face and disappeared behind a detective-like controlled facade.

For a split second in time, it forced me to smile. What did he expect . . . Chanel No. 5? Ugh! I was filled with nervous energy. My snark always grew worse when I was scared. Good thing I wasn't speaking out loud.

Fifi led Detective Justice in my direction. Broad shoulders, confident stride, there was something familiar about him other than his movie-star looks. I breathed a long and satisfying, albeit, stinky breath of air for the first time in the last half hour. His presence calmed my jitters, and his black and red pin-striped suit with coordinating shirt and tie sure made him easy on the eyes. Fifi had tried to get me to go upstairs, but I wanted to know everything she was going to say to Justice. I was glad and sad that I stayed, all at the same time.

"We meet again. Have you been heeding my advice about your aunt's case? Or is this rodent some indication of your involvement?" He slipped a notebook from the inside breast pocket of his suit jacket and flipped open the cover.

"This doesn't have anything to do with Verlene's theft." I sort of dodged his question. I didn't want to tell him about the beauty salon incident. But I did know that this didn't look like Trey's handiwork. I just couldn't convince Fifi. "Will you please take that thing out of here?"

"Yes, of course we will. Have there been any other occurrences that you would consider threatening?"

I shook my head. "No. No. Absolutely nothing. This is insanely sick for anyone."

"What about the pop-up thingy on the computer or that shiftless good-for-nothing Trey?"

Justice looked from Fifi to me. "Ma'am?"

I waved my hand. "That stupid message on the computer wouldn't have anything to do with a rodent crawling with maggots." I glared at Fifi. "And Trey wouldn't do something like this." He would have just beat me to a pulp, not threatened it. I think. I hoped. My brain just didn't want to process any more of this. I didn't know what I meant anymore. I just wanted it all to stop.

"Why don't you let me be the judge of that, Ms. Templeton," Justice said, his tone somehow firm and gentle simultaneously. He scribbled in the notebook. "What kind of messages were on the computer? Can you show me an example?"

"I really think it's just a college prank." I hopped off the stool. This was a little too bizarre to think it was all connected. Trey's computer skills began and ended with PlayStation 3. "I deleted it but I did make a copy of the property code of the e-mail that downloaded it. I'll give you a co—"

I stopped mid-sentence, not wanting to be near the box o' death. Thankfully, the CSU investigator had packaged it in plastic and was slipping it into a brown paper sack.

I continued to the desk. The smell triggered another gag reflex. My stomach ached from the muscle clenches.

Fifi hurried behind me, and whispered loudly in my direction as I bent over the computer to burn another copy of the disc while trying to hold my breath. "Sugah, you may be right about the message, but there's no way on God's green earth that you're going to convince me that Trey didn't have a hand in this."

I leaned up to give her the look of "silence is golden."

She turned to Justice. "He's a vile and evil man. And he's been trying to strong-arm Sloane for breaking off their relationship." She wagged her finger, her bangles tinkling judgmentally as they slid down her arm. "Mind my word. As sure as grits can turn to glue, that man did this."

My brain slid into the abyss. She needed to shut up before she stirred up a real hornets' nest.

"Don't accuse him when you don't know. I'm getting a feeling that we need to leave him out of this." I grabbed the copied CD and released the breath I was holding as I hurried back to the coffee bar. I couldn't hide the fact that Fifi's declaration was making me shake more than the dead rat. What could she be thinking, talking about him like that? Discussing it among ourselves was one thing, but bringing the police into it was another whole heap of hurtin'.

Detective Justice eyed her. "What is this Trey's last name?"

I hesitated. My shoulders began to quiver.

Fifi pushed by me to Justice. "Alexander. His name is Trey Alexander. And he's the scum of the earth."

"Fifi . . . don't . . ." I pulled my lips in between my teeth and clamped down.

I cringed. Justice wrote down his name. This was not a good thing. Trey was unpredictable.

Justice poised his pen on the next line. "Where can I find this person of interest?"

"I'm not sure. He moves aroun—"

"He's right down the street, sitting on that same stupid stoop he's always on, around the corner from the market." Fifi looked proud of herself for knowing the answer.

I squeezed my eyes shut and dropped my shoulders. This could not end well.

Justice held up the CD. "I'll have forensics go over this." He slid it into his inside breast pocket. "And the person of interest will be interviewed."

"Is there anything new on Verlene's theft?"

"No, not yet, but we have sent notifications to all the New York City and borough bookstores to be on the lookout for anyone trying to sell the book." He shoved his hand in his pants pocket. "This is going to be a long shot if we get a hit and catch them trying to sell it."

I wanted to tell him that I had baited the thieves, but I was afraid that he wouldn't approve. Why that meant anything, I didn't know. I could feel the cool metal of my gun in my slacks pocket. I was sure glad that my loose top covered it. I didn't want to have to explain to a police officer why I was carrying concealed without a concealed permit.

"Please let us know if you hear anything." That was all I could muster. I was a terrible liar, so it was better to not say too much and give myself away.

Detective Justice drilled his gaze almost through to my soul. "What are you not telling me, Ms. Templeton?"

I shrugged. "Why would you ask that?"

"Because I happen to read faces with extreme accuracy."

I lowered my eyes. Auh breeze! Caught. Just trying to think up an excuse was making it worse. I sighed. "Okay . . . we sorta baited the thugs and their girls."

" 'We' did what?" Justice straightened. "Didn't I tell you to stay out of police business?"

"She was just trying to help," added Fifi.

"Did either of you stop to think that this could put you in danger? That this threat could very well be from them?"

Fifi and I stared at each other. No, I suppose we hadn't thought of that.

"But if the rat was from them, then the e-mails still weren't, because they started *before* the robbery."

"One case at a time." Justice pulled out his notebook again. "Names and locations. Talk. Now."

I guess those were my walking orders. I gave him all the names that I could remember. "I do know that they come from Bed-Stuy."

"That helps. We can focus on bookstores in that area, as well." He put away his trusty notebook. "Now, please, I beg you to stay out of this case. Please?"

"Yes." I lowered my head, while crossing my fingers behind my back. Juvenile yes, but it was the only thing I could think to do to ward off the lightning bolt of God for telling a big whopper.

Justice leaned on one leg. "You're lying."

" 'Bout what?"

"About staying out of my case."

I tried a miserable imitation of being coy. "I will really try, Detective."

Justice shook his head. "You're just like Verlene."

"How well do you know my aunt?"

"Her friendship with my partner affords me the opportunity to know that she's a real pistol."

I froze. My gun suddenly tapped on my leg. Or was that my leg tapping on the gun?

"I'll try and keep a tight rein on Sloane if you'll promise to keep us in the loop on any developments in the investigation," said Fifi.

Detective Justice raised an eyebrow. "You've got yourself a deal."

I smiled back. He's a pleasant man.

Fifi walked him to the front door while I slid forward on the stool. How could one

day turn so bad in the time it took to open
a box?

Fifi sauntered back to the coffee bar, grinning. "Now, there's a man that your momma
would approve of you dating."

"You are incorrigible." I shook my head.
"Besides, a man like that doesn't need me."

"Need you? I'm sorry, sugah, but from
what I've seen, all the men that you hook
up with use you. And since when is usin'
the same thing as needin'?"

I opened my mouth then clamped my jaw
shut in a frown. I wasn't quite sure how to
answer that. It was more of a feeling inside
than something I could vocalize.

"I know how Mom felt, but do you think
I'm wrong for going out with a white guy?"

Fifi wrapped her arm around my shoulder.
"Oh, sugah, she didn't care that you were
dating a white man. She didn't raise you to
see color in people."

"I know. That's what flipped me out. She
definitely didn't like Andreas."

Fifi hugged me. "She always said the eyes
are the window to a soul, and she told me
that Andreas's soul was black as coal."

"I just don't understand why."

"Well, neither did I, sugah."

"He was never anything but nice to her."

Fifi shook her head. "She never told me

her reasons. But know this, sugah. She didn't like Trey, either."

My eyes rolled so far back in my head that I could see hair roots. "She was right on that one."

"I'll tell you what. I'm sure that no-account had something to do with this mess, especially after this morning." Fifi sat onto the stool beside me.

I bit down on my lip again. It was getting raw from all this chewing. Though glad to change the subject from death, I was not particularly fond of talking about Trey. "The more I think about it, it just isn't his style. He'd rather get his kicks beating on me rather than killing a rat." Or was I doing a really good job of persuasion on myself?

"Y'know, sugah, me and your momma used to pray real hard to break this affliction over the women in your family."

I sat up straight, letting my hands drop into my lap. "What affliction?"

Fifi sat down beside me and rested her hand on top of mine. "The women in your family have always picked men that abuse them. Your grandma did, and your momma did. It broke her heart that you were falling into the same pit of despair."

I lowered my head. A shiver engulfed me. My hand slid up to my throat. For a split second, it felt like I was being choked. But the moment passed. "I knew Daddy was no prize and he and Mom did fight a lot, but she used to hold her own. I don't know that I'd call that abuse." I shook my head, not wanting the image of my father as an abuser to solidify in my brain. "I didn't know about Gram, and Grandpa died when I was nine. Neither Gram nor Mom ever talked about it."

Fifi's hand tensed in mine.

"Let's just say your grandma used to take your grandfather's abuse for the sake of his income from the railroad. Back in them days, there was a stigma attached to single women raising kids alone." Fifi's cheeks flushed, and her brow wrinkled as though there were a thousand pounds resting on her shoulders.

I sighed. "Gram died when I was a teen. All I remembered about her was she used to say 'Pennies make dollars. Pennies make dollars.' Did you know when she died there were two trunk loads of pennies that amounted to more than eleven hundred dollars?"

Fifi smiled softly and patted my hand. "That's a good memory to have, sugah. Remember the good stuff and let go of the bad."

Let go of the bad? I remember that saying from a childhood long gone. It soothed me. I shut my eyes and lay my head on my arms. Trey would go ballistic having police chase him down for questioning. I hoped Detective Justice didn't send a patrol car or catch him doing something illegal. I'd never hear the end of it. How was I going to explain this when he came to confront me? Lord, help me, please.

My stomach clenched.

Let go of the bad.

It was inevitable.

Let go of the bad.

He would come.

22

With a wide sweep of my arm, I sprayed a thick fog of air freshener high over the counter area. The cloud of droplets floated down, misting the surfaces. Sweet fragrance overpowered the stench but didn't eliminate it. I glanced at the label on the aerosol container . . . Spring Breeze, a mixture of hyacinth and orange. Great! My top lip turned up in a grimace and I sighed. Now the store smelled like hyacinth, orange, and a dash of dead rat.

"I will not be afraid." Yeah right . . . and I'm praying out loud to myself. Good going.

We had closed up shop for the day because of the putrid occasion, so Fifi helped clean up and went home an hour early. I was alone. Fear settled over me like an extension of the mist. My finger trembled on the nozzle.

"This is not my fault." I shot another

frenzied plume of spray, as though it would scrub the words from the air.

There would be a price to pay for this betrayal. Trey was going to be hot, and not in a good way.

"I didn't say your name." I sprayed another fragrant arch. "Fifi told on you."

The thick mist caught in my throat. I gagged, and collapsed into my chair, holding my hand over my nose to block the sharp offense.

It was stupid to rationalize. Counting on one hand, only two people comprised my short list of Those Capable of Perpetuating Such Violence: Trey and my former husband. The aforementioned Mr. Templeton was apparently a money-grubber, but he hadn't contacted me personally, and I really didn't believe that he'd be hacking rodents.

Car tires screeched a long, rubber scream.

I jumped.

"Get a grip, girlfriend. It was just a car."

I shook my head. Mom always said if you were talking to yourself, you must have money in the bank. I still had no clue what that meant, but for some reason it stuck in my head now.

Bang! Bang! Bang!

My eyes stretched wide as I turned in my chair to face the storefront.

"Sloane. Open this door!"

My mouth became a desert and my knees began to give. I looked directly into the wild-eyed expression of Trey.

Bang! Bang!

I flinched.

His pounding would break the glass in the door.

My chest heaved like a jackhammer. The extra oxygen made me dizzy. I opened my mouth to speak, but no words came out. Saliva had disappeared with the fear and my tongue stuck to the roof of my mouth.

My eyes darted between his anger-distorted face and the phone. If I tried to call for help, he'd break the glass in the door and snatch me before anyone could respond. Been there, done that.

"I see you, Sloane! Open this door or I'll kick it in!"

The gun. I had Mom's gun. *My* gun. Staring into his eyes, I rose and approached the counter.

Trey stopped banging on the door as he watched me move. His fists clenched and unclenched as he short-paced outside.

Even in the dead heat of summer, my fingers had turned icy cold. I reached into my pocket and wrapped my hand around the small handle of the gun. The metal, warmed from my body heat, soothed my cold fingers. I slid the weapon from my pants pocket. Just feeling the extra weight made me feel safer, not so alone. Maybe I was feeling Mom's presence, or better yet Jesus was standing beside me. Help me, Lord Jesus.

"Don't just stand there looking at me, woman. Open this door, now!" Trey drove his fist into the solid wood.

I slid the gun back into my pocket and released it.

The frame cracked. It wouldn't take much more before it splintered and he broke in. I gripped the counter for support, trying to steady my breathing. He's going to break it down. My head buzzed. Right about now, I could use a paper bag to get carbon dioxide into my blood. Yeah, sure. Hey, Trey, just hang out a second until I get my breath back.

A madman was about to break down my door and I was making a joke. Nerves had the better of me. I wasn't thinking clearly.

"You're making me madder."

Slowly, a single step at a time, I approached the door. Think. Beads of sweat gathered at the base of my skull and rolled in a tickling rivulet down the center of my back. No longer smelling the putrid rodent,

I stank from the sweat of my own fear. I reached for the door. My trembling fingers turned the deadbolt while my other hand unlocked the knob. Think. My brain screamed for help, but no one could hear.

The door flew open and slammed against the front edge of the counter. Trey roared through the opening like a speeding train. The door bounced shut behind him. I jumped back.

"What do you think you're doing to me?" He lunged for me.

I sidestepped him and spun out of his reach. He grabbed my top and whipped me to him like a yo-yo on a string.

"Trey," I pushed off from him, breaking his grip. "It wasn't me."

He snatched my braids. I screamed. He turned my face. We were nose to nose. His breath smelled like beer and pot. He was high. No reasoning with him. All I could hope for was to get away somehow.

He cracked me across the face with the back of his hand. Stars burst in front of my eyes. I screamed and fell sprawled in the counter opening. I clutched my jaw.

He stood over me and straddled my waist. "I know you sent those cops. Cops! You sent cops to question me and my homeboys. I oughta jack you up."

He balled a meaty fist.

"Trey, I swear, it was —" I stopped short. If I said Fifi's name, he'd hurt her too.

"Was what?" Spittle showered down on me and frothed in the corners of his mouth.

I started to cry. "It was a mistake. A stupid mistake." There had to be a way . . .

"No!" He stabbed a finger at me. "Going out with that Greek guy is a stupid mistake. This one is gonna cost you."

He snatched me by the hair and pulled me to my feet.

Think. There was no getting to the front door. My eyes focused on the door behind the counter. It opened onto the stairwell leading up to my and Mom's apartments. Panic. I hadn't been up those stairs since the night they brought Mom's body down on the gurney.

Breathe. Shaking fingers reached in my pocket. I whipped out the gun and held it out in front of me with both hands.

"Get away from me!" Tears streamed down my cheeks. My hands shook like a paint shaker.

Trey stared at me as though he couldn't quite understand what I was doing.

I took that moment of stoned confusion to back away from him. I retreated behind the counter.

He charged.

"Stay back or I'll shoot." But could I really pull the trigger?

Trey skidded to a stop at the edge of the counter. "You don't have the guts."

He advanced, wild-eyed, his face distorted by rage.

"I mean it, Trey. Another step and I'll shoot." I reached for the knob, pulled the door open. I could lock it from the other side, and maybe have enough time to get upstairs before he broke it down.

He ignored my plea and kept coming.

I closed my eyes, gripped the gun tight, and squeezed the trigger.

The air exploded. Trey howled. He lunged and slapped the gun from my hand.

The acrid smell of cordite stung my air freshener–assaulted nostrils.

I whirled to my left and sprinted through the doorway. Which way? Straight ahead to the locked outside door or up the stairs to my apartment? I sprinted up the stairs without closing the door. Third step up, my foot slipped off the edge of a tread. I slammed face first into the wood. Using hands and feet, I scrambled upward.

The vise-like grip of his hand claimed my right ankle. He yanked me down the steps. I screamed, twisting myself over. I kicked at the hand with my free foot. My flailing arms tried to stop my descent.

"Let go! Let me go!"

"You shot me. I'm gonna kill you!" He dragged me down the stairs calling me every name he could think of and then some.

The back of my head whacked on the treads. Sharp, stabbing pains shot through my hips as I slapped onto each descending step. "Please, Trey," I wailed. "Let me go. I won't tell. I won't."

I thumped down the last two stairs. He pulled me out the door and back into the store. In the bright fluorescent light, I could see a stream of blood oozing from the left arm of his white T-shirt where my shot had connected with flesh.

He pulled me by the foot. "I've had about as much of you as I can stand. You're done." He turned his back to me and continued dragging.

As he pulled me toward the storeroom, I knew I was going to die. My hands clawed the floor, trying to get a grip on anything. Under the edge of the desk, my fingers connected with the gun. A split-second decision seemed like it took five minutes. I had to shoot him or I was going to meet my mom.

I took aim at his other arm. This time I

didn't shut my eyes. A veil of calm slid over me. My hands steadied and I slowly squeezed the trigger. As though every frame were in slow motion, the percussion slapped my ears. A slight wisp of smoke curled out of the barrel. The round thunked into his shoulder. A small spray of blood shot out from the entrance wound. The red puddle expanded around the new hole in the other arm of his shirt.

Trey bellowed like a gored bull and let go, turning to face me.

I scrambled to my feet, planted them in a shooter's stance, and glared at him with the gun pointed in his direction. Calm.

"Get out of my store. Don't ever come back and I won't call the police on you."

"You shot me. Twice!" he screamed, barely able to raise the newly shot arm to the wound in the other shoulder.

Slowly my shoulders rolled back. I straightened my posture and stared at him. I took sight down the end of the short barrel as I raised my aim.

"If you come at me again, I will shoot you in the head. Get out of my store, and don't come back."

For what seemed like an eternity, we stared at each other. *Please, Lord, don't let him force me to shoot him again.*

Trey seemed to have a moment of clarity in his drug-and-liquor–induced fog. He turned and stumbled out the door, leaving it open.

I scrambled to the door, set the locks, and ran back behind the counter. My bottom lip quivered as I backed myself into the corner beside my desk and slid to the floor. I covered my face with my hands and wailed.

Overwhelming dread pounded in my ribcage.

This wasn't over.

23

Radiating sunshine and humid air followed Fifi inside Beckham's Books & Brew. Humming, she removed her key from the lock and reached to turn off the alarm panel. At that moment, she noticed the alarm was off and the store lights were already turned on.

"Hey, sugah, you're in early today. That's a new record," yelled Fifi over her shoulder as she flipped the window sign to OPEN. Her PhotoGray glasses cleared as they adjusted to the fluorescent light.

She turned toward the room. Two chairs at the front table were overturned. Her brow furrowed.

Fifi removed her glasses and set them, her purse, and keys on the counter. "Sugah, what's this mess all about? You get mad at the furniture or something?" Her voice echoed in the empty store. No one answered.

She put her hands on her hips and huffed.

"Sloane! Okay, you're starting to worry an old lady now. This ain't a nice thing to do to my ticker." The silence felt deafening.

She scanned the rest of the room. A trail of dark droplets on the polished hardwood floor caught her attention.

She reached down with trembling fingers, hesitated, then touched one of the spots. Her fingers came away clean. The circle, the size of a dime was dried. Fifi lifted her gaze and followed the trail until it disappeared behind the counter.

Fifi's legs seemed shaky as she rose and slowly reached for the counter. She peered over the surface.

Sloane was sitting on her haunches wedged between the desk and wall. Her head was down with arms resting on her knees.

Fifi hurried around the counter and dropped to her knees. "Sloane? What happened?"

No response.

Fifi put her hand on Sloane's arm and shook gently. "Sloane, sugah?"

No response. Fifi checked for a pulse. It was slow but steady. She shook Sloane again and still no response. Was this a coma, or was Sloane just unconscious?

Her gaze moved over Sloane's arms and

she pulled back so fast that she toppled off her knees and onto her bottom.

Camille's gun rested in Sloane's right hand, hanging limply over the edge of her knees.

Fifi's hands went to her mouth. "Sugah, sugah, what have you done?"

Somewhere in the muddy haze of my brain, I watched Fifi through the wall of braids covering my swollen eyelids. Every muscle in my face throbbed.

Just the touch of her fingers radiated pain up my arm. But I couldn't coordinate my functions to speak. My tongue stuck to the roof of my mouth. Was my nose broken?

In a controlled quiver, Fifi spoke. "Sugah . . . Please, tell me what happened. Talk to me."

I mumbled something that even I didn't understand what I meant.

"Honey, I can't understand you . . . Speak up."

Slowly, I lifted my head a few inches. The cascade of braids parted in the middle and fell back to expose my nose and part of my eyes. I cleared my throat, pried my tongue loose, and rolled it around in my mouth to spread what little saliva I could muster.

"I said . . . someone besides Trey is trying

to kill me." My words came out monotone. I saw without seeing. I felt dead. But I was breathing and Fifi was talking to me, so I knew that I must still be alive, or doing one great imitation.

Fifi pulled back her chin. "What in the world are you talking about? Why are —"

I flicked up my right hand signaling for silence. I grimaced. The pain of moving a body part was over the top. I leaned forward to rest my head against the hand. My forehead came in contact with the warm metal of the gun. I needed a moment to process the new ache.

Without looking up, my other hand searched the floor. My fingers came to rest on the plug for the monitor sitting on the desk. I inserted it back into the power strip beside me.

With eyes still downcast, my hand pointed up in the direction of the monitor. "Look."

Fifi craned her neck to look over the edge of the desk. I didn't need to look up to know what it said.

Searing yellow letters spread across the center of the black screen proclaimed *GET OUT OF TOWN OR DIE!!*

Fifi scrambled to her feet and stormed toward the computer.

"Leave it!"

"But, Sloane, that is horrible. It has to be some sicko prank."

"Ya think? And what do you suppose the dead rodent was, a birthday present?"

With small, deliberate movements, I raised my head to look at Fifi. I shut my eyes once or twice, wincing at the stiff tendon pulling in the back of my neck. The braids slid back to expose my whole face.

Fifi's eyes flew open wide and a sob caught in her throat. "Oh my Lord, child! I'll call 9-1-1."

"No! No more police or publicity."

For the first time in the last ten hours, I noticed the stiffness in my face when I opened my mouth. With my hair no longer blocking my sight, I realized the vision in my right eye was constricted and blurry. I carefully moved my fingers over the swollen and painful flesh.

"But . . . but . . . What happened?"

"Trey happened. He sorta became a self-fulfilling prophecy."

"Sugah, you're not making sense."

I squeezed my eyes closed. "Well, Trey *wasn't* trying to kill me until *after* we sent the police to question him about threatening to kill me."

"Is that why you're holding the gun?"

Fifi's hand went to her own throat and she sobbed.

I waved the hand with the gun as though they were a single welded unit and sighted down the top of the weapon at nothing in particular. "I shot him coming." I tried to wink but flinched at the pain in my jaw. "And then I shot him going."

Hands flew to Fifi's face. "Oh, Lord, help us! Is that his blood trail on the floor? Where is he? Sloane, what have you done?"

"It was only in the arms. The first time I closed my eyes 'cause I was scared to look at him and actually pull the trigger. So I guess he's lucky I didn't get him in the head. You know, you were right about that keeping-the-eyes-open thing."

Fifi reached out a shaking hand to touch my bruised face. "I can't believe one of the neighbors didn't call the police last night."

"There were only two shots. They were spaced a few minutes apart, and I wasn't screaming or anything. So even if someone did hear it, they couldn't have gotten a bead on where it was coming from."

"But we know just about every shop owner in this block!"

I shut my eyes. "And they're all old and can't hear. You can barely hear anything that goes on outside from in here. This building is old and layered in brick. What makes you think you can hear any better out there?"

I struggled to get up from the crouched position I had rested in for almost ten hours. I grunted. Muscles rebelled, denying me the ability to flex. My torso ached from bouncing down the stairs and each motion brought a fresh stab of pain. I thought I might have to go to the bathroom.

"I finally, *truly,* defended myself and, God help me, it felt good." Tears welled up in my eyes and splashed down my cheeks, hanging up on my swollen lip. "And you know what? If he hadn't left, I'd have shot him again." Yep! That I was sure of. I was cured of my fear. I could defend myself now.

I groaned and huffed out air as I stood, bracing myself on the desk, and forcing my knees to straighten. I laid the gun on the computer mouse pad. Every part of my body had an ache, a shooting pain, or stiffness.

I pounded my fist on the desk. Good, make something else hurt. "I will *not* be a victim anymore."

"Oh, sugah, where is he? Where's Trey?"

I shut my eyes and lowered my head. "He is probably with the stitcher he has over on Clermont."

"Stitcher? What's that?"

"That's the guy who sews them up when they get cut in a fight or shot. No hospital or police reports that way."

I forced myself upright. My back cracked in several spots as my spine realigned. I turned to face the door at the end of the counter, the one leading upstairs. My eyes squeezed shut, then popped open and stared. The pain and degradation of being pulled down the stairs by my feet flooded my senses.

Fifi followed my gaze to the open door. "Why is that door open? You haven't used those stairs since your momma died."

I lowered my head, speaking in a hushed whisper.

Fifi moved closer. "What?"

"I was trying to get away." I pulled myself up straight. "But I'm not running anymore."

I took a step toward the doorway. Stopped. My brain couldn't make my feet go up those stairs while I was thinking clearly.

My heart thumped hard. I turned away, moving to walk around the counter. I swore. My fist slammed onto the counter again. Another shooting pain radiated up to my elbow. "I can't take this! I can't go back to that. I'm a failure. How can he bear to look at me?"

I collapsed into the leather chair. The

force of my movement slid the back of the chair into the desk with a resounding thud. The bruised muscles in my body screamed for relief at being jarred.

Fifi rushed to me. "Who, sugah? Who can't bear to look at you?"

"Jesus."

Fifi pulled back. "How did Jesus get into this conversation?"

"You wouldn't understand."

"Try me. And granted I don't go as overboard as you do, but I do go to church on Christmas and Easter." She snorted with laughter. "If I went any more often than that, the ceiling would fall in." She put her hand to her chest. "Lawd o' mercy, God knows my heart."

I diverted my gaze from the floor to Fifi. I so wanted to give a snarky reply like "yeah, the Lord knows our hearts are continually evil," but I just didn't have the energy. Instead, I lowered my head again.

Sigh. "I'm supposed to be a Christian. I'm not supposed to be acting like this." I made a waving motion with my hand as a groan escaped my lips. "I mean, my goodness . . . I shot Trey."

"You were defending yourself."

"I could have killed him."

"It would serve him right."

I snapped my attention back to Fifi again. "Do you have any clue how long it has taken me to let go of that kind of attitude?" I shook my head. "I'm supposed to be a new creation in Christ, and here I am shooting people and declaring that I won't be a victim anymore. I sound like the hoodlums I can't stand."

Fifi screwed up her top lip. "What the . . . a new creation? Sugah, are you sure about the church you're going to? It sounds like a cult or something."

"Ugh, that just means that since I've accepted Jesus into my heart, I'm supposed to be a new person, and not act like the old me."

"I've known you since you were a little girl and the old you was just fine."

"No . . . no, I wasn't. I didn't need God. I didn't like God. And I didn't even trust God very much."

"Well, your ma was a good Christian woman."

"That only came after Dad died. Before that, she used religion like a weapon."

"I never saw that."

I gulped back the lump threatening to close my throat. "Daddy was one denomination, and Mom was another. Daddy didn't like her church and wanted me raised in

269

his. Mom refused and raised me in a whole different church altogether. And the best, or worst part, depending on how you look at it, is that neither one of them ever went to church with me."

"Well, good gravy! All I know is she went to church every week after your daddy died, all the way up to her passing."

"I know." My voice went small. "But by the time she straightened out with God, I was all messed up. It took a lot of praying, soul-searching, and help from the Lord to get me where I am today, and I don't want to slide back to the kind of person I was in those days."

"She was proud of you, girl."

I rose from the chair again, grimacing under the weight on sore muscles. I had to get out of here. Have a chance to think. Feel safe again. And go to the bathroom. "Call Brinks and have them get Broadview over here to wire this whole place for security. The store, my apartment upstairs," I pointed at the door, "and especially the outside door in that hall. Have them put control panels in here, out in that hall, and up in my apartment. I'm going to get a good soak in the tub and try to get cleaned up."

I snatched my keys from the desk and my cell phone from its dock, and turned to look

Fifi square in the eyes. "And don't you dare call the police again. They've caused me enough trouble for one lifetime."

"But sugah, maybe Griffen Justice could help."

"Yeah . . . help . . . Right! Help put me in my grave. Please. If you love me like you say you do, let this go. I'll handle it."

"How are you going to do that?"

"I don't know, but I will. I need time to think."

My nose prickled. I sneezed. My whole body screamed with pain. I shut my eyes and stood there, pulling it all back together. I needed all kinds of help.

24

I limped out the front door. My eyes
scanned up and down the street. Granted,
it was early morning, and usually Trey
would be sleeping off the previous night's
party, but last night was different. I could
never take anything about him for granted
again.

I didn't see him or any of his boys on the
street. *Thank you, Jesus.* I didn't fool
myself, though. The proverbial other shoe
would drop sooner or later.

Whether from sheer determination or
pure adrenaline, my body pushed the numb-
ness out of my joints, and straightened me
to an upright position as I walked around
the building. I didn't want to run into
anyone while walking like a mummy.

I climbed the stairs. The aches in my
posterior magnified with each muscle con-
traction as my legs moved me upward.
Okay, so maybe not all the kinks had left. I

concentrated on cleansing breaths to keep from crying out in pain. Going down the steps would be easier, or at least I hoped. Someday, I really needed to install an elevator. But it was the only exercise I had to ward off the Red Velvet hips.

By the time I reached the third-floor landing, beads of sweat coated my forehead. I dragged the back of my hand across the wetness, so I could see to use my key. I locked the door and leaned against it, releasing the breath I had unconsciously held. Safe.

My hand moved across the surface and contacted the swinging chain. I slid it into place. A twinge gripped my chest. That wouldn't be enough to keep Trey out. I needed deadbolts.

A shiver passed down my arm as I looked at the light coming through the narrow glass pane. Why hadn't I ever noticed that before? The front door to my apartment has the same glass panel. A body would never fit through it, but a hand? That's all it would take to unlock the door.

Panic pushed up from my legs and zipped up my torso.

Knock it off! I have figured out worse situations than this. Sure, they didn't include shooting anybody twice, and they never included multiple death threats. But I hadn't been as strong then as I was now, so I figured the ratio of trauma to tenacity worked out the same. I'm really smart, and extremely capable. I would learn to operate in this new environment and the Brinks guys would know how to handle the window. We all had our own areas of expertise.

The self-pep talk had the desired effect. My pulse dialed down to normal. I pushed off from the door and forced myself to trudge up one more flight of stairs to the sanctuary of my bathroom.

Nothing was more luxurious this side of heaven than a pampered soaking. Mom always thought the expense for top-of-the-line bathroom fixtures was frivolous. But I had the money at the time, which was another reason for me to lament giving up my job in the CC unit. It paid very large bucks.

I slid back the double-glass doors, and turned on the heat lamps over the tub. I dialed the settings for a hot bath. I watched the rushing water swirl a rapid circular pattern that pushed steam curls up to fog the walls.

Rapid circles. Just like my life. Rapid circles. Driven to fear by one violent man after another.

But this time I broke that pattern. I would

not be afraid. The corners of my mouth turned up, and the resulting pain that stabbed my face diverted my eyes from the water. I caught my reflection in the mirror before it was obliterated by the encroaching steam. Ugh! I looked terrible.

I rummaged through the medicine cabinet and found a bottle of Advil. I gulped down two of the brown caplets with a cupful of tap water and prayed the swelling would go away before anyone noticed.

I slipped from my clothes and slowly submerged myself in the blissfully hot water. Leaning back on the towel padded headrest, I engaged the hydro-massage system and aimed the jets at my back. Just as I began to relax in the soothing current, I noticed my cell phone sticking from my pants pocket on the floor. I leaned over and pulled the leg of the pants closer so I could grab it. I pushed the ON button. Two missed messages.

Both were from Andreas. He had called to tell me that he had returned from Manhattan late, he loved me, and goodnight. The second was to tell me that he realized he had a full schedule for today and I might not see him.

I breathed a sigh of relief. This could work to my advantage. I'd need to avoid him until my face started to look better, or I came up with a good excuse for looking this bad. If he found out about Trey, there might be a war.

I still had a would-be killer out there, and I wasn't going to figure this out sitting in this tub.

25

Andreas Comino flipped through the report in front of him, backed up a page, and jotted a note in the margin — *multiple prolonged doses produce psychotic episodes.* He tossed the blue folder back onto his desk. It landed on top of four other blue folders and skidded into his Beckham's Books & Brew coffee mug, sloshing the weak coffee his secretary had made onto the edge of the folder. If he hadn't needed to be in early, he could have stopped at Sloane's to get a decent cup.

He dabbed the liquid off with a tissue and turned to stare at a picture of him with his arm wrapped around Sloane's shoulder. He reached for the frame and traced his finger along the outline of Sloane's face. She was the pot of gold at the end of his rainbow. His face softened and the tension relaxed in his shoulders.

He glanced at the clock on the marble

mantle just as it chimed nine a.m.

His intercom buzzed.

He pushed the button. "Yes, Erin?"

"Doctor Comino, your nine o'clock is here."

"Erin, pick up the phone, please." He let go of the button and picked up the receiver.

"Yes, Doctor?" answered Erin.

"Are we sure who this is?"

"Yes, Doctor."

"Give me a minute and then show her in."

He replaced the receiver in its cradle, rose from his chair, and walked to a panel situated in a wall recess behind the front door. Opening the small painted metal door, he rotated the numbered disk to the digit ten. The timer began its soft audible tick. Comino shut the door, and strolled to the long expanse of floor-to-ceiling windows. He pulled the cord and closed the heavy burgundy drapes, then returned to his high-backed leather chair.

He shuffled through the blue folders once again, selecting the one with an orange paperclip hooked on the cover. He opened the cover, disengaged the clip, and slid several pages off to the left as he picked up his pen.

A soft tap sounded on the door.

Comino looked over the top of his reading glasses. "Come in."

The door opened, and a woman with frightened eyes poked her head around the door. "May I come in?"

He laid the pen down. "Yes, of course. How are you feeling today?" He sat back in his chair and swiveled toward her.

"I . . . I'm fine." With downcast eyes, and shoulders hunched, she wrung her hands.

"Come and sit down." He offered a slight smile.

She looked around the room with a halted gaze. "Where? Here or on the couch?"

"Wherever you like."

With small, quick steps, she crossed the thick carpeting to the couch and reached out to touch the burgundy brocade material. "This is lovely. When did the new living room furniture come?"

"This is not —" Comino clamped his lips shut and picked up the folder, along with his pen. "Why don't you sit on the couch today?"

The woman seated herself to the far right, her back against the arm.

Comino sat in the chair opposite that end. "Have you finished the medication I gave you?"

"Yes, and now that I am finished I want to come —"

"We have a new course of medication for you."

She frowned and blinked her eyes as though something was waving in front of her face.

He watched as she continued to wring her hands and cross and uncross her ankles.

Today she had dressed appropriately and her shoes were as shiny as the pennies in the tiny leather slots on the tongue of each shoe. Her hair was a bit askew, but understandable, given the way she kept fiddling with the tendrils around her face when she wasn't wringing her hands.

Suddenly the room went dark.

The small red security light glowed in response to the loss of power, flooding the room with scarlet light as though it were blood.

The woman screamed and slapped her hands to her eyes. "Light! There is no light! Agh . . . I'm afraid of the dark."

"Take your hands away from your face and you will be able to see," Comino spoke calmly in an even tone.

She looked out from behind her hands. "No, no, no . . . it's still too dark. The monsters will come. The monsters will come."

She jumped up and bolted for the door.

Comino pushed the button at the edge of his table panel.

An audible thunk echoed from the door.

The woman jerked on the knob. Nothing happened. She turned, throwing her back to the door as her breath came in short, jagged spurts. "Let me out! The monsters will get me."

Her voice lowered, turned raspy as her breathing became labored. "Open this door."

She pounded her fists on the heavy oaken door. "Monsters are in the dark."

Comino turned to face her but held his position. "You can see me. There is no need to be afraid."

She screeched like a wounded animal and pounded harder. "You're trying to kill me."

"Calm down. Breathe slowly. Concentrate on my voice." Comino pressed the second button on the small panel and shut the lid.

The lights came on in the room.

The woman slumped against the door. "The monsters want me. The monsters want me. Did you see them? They are in the dark. Did you see them?"

"No, I didn't see them this time, but I think we can help send them away." Comino pulled an amber vial of white capsules from his jacket pocket.

26

The digital wall clock over the sink mirror read 11:15 a.m. I'd spent a couple hours in the tub. Did I fall asleep, or was I just that zoned out?

I remembered several prolonged bouts of crying. Okay, so the waterworks weren't very satisfying because I was in water. Why do tears only feel good when they are falling on a linen or silk blouse? It must just be the drama.

The Niagara Falls imitation gave way to a couple ranting jags. When was I going to learn that yelling at God was about as fruitful as yelling at the wall clock? "Lord, I'm trying to understand your reasoning. But frankly, when I was bouncing down those stairs, the only thing I could think, was 'Lord, don't let him kill me.' " I thought a minute and grimaced. "I guess you did answer that one." Okay . . . one for you.

With the tub-heating thermostat set, it

had kept the water at a comfortably warm temperature to soothe out my kinks. The plan worked and, along with the Advil, I was beginning to feel human again. I sloshed myself upright. Water slurped over the side and onto the tile floor. I stared at the puddle as though it had done that just to tick me off.

"Lord, why Lord?" My hands slapped the surface of the water, splashing more onto the floor. "Why am I going through this with Trey?"

I looked up at the ceiling as though I suddenly developed x-ray vision and it would afford me a view of the heavenlies. Raising my neck made me wince. "Okay, so what am I supposed to do now? Sheesh, I can practically hear you clearing your throat and tapping your foot at me."

I'd come a long way since I returned home. I couldn't take all the credit. Mom took me to church a couple of times a week and read the Bible with me. Sigh. I missed those times. They had been few and far between these last few months without her. I felt like I was drifting back into my old self.

So how's that working for you?

I shook my head. Did I really just hear God say that? Was it out loud or in my head?

283

And then there was some self-admonishment thrown in for good measure. I was a certified candidate for a rubber room. I'm losing my mind, sitting in the tub, naked as a jaybird, having a conversation with the Lord, the God of the universe. Ugh! Get up and get dressed.

I looked at my hands, now achy prunes, and huffed out a puff of air. Expanding my cheek caused a wince, but the pain was dull. I stepped from the tub and wrapped myself in a fluffy cream-colored terry cloth robe.

I padded into the bedroom on fuzzy, quilted slippers. Every step led further and further away from the fog in my head.

High time to put on my big girl pants and take command of the situation. God, with your permission, please.

Why would anyone want me dead? What had I done?

And better still . . . how was I going to figure out who was responsible?

Fifi sauntered into the storeroom to pick up the last of her supplies. She had cleaned and reloaded Sloane's gun and safely placed it back in the drawer below the register. As she reentered the store with the gun-cleaning kit in hand, the bell jingled. She looked up to find Detective Griffen Justice approaching the counter.

She glanced down at the kit and, using a fluid continuation of her forward motion, shoved the kit under the counter between two small boxes and continued her stroll to the front.

"Well, Detective, what brings you here this early in the day?" She pasted on a demure Mona Lisa smile.

Justice looked down at his watch and frowned. "Officially, it's afternoon since it's almost one o'clock. But that makes no never mind because I came to return Miss Templeton's disk."

Fifi raised an eyebrow. "Have you investigat—"

I opened the front door to the bookstore and limped in wearing brown drawstring linen pants and a black and brown animal print caftan top. The looseness of the top hid the slight bend in my posture. I had let my braids flow free so they masked most of my facial swelling. I glanced up at the man standing at the counter with Fifi. Great! Griffen Justice. Just what I need right now. I pulled myself up to my full height before he turned around. Believe me, the popping noises in my spine were loud enough to scare birds.

I cut my eyes at Fifi and frowned. If that woman called the police again, I'm going to have some definite attitude. I glanced back and forth between the two of them and attempted to walk normally.

"Detective, what can we do for you today?" I glared at Fifi as I passed behind Justice and came behind the counter. He didn't have any muscles to speak of, but he sure was easy on the eyes. I guess detectives didn't get much time to go to the gym. Too busy chasing criminals who, ironically, spent most of their time in the gym building muscles.

"I'm afraid we've hit a brick wall with the e-mail sample you supplied." He extracted the disk from his inside suit pocket while staring at my face.

Could he see the swelling around my eye? I reached out with my right hand but pulled it back and carefully extended my left hand to accept the CD. Bruises covered the knuckles on the right that I didn't want him to see or question. "Did you find anything usable?"

"We do know that it didn't come from an account with the ISP that it was routed through. It used a sophisticated set of bounces that we are not able to follow with the equipment available to us." Justice continued to sweep his glance over my face.

I recognized that look and snapped my head down to flop the braids closer to my nose, hiding the bruise that I had attempted to camouflage with concealer. "Onion routing isn't so difficult to decipher."

Justice squinted. "Excuse me? Onion routing?" I broke his concentration on my face. Good.

I attempted a smile but spent more energy masking the painful pull to my face. "It's using cryptography in a multilayered manner to impede Internet traffic analysis."

He raised both hands and chuckled. "Okay, you've just gone over my head just like our tech did. I give."

Fifi tapped on the counter with her glossy fingernail. "But I see it on TV all the time. Crime scene investigators have all that high-tech equipment —"

"Not in the 88th. Our forensics lab is very small." Justice shook his head. "We don't have the money for manpower, let alone equipment. We'd have to send it to Manhattan for further analysis, but as backed up as they are, it could take months. And that's only if they wanted to spend the money on the investigation at all."

I nodded softly so as not to disturb my hair cover. "I understand. Our lab at NYU cost several million dollars, and we still didn't have the latest equipment."

"You can't repeat this," Justice leaned closer, "but if you can get me more tangible proof, I can put the muscle behind it to get it sent to Manhattan."

Even though his effort was useless at the moment, I felt better that he at least wanted to help. Or was he just trying to get a closer look at my face? "Thanks."

Fifi put her hands on her hips. "What about the rodent and the box? Did you check them for fingerprints?"

Had he just rolled his eyes?

Justice shook his head and jammed his hand in his slacks pocket. "Your rodent friend received an unceremonious burial in the Dumpster along with the box."

Fifi chimed in. "But that was evidence. All those shows on TV —"

"You can't fingerprint a rat." The detective cut Fifi's procedural perception off gently. "And the box was no help because everyone at UPS, and even you, had handled it. The label was investigated, but it was just a cash drop-off package at one of the services across town. The only thing we had that no one but the perp could have handled was the knife. And it didn't have any prints. So we've hit a dead end until something else happens. Sorry." He shrugged.

Fifi pulled back her chin. "What do you mean until something else happens?"

"Technically a couple e-mails are not a credible threat."

"But there were a lot of e-mails." Fifi turned to the computer. "Where did that one go from this morning?"

"It's gone. I deleted it." I glared at her. If she kept up like this, I might have to appeal to her compassion and ask her to just shoot me instead. Why does she keep pushing it when I tell her to let it go? Thankfully, neither of them seemed computer savvy enough to know I could retrieve it if I wanted to.

"Were there others that I didn't see?" Justice looked me square in the face.

"Most of them we deleted. Like you said, Detective, they aren't serious." I wasn't about to let him see the latest threat. Just in case it actually was from Trey. If they sought him out again . . . I suppressed a shudder. *Don't think about that. Not now.*

"And the dead rodent? *That* wasn't credible enough?" Fifi's eyes widened.

I dropped my head. *Let it go. Let it go. Let it go.*

Justice shook his head. "Nothing ties them

289

together."

"So you're saying she has to be attacked —"

I stomped on her foot.

"Ouch!" Fifi glared at me.

I raised a sore eyebrow. "Sorry. I didn't see where I was stepping."

Justice looked back and forth between the two of us.

"We will call you if we find any more evidence, Detective Justice. Thank you for coming." I tipped my head to obscure my swollen eye. I wanted to ask him about Verlene's case but I couldn't risk the extra time, what with him looking at me so intently.

He waved as he left. "Ladies, good day."

Fifi slapped the counter. "Sugah, did your brains fall out your ears when that no-account dragged you down the stairs?" Her eyes shot open so wide I could see the whites all the way around her eyeballs.

"Why? Because I wouldn't let you open your mouth about Trey? Or about me shooting him? I could get hauled in for that ya' know."

"So you're just gonna wait for him to come back and finish the job?"

"Don't go all melodramatic on me. He won't be back." Yeah, sure. That's why I was installing more security.

"At least you *hope* not. I've cleaned and reloaded your gun, just in case." Fifi gestured toward the drawer. "Now put it in your pocket."

I hesitated. Did I really want to go there? If I chose this path, it would ratchet up the stakes. My hand rested on the pull for the drawer. I slowly opened it. The gun lay there, taunting me. *I am your new best friend,* I heard it say. I slammed the drawer shut. The gun slid the length of the drawer, hitting the back with a thump.

Fifi touched my shoulder. "What's the matter?"

"I shot someone with a gun."

"Is there any other way to shoot them?" A smirk crossed Fifi's lips.

I snapped my head toward Fifi. "I could have killed him." I lowered my head. Sadness tugged at my heart. Was I becoming violent like him? Or am I just becoming brave enough to protect myself? Could I even be one without the other?

A tear splashed from my eye to my cheek. I scrubbed it away with the back of my hand. Pain shot though my face.

"Considering what you look like now, he should count himself lucky that you only popped two holes in him." Fifi acted almost happy.

I shook my head. "I don't think I could do that again. There was so much blood."

"You'll learn."

"Learn?" My eyes went wild. "I don't want to learn! I don't want to have to pick up a gun and shoot someone again. This is not the Wild West!"

"As we say down home, there comes a time . . ." Fifi tipped her head.

"A time for what? Violence? Violence begets violence." I ran my hand across my forehead.

"All I can say is that when you turn on the lights, the roaches run everywhere. Sugah, you've obviously done something to someone that is pushing all these buttons. You just need to figure out what it is."

I gestured to my face. "Let's not forget that this beating was caused by you siccing the police on Trey."

"I'm talking about this whole thing. The threats. The rat. Who would like to get rid of you?"

"My fan list seems to be growing every day. Let's see . . . Coltrane Realty wants me gone."

Fifi frowned. "Robby would not try to hurt you."

She and this Robby thing were beginning to bother me. He was way too young for her. It felt creepy. "Yeah, right. I wouldn't put it past him. Then, there's our two professors and that stupid book."

"Nah, what would they have to gain if you were gone?"

I shrugged. "I don't know. Maybe they think dealing with you would be easier." I laughed a little nervously. "And then, there's you."

Fifi dropped the papers she was picking up from the desk. "Me? Sloane. How could you say such a thing?"

"Because you've said more than once that I should go back to my computer job and sell you the store."

"But that was the deal between your momma and me, and you know it." Fifi looked over the top of her reading glasses. "You never wanted to be here when she was alive."

"I changed my mind." I really didn't want it, but I didn't want to leave the last of Mom either.

Fifi looked at me. Her eyes went downcast, and she leaned against the counter.

"Sugah, please put the gun back in your pocket. Remember, we have other hoodlums to be on the lookout for. I'm packin' mine."

She slapped her hip pocket.

I had already forgotten about the thugs we were possibly expecting to try to sell Verlene's book. Reluctantly, I opened the drawer and wrapped my hands around the cool metal, bringing it out into the open. It smelled of fresh gun oil and gleamed shiny bright. I stuck it in my pocket. The last time I had done this, it had saved my life. I guess I was going to have to learn to like it.

I slid onto the chair at the desk, pulling the keyboard over in front of me. I tapped a key. Nothing happened. I flicked the switch on the monitor. Still nothing.

"You told me not to touch it, and I couldn't let customers see that, so I pulled the plug." Fifi bent down and plugged the monitor in. The screen blinked on with the death threat.

I glanced around to see who was close enough to read the screen. Barbara was sitting in her regular spot on the other side of the room between the fiction section and the coffee bar.

I motioned toward Barbara. "How's she seem to be doing today?"

Fifi sighed. "You've just been beaten senseless and you're worried about that nutjob? Give it a rest, sugah. Worry about yourself for a change."

"I can take care of myself, and she can't."

Fifi stage whispered. "Don't look now but here comes your charity case."

Barbara approached the counter.

I whipped my head around, disturbing the braid facade.

Barbara gasped and gripped the counter. "My goodness, Sloane. Your face! I'm so sorry. Is he beating you too?"

My chest clenched and I started to sway forward in the chair. "W-What are you talking about?" There's no way this woman could know about Trey.

Fifi touched my arm to steady me.

Barbara stood staring and wide-eyed. "M-My husband . . . is he beating you too?"

Fifi and I expelled a collective sigh of relief.

"No, honey, your husband is not beating me." I brushed the braids back over my swollen eye. "Is someone hitting you?"

Barbara's eyes darted around. "No, I don't provoke him." She shook her head in small, jerky movements. "I want to be a good wife."

Fifi pushed past my chair and over to the counter.

"Barbara, can I help you with something? Sloane has work she needs to get done." Fifi turned and glared at me.

"I-I just wanted to use the computer. But it's not coming on."

I looked out into the room at the dark monitors.

Fifi reached behind me and clicked off the button on my monitor. "Have a seat at your table, sweet pea. They'll be running in a jiffy."

Barbara nodded her head and padded back to her table, scuffing her loafers on the hardwood.

Fifi gestured and shook her head. "The woman can't even pick up her feet when she walks."

I squinted, and looked at Fifi from the corner of my eye. "You need to be more compassionate with people in her condition, Fee. She ain't all there."

"Listen, sugah. Your momma and I ran this store right fine all these years, and we never had to adopt no vagabonds." Fifi waved an arm. "She hardly spends a penny here, and all she does is sit there all day. I'll tell you, if your ma was still alive —"

I felt a twinge in my chest. If one more person challenges my personal decisions, I'm going to blow a fuse. "My mom isn't still alive. And I'm the one in charge now."

"Need I remind you that this store was *our* dream? You never wanted anything to do with it or the book trade." Fifi put her hands to her hips.

"Well, I do now." That was the second time today that she'd said that. Was she just digging at me, or was there an underlying problem? If I'd had druthers, running a bookstore would not have been among my choices for a profession.

"That newfound interest wouldn't have anything to do with the boatload of cash that the book auction is going to bring, would it?"

"You think I want to keep the store for the money? The book wasn't even a consideration until just this week." Who was this woman? Fifi had never acted this way in all the years I'd known her. Mom always said money did strange things to people.

"So is that why you're stalling on selling the store to me? Before your momma died, you couldn't wait to get one of your computer jobs and get out of here." Fifi waved a hand at the computer. "That *thing* is what you like. You don't care about books. Unless they're ones that can make a lot of money."

I needed to end this conversation before I said something I'd regret. I turned back to the computer. "This conversation is over."

"I have dreams, too, you know."

I raised a hand and shook my head.

Fifi moved forward. "You need —"

"You need to get out of my face. Now! Leave me alone, please." I just couldn't take anymore of anybody or my head would blow off.

Fifi set her jaw and stomped off across the store.

I clicked on the monitor, sectioned off and locked the Administrator node, then booted the computers for the store.

I didn't like the thoughts running through my head. Fifi was not money grubbing. She would not threaten me or try to run me out of town just to get her hands on the store. Would she? I thought about it for a minute and then shook my head to clear away the thought. No, that was ridiculous. The enemy was playing tricks in my mind. Thinking that Fifi would hurt me was as absurd as thinking Andreas would hurt me.

"I'm sorry."

I tensed and swiveled around in the seat. With my heart pounding against sore ribs, my already fragile core was being pushed to the brink of anxiety.

Fifi stood at the counter, her shoulders sagging. "I'm sorry for upsetting you, sugah. I know you don't want the store for the money."

"I believe you. This has got us all crazy and disoriented." I chewed on my bottom lip. "I'm sorry I talked to you that way."

Fifi hurried to my side and wrapped her arms around my shoulders. "We'll figure this out, darlin'. It will be okay."

I wanted to flinch from the pain, but I didn't want to further damage our relationship by making her feel unwanted. I put my hands up to my face and sobbed.

It wasn't going to be okay. It just kept getting worse.

27

I winced at the stiffness in my joints and wondered if this was what being old felt like. Same pain, different game. The Advil was wearing off. I rummaged through the desk for more and downed a couple with a slug from my carbonated black cherry water. I shifted in the seat, trying to stretch my back as I waited for the Skype video call to be answered.

"Hey, Sloane! Speak to me, girlfriend. What it is?" The center of the screen filled with the smiling face of a thirty-year-old male of Chinese descent with shoulder-length black hair and heavy, black-rimmed glasses wearing a black Jimi Hendrix T-shirt. His given name was Jimmy Chen, but with his near-perfect ability of tracking a computer signal around the world, he had acquired the nickname in computer circles of Globe Trotter. To his close friends, it was Trotter for short.

I grinned back. "Hey, Trotter. How ya doin', dude? Long time no see."

He raised both hands. "Girlfriend, I'm still workin' it at NYU-Poly where you left me. How are you likin' the sticks?"

I laughed. "Brooklyn is not the sticks, bucko. And you'd be in Brooklyn to, if you hadn't been working on your doctorate at the Broad Street campus when they started the government program."

"R-O-F-L-O-L . . . That's true but Fort Greene is not Manhattan!"

"Yeah, whatever. You can roll on the floor and laugh out loud if you want to. Believe me I'd love nothing better than to be back in Manhattan, working in the Cyber Crimes lab. But after leaving Mr. Templeton, I needed a break."

"I hear ya. So, you keeping your skills up-to-date for a mega-comeback?"

"That, my friend, is the reason for my call. I've started getting e-mail death threats."

"Word!" Trotter leaned into the screen. "Who would dare try to hurt my warrior princess?"

"Don't know, dude." I shook my head. "I need your help. The real estate here doesn't have the juice to give me the four-one-one." I'd have given anything to be back in that lab, where I had him to mentor me through these kinds of processes. I had been the info guard dog while Trotter could run circles around any program made.

"I'm on it like white on rice. Whaddaya need me to do?"

"I have one of the hot e-mails on my machine. The police here aren't much help because they can't follow the bounces. Can you?" Sheesh. Already I had forgotten the routing steps to access the data. If I stayed in this book world much longer, my basic computer skills would be about as cutting edge as a rotary phone.

"BRB." Trotter flicked switches outside my field of vision, but I could hear them all the same. "Okay, back! Your wish is my command, O Warrior Princess. Wanna let me into your machine?"

"Sure. Hang on, and I'll create the link." I tapped out several commands. At least that hadn't eluded me. I would have been very embarrassed if I had had to ask him how. "I erased the e-mail attachment from my machine, but it's got to still be there some-where. There haven't been any more e-mails, but I'm still getting messages. Maybe it's a time release."

Trotter tapped for a few minutes. "Here's the lab scan."

Several charts appeared beside the Skype

screen. I watched the data scroll by and wondered how hard it would be to create my own IT setup, piecemeal, in my apartment office.

"To start with, it looks like you've got a rootkit on your machine. Very sweet."

"I wouldn't call this junk *sweet.*"

"*Au contraire,* but it is." Trotter was tapping keys like a woodpecker drilling a tree. "It even has a built-in back door. Yesterday's e-mail triggered the next-level message."

"A backdoor? How long has it been there?" I'd missed the signs. I hadn't been paying attention to the symptoms of the messages. Who would hack a bookstore? I was getting way rusty.

"Looks like a couple months. I'll clean it out when we're done here. Now for the route . . ." He continued the furious keystrokes. "OMG, girlfriend, whoever this person is really knows their way around cybercrime. I was thinking you had a script kiddie but this looks like a real black hat."

I rubbed my chin. "I had a bad feeling that it wasn't a kid just messin' 'round."

A few more keystrokes and his smile trailed off. He began his Slow and Serious Nod, like when a Zen master is bested by his student. "This, my warrior princess, classifies as a gen-u-ine cyberstalking."

"Why do you say that?" That didn't fit anyone I knew. But then again, I had been pretty sure that no one wanted to kill me, either.

"They're using Creeper to bounce the signal."

My chest tightened. "But that distribution system of relays is manned by volunteers all around the world. Ordinary people wouldn't know about it."

"Here, I'll give you the graphics too." Trotter tapped on his keyboard.

Several more charts popped up alongside the Skype video screen. The largest frame labeled *Hub* showed a flattened world map with a straight-lined signal bouncing to nine points in the United States, South America, England, Sicily, Australia, Indonesia, and three spots on the continent of Africa.

Trotter clicked out more taps on his keyboard. "Thing is, it's getting more and more popular. Bloggers, journalists, human rights workers, freedom fighters, and even ordinary people are using it now."

"So where's that leave us?"

"It leaves us . . ." He had lapsed into concentration on deciphering the signal. I knew that run-off pause well. "Hah! It leaves us with the *answer.*"

I sat forward.

"Whoa, girlfriend! The signal is coming from your own ISP." He tapped some more.

"There's a lot of real estate involved with my ISP. It covers most of Brooklyn."

More tapping from Trotter. "I'm on it like a rat on a Cheeto."

A shiver radiated from my core, causing my head to quiver. "Please don't say rat."

"Uh . . . okay." He click-click-clicked a wireless mouse, then blew out a breath. "All right, you have fifty-six zip codes, but only three area codes. Newer landlines are on nine-one-seven or three-four-seven. So the winner is . . ." Trotter drummed a measure on his keyboard. "Seven-one-eight area code! That includes your neighborhood."

A chill ran up my back and across the top of my head. The killer could be a neighbor. "Wait a minute. You said it's been there a couple of months. I haven't been running the store that long. My mom owned it a couple months ago."

"Is that right? So maybe this isn't about you personally. How is Miz Camille doing?"

An invisible fist squeezed my heart. "She's passed on."

28

I sat at the computer for another ten minutes, elbows on the desk, and head in my hands. I kept repeating, "Mom didn't have an enemy in the world," as though saying it enough times would bring a lightning bolt of an epiphany.

Why would someone want to hurt Mom? My hands trembled.

Mom, I need you to tell me what to do here.

Other than Fifi, the only person I trusted was Andreas. But if I told him about everything, what if he thought I had too much baggage and left me? Tears formed in the corners of my eyes.

A hand touched my shoulder. I jumped, nearly tipping the chair.

"Sorry, sugah." Fifi motioned behind me. "The men are here from Brinks to install the security system."

Fifi lowered her head to come in line with my face. "What's the matter? Are you having pain somewhere?"

"No, I just . . ." I looked up at the men standing behind Fifi and waved her off. "Get them started on the job, and I'll tell you later."

Fifi glanced at me again. "Are you sure?"

"Yeah, later. Tell them to give me control panels at the front and back doors to my apartment," I grabbed my keys from the tray on the desk and tossed them to Fifi. "And tell those guys to put captured-key dead bolts on the apartment doors, and a new lock on the outside door that goes up the front. They might as well put a new lock on the basement door too."

"Yes, ma'am," Fifi swiped the keys from the air and led the two men to the phone line access panel in the storeroom.

The bell jingled on the front door.

Rob Landry and another man entered. Tension radiated from the back of my neck, down through my arms, and snatched at the pit of my stomach. I closed my eyes for a second to collect my thoughts, grabbed a gulp of my water, and then rose from the seat.

"Miss Templeton . . . ?" Just hearing his voice set my teeth on edge, like fingernails on a chalkboard

I bit my lip. Remain civil. "Mr. Landry,

why have you graced my doorway today?"

"I came to acquaint you with the new associate who will be taking over —"

"Taking over what? Harassing me?" So much for civility.

Rob's face turned crimson and he lowered his eyes.

My new victim wore a black suit that, judging by the way it hung on his bony frame, I'd have guessed that at one time he was about fifty pounds heavier. He appeared to be fortyish, balding, with a beak-like nose, close-set beady eyes, and skinny lips. The perfect picture of a carrion-eating bird.

The new man moved in front of Rob. "I'm sure it is not necessary to have that tone with one of our procurement associates. He is only doing his job."

I almost called him Mr. Vulture, but managed to keep myself in check. I leaned forward with my fingers on the counter spot where Mom had worn a groove. "Excuse me, *you* are in *my* store, and if *you* don't care for *my* tone," I motioned with a hitch of my thumb, "there's the door."

"My name is David Bar—"

"I don't care what your name is. I'll tell you what I've told Mr. Landry repeatedly: *no!* I *do not* want to sell this building. I *will not* sell this building."

"Considering the monetary remuneration Coltrane Realty is offering, that is a foolhardy decision."

I bristled. Heat crept into my cheeks, and my voice rose. I was headed for an *Exorcist* movie moment. "What part of N-O do you *not* understand?"

Rob Landry touched the man's arm. "I've told you that Miss Templeton is adamant about retaining her property rights."

"No, playtime is over." Vulture man shook off Rob's touch and stared at me.

I pulled back at his aggressive posture.

"Let's face it, this is more money than most of you people will ever see. Quit stalling, and take it. Buy another building in a cheaper neighborhood."

"You people?" My voice rose an octave. "Oh no, you did *not* just say *you* people to me." I started around the counter. "This conversation is over."

The storeroom curtains parted and Fifi rushed out. "What in the world is going on out here? It's loud enough to raise the dead." She glanced at Landry. "What's going on, Robby?"

Landry turned in Fifi's direction. Relief washed over his face. "I'm afraid Ms. Templeton misunderstood my associate's intentions."

"I didn't misunderstand anything this cretin said." I stabbed a finger in vulture man's direction. "Get him out of my store. Or do I need to tattoo N-O on his forehead with my stapler?"

"No, ma'am, that will not be necessary." Landry touched the other man's arm again.

The man jerked from his grasp. "Listen . . . this project is considerably larger than your one little building, and this *will* end satisfactorily for Coltrane Realty. I was just trying to save you the time and heartache involved in litigation."

Fifi stormed to my side. I held out my hand to keep the red-hot redhead in check.

"You threatening me with court?"

Vulture smirked. "Since the state and federal government are involved in the neighborhood revitalization, this property can be claimed by eminent domain."

"Eminent domain was taken off the table at the Concerned Citizens meeting," I said. "We proved that the Historical Registry is interested in a lot of these buildings and the feds didn't want to get involved."

"There's a resolution to restore it."

My newfound bravery resisted the urge to slap his smirk into next week. "You seem to forget there is a neighborhood alliance against this urban renewal. We'll keep you

310

in court till I have grandchildren."

Vulture's smirk disappeared.

"Now. Get. Out. Of. My. Store."

Rob Landry touched the man's arm again. "Dave, I think we should leave."

Vulture brushed off Rob's hand and stormed out the door, leaving it open.

Rob had the decency to look chagrined. "I'm sorry, Ms. Templeton. You won't see me again. I've taken another assignment in the company. And I truly regret any agitation that I have caused you. It was not my intention." With that, he smiled at me, nodded at Fifi, and left.

I turned to Fifi. "Can you believe that? The jerk threatened me with litigation. I'm done being pushed around by them too."

Fifi grimaced and rubbed her forehead. She opened then closed her mouth with a sigh. "I hate to bring it up, sugah, but their court-talk reminded me about your ex-husband's lawsuit. Did you call the lawyer?"

"This is the last straw." I paced the length of the counter. The added adrenaline had overcome the stiffness in my joints. "You have to leave me alone about that. I've got enough problems at the moment to last a lifetime."

Fifi backed out of my way.

"Who do they think they are? All these

men, especially Templeton. Just because they're bigger and stronger, they think they can push me around."

"Uh, Sloane, I don't think —"

"That's the problem. Everybody thinks I'm a pushover. Well, no more!" With a violent sweep of my arm, I cleared the top of the desk. Pens, pencils, ordering spreadsheets, and folders full of paper rained to the floor as organized chaos. The momentary rage abated. I slumped to the chair, pounded a fist on the desk, and began to cry.

Fifi gingerly stepped over the paper carnage and wrapped her arms around my shoulders. "Sugah, what's the matter? I've never seen you like this."

I shook my head, sinking into her shoulder. "There's too many things in my head."

Fifi used her foot to push a path in the mess, pulled the chair over from the desk, and slid onto the seat in front of me. "What things?"

"My lack of a real career for one thing. I didn't realize how far behind I was getting until I talked to Trotter."

"That set you off like this?"

"No . . . there's Trey, Andreas, Mom dying, the building, Templeton, Verlene, Barbara, and now this." I gestured at the computer.

Fifi looked bewildered. "Am I missing something?"

"This computer thing isn't a random joke. It's some high-tech, serious stuff, and it's been going on for at least three months."

"Three months?" Fifi pulled back her chin. "So you're saying this was active when your momma was here."

I sniffed back the tears. "And now Mom's dead. You don't think there could be a connection do you? They said she died of a heart attack. Right?"

"I don't think this had anything to do with your mom, other than them trying to worry her to death."

I lifted my head. "You may have something. This Coltrane Realty thing started about three months ago. And that guy that came with your *Robby* today was certainly a piece o' work." I pointed toward the front door. "He . . . that was a real threat."

"Did your friend figure out who sent the e-mail?"

"Nah, he pinpointed it to this neighborhood, but that's as close as he could get."

"What about the e-mail address? You can't use that to find them?"

"They used a mask. That's why you

313

thought it was the bank. There's only a Gmail address behind that."

Fifi clapped her hands. "Well, then you have them, right?"

"No . . . it's not that easy. You don't need your real name to create an account."

"But, sugah, they track people down all the time on TV."

"Yeah, and that's the only place you would. You'd need a subpoena and a ton of evidence and a ton of time. I could walk to Google headquarters in California faster than they'd even *think* about telling us where that account originated."

Fifi glanced down at the floor as I talked. Her head shifted to the side to read the page lying under her feet. She bent over and picked up the page. "Uh, Sloane . . . did you read this?"

29

"No, I've been carrying it around for weeks but couldn't bring myself to go through it. It's like that will somehow make her more gone than she already is." My glance traveled across the mess of papers strewn on the floor with my focus coming to rest on the open green folder. I averted my eyes. It mocked me. It looked as though it had belched out the estate paperwork, just to spite me.

Fifi frowned as she read the page. "This page says that your mom wanted some guy named Bakari Ahmed to get a cut of the profits from selling *Histoire de la Magie.*"

My head snapped around. "What are you talking about? Who's bakery?"

"Baa-kari . . ." Fifi said it phonetically like a sheep sound. "I remember that name." She scanned the page and flipped it over. "That's the guy who talked Camille into going to Europe to buy the book. I thought she was nuts because she didn't even know him."

"That just doesn't sound like her." I reached down and swept the papers together into an unorganized heap, depositing the mess back on the desk.

"He was the son of a friend of your grandfather's or something like that. I tried to talk her out of it, sugah, but you know how your ma was when she had an idea in her head." Fifi held out the page. "This looks like contact information. He's the one who started this book thing, so maybe he knows something about those two professors."

I took the page and stared at the words. It was in Mom's handwriting. Her fluid graceful strokes of cursive always made me wish I had spent more time on my own penmanship. I had rationalized the deficit like most other computer people do . . . penmanship was an archaic, soon-to-be lost art. Now I regretted not spending more time at it. My chicken scratch looked like a doctor's bad writing.

The tips of my fingers touched the elegant lines, tracing each word as though it would magically draw Mom closer. "If Mom had this paper in the lawyer's hands, then you'd better believe she was serious about sharing the money. I'll call him, if for no other reason than to announce the sale."

Fifi frowned. "Where is he?"

"Cairo, Egypt."

"What time is it in that part of the world?"

I turned to the computer, clicked the mouse to open a browser window, and typed in the Google Search box, *Time difference between New York and Cairo, Egypt.* "Six hours ahead."

"So it's 2:30 p.m. here. That would make it —"

"8:30 p.m. there . . ." I already had the handset, dialing the international code and the number from the paper lying in front of me.

The phone rang, unanswered. Tinny computer tones echoed in my head. I was just about to disconnect.

"Hello." An anxious male voice filled my ear. "Madame Camille, I had misplaced your number. Thank Allah that you contacted me. There is great danger. You must —"

"Umm . . . this isn't Camille. I'm —"

"You are not? Why are you calling me from her store?" The voice went up an octave, displaying palpable fear.

"I'm Camille's daughter, Sloane Templeton. I'm sorry to say, but my mom is dead."

"No . . ." The groan seemed to emanate

317

from the center of the man's soul. "When? How?"

I shivered. Maybe it was the level of anguish in this total stranger or, more likely, that it mimicked my own, unexpressed sorrow. I didn't know if I'd be able to rein it back in once I let it out. "Mom passed away three months ago. It was a heart attack."

"Are you sure?" Ominous words, yet the melodic lilt of his Egyptian accent strangely soothed me.

I pulled back from the phone and stared at it.

Fifi made a face. "What's the matter?"

I waved her off, and put the receiver back to my ear. "What kind of question was that?"

"A very important one, Ms. Templeton. Many deaths have been attributed to the book. I have been in hiding because of just such a threat."

"My mom died of a heart attack." Speaking the words solidified the premise in my consciousness.

Concern rippled across Fifi's face. She sat forward and clutched at the receiver trying to get her ear near the phone to hear the other end of the conversation.

I tipped the receiver so we could both hear. "But if she hadn't, where would this threat have come from, and why?"

"Dr. Carlton Mabry and Dr. Lucius Barlow."

Fifi whacked me in the arm and pointed her finger while mouthing the words. "I told you so."

"If you don't mind me being blunt, how do you know my mom?"

"Your mother . . . a very lovely woman . . . was a friend of my father's. She helped him out of a difficult situation with an antique book four years ago, and on his deathbed, Father made me swear to pay back his debt to her. I happened to be privy to the location and renewed interest in *Histoire de la Magie* and, at the time, thought it would be an excellent way of repaying my father's debt. But I erred in my judgment, not realizing the danger involved."

"Are you telling me that leading my mom to buy a book ultimately worth twenty or thirty thousand dollars paid back a debt of your father's? What kind of debt was worth that much money?"

"Twenty or thirty thousand dollars?" Bakari Ahmed's voice ticked up another octave. "Ms. Templeton, your mother paid twenty thousand dollars to buy the book. *Histoire de la Magie* is easily worth one million dollars, if not more."

My jaw dropped and Fifi's eyes bugged as we stared at each other. We scrambled to get both our ears closer to the receiver.

"Come on. You're telling me that you turned my mom onto a book that was worth a million dollars? Why not keep it for yourself?"

"Because the deal that your mother saved for my father was also worth the same."

I stared at the surface of the desk. Processing that many zeroes drained my fragile mental resources, but I had Fifi as a witness. Those were his exact words . . . *one million dollars.* This wasn't a dream. What had Mom gotten into?

A clicking sounded in the receiver several times then stopped.

"Ms. Templeton? Are you still there?"

I inhaled and puffed out a deep breath of air. "Yes . . . I'm still here. How do Barlow and Mabry play into this situation?"

"I was the chief pit crew boss on their Giza dig last year."

"*Their dig?* As in *together?* I thought they were rivals." I rubbed my brow.

A rustling sounded in the receiver. I looked at Fifi. She shrugged her shoulders.

Loud voices. Indistinguishable words. A sharp crack. A scream.

The phone went dead.

"Bakari? Hello? Are you there?" Dead air space. I looked at the phone for a moment before clicking the off button and returning the receiver to its docking cradle.

"Where'd he go?" Fifi sat on the edge of the desk.

"I don't know. You heard exactly what I did."

"He said those two guys were on the same dig. If they're partners, what's going on here?"

I tapped the point of a pencil against the desk blotter so fast that the tip snapped off. "I want to know why he would question Mom's death."

30

When the phone rang again, Fifi and I scrambled to grab the receiver. I snatched it first. "Hello. Bakari?"

"Ms. Templeton." The weak voice whispered in a raspy tone. "There's not much time left. I have been shot."

I stiffened. "Shot! Where are the authorities? Are there police?"

A gasp, and then a moan. "No, help now. Please . . . listen." A gurgling sound. "They triangulated my cell phone to find me. . . . I have neutralized my assailant. . . . As long as you have the book in your possession, you are in danger."

"I'll call the police, or Interpol, or something. Where can they find you?" My eyes misted. This man was dying in my ear.

He ignored my plea. "You must *listen* to me!" *Gag, cough.* "There are three ciphers."

"Bakari, stop talking about the stupid book. Please, where are you?" I pushed back on the chair and paced. "Let me get you help."

His voice grew tired. "My time is done. My path is to my reward with Allah."

"Tell me who did this!" I screamed.

My glance darted around the store. Several customers looked up from their reading. And one stopped in mid-sip at the coffee bar, but Barbara continued typing at a furious pace, her eyes trained on her monitor. I motioned them that it was all right.

"A letter that will come to you from my successor."

"What? Why?"

"The . . . the secrets . . . the Sphinx and Orion . . ." He gurgled a wet cough.

"What? What are you talking about?"

A clunk.

"Bakari . . . Bakari?" No sounds. Just quiet, hollow airspace. "Bakari?"

I shoved the phone at Fifi, who fumbled to grab the receiver.

Fifi pulled the receiver to her ear. "The call hasn't disconnected. I hear labored breathing." She held out the phone to me. "Listen . . ."

I snatched the phone and pressed it to my ear. A cough . . . a moan. I shoved the phone into Fifi's hand and pulled the keyboard in front of me. A few clicks and the Skype call began to ring.

Trotter's grinning face flashed on the screen. "Helloooo, Warrior Princess. Greetings from the Big App—"

"Trotter, no time." I leaned into the monitor as though close proximity would telegraph the urgency. "My store landline is connected to a cell phone in Egypt. I need to know *where* in Egypt."

"LOL, girlfriend, are we chasing the brute that gave you that shiner?" He reached forward and touched the screen from his side as though he could connect with my black eye.

I consciously tilted my head to the left, flopping braids over my right eye. "This is an emergency, man, stop screwing around. There's a guy dying on the other end of my phone."

Trotter's face registered the emergency. He retracted his finger and expertly tapped out commands on his keyboard. "Does the store still have the same number?"

"Yes."

Trotter grinned. "Girlfriend, you don't have an iPhone." He clucked a scold. "You are falling behind the rest of the modern world. I knew letting you go back across the river was a mistake."

"Trotter, not now!"

He rolled his eyes. "I can find the phone within five feet of its location but to do anything about it you'll need the police."

I moaned. I hadn't thought of the next step. "You have the maps. Find a nearby police station."

Fifi grabbed my arm. "A police station? Don't you watch the news? You're talking about Egypt. That's going to be next to impossible."

I jerked away from her grasp. "What's wrong with you? A man is dying." I looked back at Trotter.

He flicked another piece of equipment on and chuckled. "My princess, the country of Egypt . . ." He reached out of sight and then came back. ". . . is not like small-town USA. You'll be lucky if you can get the police to answer the phone, let alone actually go on a wild goose chase caused by a hysterical American woman."

"I'm *not* hysterical." I glared at Fifi, then sat back. Maybe it did look that way. "What else can I do?"

"Okay, I'm triangulating. If the signal lasts, we may catch a break." He watched the screen intently. "What can you do? Hmm, good question . . ." His voice trailed off as he concentrated. "Interpol. You need Interpol." He cursed under his breath. "The signal is being overrun." He tweaked more settings.

Fifi touched my arm. "That's the International Police. Sloane, these are obviously dangerous people. What if they come after us?"

"They may have already done that." A shiver waved across my chest. I replayed the day I found Mom's still-warm body. My shoulders slumped. I leaned into the monitor again. "How do I call Interpol?"

"You don't." Fifi and I whirled from the computer to face the male voice. "I do."

Detective Griffen Justice approached the counter with his hands shoved in his pockets and a quizzical expression on his face. We were so involved that I didn't even hear the bell.

"Who said that?" asked Trotter.

I turned back to the screen. Trotter craned his head as though he could look around the corner.

"Hold on." I held up a hand and swung back to Justice. "What do you mean, you can get Interpol?"

His hands slid from his pockets as he moved around the counter to stand at my side. "I'm sorry that I eavesdropped on your conversation. I have contacts at the U.N. Now, why do you need Interpol?"

Fifi jumped up, propelling herself toward us. "Detective, please tell her not to get involved." She held out the quiet phone. "There's a man on the other end of this phone, in Egypt, who is probably dying because he's been shot."

A frown creased Justice's face. He accepted the phone and pushed the receiver to his ear. "Hello? Can anyone hear me?"

"I think he may be dead. He hasn't said anything for several minutes." I leaned over on the desk, resting my forehead on my hand, partly out of frustration, partially to keep my right eye from Justice. I watched Trotter working on the screen.

The bell on the front door jingled.

I glanced over my left shoulder and leaned back to look around Justice. My spirits sank further. *Andreas.*

He strolled through the sun-emblazoned doorway, casting an impressive silhouette of darkness.

Normally I would have been thrilled as all get-out to see him, but hiding my aches, pains, and black eye felt awfully labor intensive.

Andreas peeled off his sunglasses as he reached the counter. He glared at Detective Justice standing next to me, and moved around the counter to join the group. *Please don't let this turn into a testosterone battle of wills, Jesus.*

Justice shook his head and handed the phone back to Fifi. "I don't hear any movement. Give me a rundown of what's going on here." He glanced at Andreas, standing next to him. "I'm sorry, can I help you with something?"

Andreas lifted his chin.

Fifi laid the receiver on the desk beside me and moved to the other end of the counter to wait on a customer carrying an armload of books.

"Detective Justice, this is Dr. Andreas Comino." I tried not to expose the right half of my face. "Dr. Comino is . . ." Auh breeze! My brain vapor locked. What do I call him? ". . . my significant other."

Justice nodded.

Was that mouth twitch a frown?

Andreas returned the nod and stepped around Justice, approached my side, and began to massage my neck. I winced under the touch. Sore muscles screamed at the pressure. But I snickered at the obvious machismo display of Andreas marking his territory in front of the detective. My Greek had a little bit of a jealous streak going on. I'd never noticed that before. With a careful head movement, I smiled up at him and leaned into his hand, while inwardly the massaging fingers tortured my painful neck muscles.

"My mom's papers contained a legal document that gave a portion of the proceeds from the sale of a particular book to a gentleman in Egypt." I held out the paper to Justice and tried not to grimace from the pain radiating up my side and into my shoulder. "We were talking on the phone. He was attacked, and now I think he is dead."

"Holla!"

At Trotter's victory cry, I moved attention back to the screen. "Give it to me."

Trotter leaned into the screen and grinned. "Dude . . . it looks like it's gettin' kinda busy over there with you. Are you having a party without me?"

I didn't return the playful banter. "Not now, Trotter. The location please."

The smile melted from his face. "Sorry, warrior princess. The location is four-point-two miles southwest from the Cairo city limits. An access road dead-ends at a warehouse. Infrared imaging shows him in the northeast corner of the building. Here's the GPS coordinates."

A file scrolled in a pop-up on the left side of the screen.

"How do you have infrared capabilities?" Justice leaned down to the screen and jotted several notations from the short file.

"I just borrowed a feed from —"

"Five-oh, Trotter, five-oh." I scrunched up my face and raised my right hand in a cut-throat motion to my right where Justice couldn't see.

Trotter grinned broadly, exposing perfectly white teeth. "Girlfriend, you playin' with the po-po. Well, if that don't beat all."

I slapped my head into my hand. Great. On top of all the other problems, now pilfering government services could be added to the list.

Justice straightened up from the screen and nodded at me after making his last notation. "We'll talk about this later." A slight grin creased his face.

Something in his tone suggested maybe jail wasn't in the offing after all. I tried to read his body language as he exited from behind the counter. He flipped open his cell phone and turned his back to the assembled group.

I glanced up at Andreas, and did a double take. He was staring at me intently. His jaw set in a grimace. Okay, so maybe it wasn't jealousy, but that looked like it could be irritation.

The right side of his mouth slid up, dimpling his cheek. Was that a smirk? *No.* It had to be a smile. Right?

"You're awfully quiet, hon. Something wrong?" I lifted my chin to look into his eyes, still careful to keep my swollen eye from his view.

Andreas rubbed the back of my shoulder. "I had just hoped to get a little time with you alone. But that's all right. I'm content to watch and absorb."

31

"We're in luck." Justice turned back to the group as he snapped his cell shut. "There's a field team, less than five miles away, in Cairo. They have what you'd essentially consider an EMT team that can be deployed with the operation. They're on the way."

I let out a sigh. Maybe they would find Bakari alive, just unconscious.

"Hello, remember me?"

I swiveled toward the computer screen. "I'm sorry, Trotter. Help is on the way."

"Good . . . then I'm outta here before your po-po decides to . . . ," Trotter wiggled a finger toward Justice and whispered, ". . . ask me for ID."

The screen went blank.

I swiveled toward Fifi. The feisty redhead, uncharacteristically quiet, sat on the edge of the desk beside me.

"What's the matter? I'm not used to you not having anything to say."

332

"I missed most of the conversation waiting on a customer. But if I remember correctly the last thing I said was, 'Don't get involved.' I swanney! Sugah, you've disregarded *all* my advice so far. So what more is there to say? This can't lead to nothin' but more danger. This situation has more stink than a chitlin'." Fifi shrugged, and dropped her hands into her lap.

"More danger? What is she talking about?" Andreas swung my chair to face him.

I looked up at him, trying to think of a way to explain. In that instant, I realized he could see my right eye, and so could Justice. Auh breeze! Caught!

"Honey, what happened to your face?" Andreas cupped his hand under my chin and tilted it up for a better look.

My eyes darted between Andreas and Justice as I searched for an excuse.

"Books! We were adding inventory to one of the higher shelves, and wouldn't you know? It dislodged several big ol' moldy volumes and they hit her right in the face." Fifi said as she turned my chair, pulling my face from Andreas's grasp.

I breathed a sigh of relief at the perfect excuse. Why didn't I think of that? Jesus forgive me. I'm going to rot in hell for lying. I just can't tell the two of them about

333

Trey. "Yes, well, you know me! Just so clumsy sometimes. Fifi even warned me to be careful too."

"Yes sirree, Bob, this sweet li'l heifer never pays any attention to me." Fifi slid her arm around my shoulder and pulled me close, and away from Andreas's stony gaze.

I flinched at the pain in my shoulder but looked up at Justice. He glanced back and forth between me and Fifi. I had seen that look before on Mom's face. He's not buying a word. *Please don't ask any more questions,* I pleaded telepathically.

Justice cleared his throat. Apparently, he didn't accept incoming calls. Okay, then. Fine.

Change the subject.

"So tell me, Detective, what brings you here again?" My words trailed off. Auh breeze! Sheesh, me and my big mouth. Andreas hadn't known the police were here the first time. Until now, that is.

"Again?" Andreas slipped his hands under the flaps of his suit jacket and into his pockets.

If I started telling him everything, how could he see me as anything *but* a liability? Lie number two had just about finished brewing. I hoped Justice would play along. "Yes, the detective was here —"

The familiar prickle pulled at my nose. I sneezed into my arm. Good save. That got me out of the subject.

The front door opened and the two technicians from Brinks stepped into the store loaded down with their toolboxes and electronic equipment. The shorter of the two men set his toolbox on the floor and slid a coil of wire labeled Romex from his shoulder and onto the box. The taller and wider of the two approached the counter.

"All done, ma'am. The new system is installed. It's the same as in here, so I left you a refresher book on setting the codes. Here are two sets of keys for the new locks." He slid the key rings across the counter to Fifi.

"Thank you." Fifi plucked the keys from the counter and tossed them on the desk. Both slid toward the back edge of the smooth surface, tinkling as they tapped my mug and then the key tray.

"New locks and the police?" Andreas eyed the men in Brinks Security uniforms as they left. His gaze alternated between me and Justice. "Did you have a robbery or something?"

Aha! Relief washed over me as I rose from the chair. "I had an additional security system and locks installed upstairs today.

Just precautionary after Verlene's fiasco."

I needed Justice to take my cue and stick to that subject. I turned to him. "But I'm confident that this busy detective was about to tell us some new development in Verlene's robbery." *Please, please stick to the script.* "And thank you for getting us help in Egypt."

I hoped that the babbling would cover up my earlier gaffe, and that Justice was not here with any info on the rat.

He hesitated for a second then looked directly at me. "You're welcome." His eyes softened. What was that about? He continued. "I came to relay a development in your Aunt Verlene's case, like I promised."

Heavy sigh. Thank you, Lord.

Andreas moved forward. "What happened to Verlene?"

"You were in and out of here so fast yesterday, that I didn't get a chance to tell you. She was robbed at home, at gunpoint, the day before yesterday."

"Is she all right?"

"Yes, she's mostly just annoyed that she wasn't more careful with locking the front door." He was so sweet to care about Verlene! He barely knew her.

"Is that why you are changing your locks?" Andreas looked genuinely concerned.

No, not exactly, but . . . hmm. Did it count as a lie if you didn't actually say it? "I was nervous that my security was not up to par." That was a true statement.

Andreas put his hand on my shoulder. The pain in my neck muscle shot up through my head and I reflexively scrunched my neck, relieving my shoulder of his hand.

He stared. Great. Now he thinks I don't want him touching me.

Justice stared. There's an odd look on his face that I can't decipher.

Fifi stared. *Girlfriend, if you say a word to either of them we are going to throw down.*

I glanced at each of them in turn. "What? I want to sit down." I reached for the chair and slid onto it. "So what development do you have, Detective?"

"There were two hits in Bed-Stuy at local bookstores."

"So then you have them. Or at least you know who they are?"

"No, unfortunately, neither owner was interested in antique books so they didn't get their contact info." Justice pulled a folded sheet of paper from his inside breast pocket and unfolded it. "But both of them later received this flyer that the patrols were handing out, and that's why we got the calls."

I accepted the flyer and scanned the details. Somehow they had even come up with a pretty close facsimile picture of the book. "Yeah, I wouldn't expect them to be stupid enough to leave their names and numbers anyhow. I mostly just prayed for a takedown."

"Well, the flyers have been distributed in Bed-Stuy. All we can do is hope."

"But we didn't get any here in Fort Greene. Or at least I didn't."

Justice slid one hand into his pants pocket. "We started on their home turf first. We figured they'd be more comfortable trying to fence it that way. Besides, there are only two stores in the Greene that would buy antique books. I'm visiting them after I leave here."

"Then including me, that's three."

"Including you what?"

"I buy and sell antique books here."

Justice lowered his head and raised his eyes. "Very interesting. I wasn't aware of that. You stay out of this, and call me if there's even a hint of trouble."

He looked so serious that I couldn't resist. "Aye, aye, sir!" I signed off on "sir" with a quick salute.

Andreas drilled dagger looks into Justice. I felt the urge to explain . . . something . . .

anything. "Detective Justice is being so nice to us because he is the partner of Verlene's *friend*, Detective Derby Weller."

Andreas remained tight-lipped, not acknowledging the explanation.

Justice gave a flatlined smile to Andreas and nodded to me and Fifi. "I must be going. Please keep me informed." He started to walk away but turned back. "And please stay out of trouble. No more confronting criminals." He turned to the door and left.

Well, thanks for nothing, buddy. I could feel Andreas's eyes on me. Here it comes . . .

Andreas looked me. "Confronting criminals? What criminals?" He glanced at his watch.

I winced.

He didn't miss a beat. I could tell he was in a hurry. The watch thing always gave him away. If I could stall long enough, he'd go back to work.

"Sloane!"

I jumped. "Okay. We just happened to run into some women at the beauty salon."

He looked at his watch again.

"I had my hair done there. Hey, you haven't said anything about my new hairstyle. I think it's really chic and for my age I think that I carry it off well." Now that I thought of it I was sorta miffed that he hadn't commented on it yet.

"Listen, I'm late for an appointment."

I smiled. It had worked. Safe for now.

At the door, Andreas turned and pointed his finger at me. "I want a full accounting of this situation when I return. I'll be back in a couple hours, and you'd better be ready with the rest of the explanation." Andreas breezed out the door.

But hold up! Excuse me? What was all that "I want a full accounting or else" attitude about? I frowned. What had I become? A wayward child? Come to think of it, I wouldn't even let my own daddy, God rest his soul, speak to me like that. Why was life conspiring against me today?

32

Business was slow this week. It was hot with extreme humidity and everyone preferred the beach to staying in town. Even Barbara had left for the day. I wonder where she went because she usually acted as though this was her only place to go. I had never asked her again where she was living. I was afraid that the answer would be her car. I didn't want the responsibility once I knew she didn't have a home. Why did I always feel responsible for other people's welfare?

I absently glanced up as I thought.

Fifi stared at me, arms crossed.

Her rigid Gestapo stance caught my attention. "What?"

"I can't believe how you get away with this stuff." She shook her head and almost bent over laughing. "You double-talked both of them and I don't think either of them caught on."

I tipped my head. "I dunno. I think Justice

was on to me, but Andreas is pretty easy. He's always distracted by his practice." I chuckled. "If I didn't know better, sometimes I'd think he doesn't care!"

Fifi scrunched up her nose. For a blooming second I thought the rat had returned. "Yeah, right." Her face straightened. "You heard from Verlene today, sugah? She's usually 'round here long before now."

"Come to think of it, I haven't. I should check in, just in case she's worked her way into more trouble."

Fifi picked up a stack of books and headed toward the nonfiction section.

My chest tightened. I'd been so self-absorbed with my own problems that I hadn't even noticed her absence. I should have. Time had just gotten away from me. I reached for the phone and dialed with shaking hands.

One ring, two rings . . . where is she?

My throat started to close.

Three rings.

Verlene picked up on the fourth ring.

"Where have you been?" I was close to shouting. Well, okay, it was probably closer to the eighty decibels of a garbage disposal, but at least I was trying to remain calm.

There was a moment of silence.

Verlene cleared her throat. "Sloane, are

you all right, honey?"

"Of course, I'm all right. But I need to know that you're safe." It suddenly occurred to me that if she saw the condition of my face at this moment, there'd be a whole 'nother conversation going on and it would be *my* feet to the fire.

She chuckled. "I got robbed, honey, not beat up."

That hit a nerve.

"What are you doing today?" I was careful not to invite her over. It would take a few days to cover these bruises. Unless I was ready to lie some more. *God, I really need to repent to you. I know you have a lot to say about my behavior lately.*

"Honey, I'm creating a gourmet recipe for deep-frying a turkey."

"A turkey?" Good grief! That happens in one of those big cookers. Ack! "Verlene . . . is that why you bought all of that cooking oil?"

"Yes, my darlin', it is. Now I have to get back to the cooker. My oil is heating."

"Verlene, where do you have that cooker?" *Please don't let her say it's in the house.*

"It's in the backyard. Gotta run. Luv ya, honey."

"Verlene!" The phone disconnected.

I rested my chin in the palm of my upturned hand as I leaned on the desk. I need to go see what she's up to, but I can't go looking like this. I huffed and ran my hand across my forehead. She's going to burn down her house. And then I'm going to have her living with me. I know it, sure as shootin'. Ugh.

Fifi walked back to the desk.

Speaking of shooting . . . "How often do you go to that shooting range?"

"It costs money for every visit, so we only go there once a week. Why?"

I leaned back in the chair. "I was thinking that I need more practice."

Fifi smiled. "Well, I never thought I'd ever hear you say that, sugah. What brought about this change of heart?"

I shrugged, remembering last night. "I need to learn not to close my eyes."

Fifi burst out laughing. "I could say that should be a necessary requirement, but you didn't do too bad last night."

I put my hand up to my mouth, and closed my eyes. "I should be saying that I can't believe it has come to this, but I *do* believe it. The strangest part is that I feel . . . well, calm."

I had probably been knocked senseless last night. No brain, no pain. No sense, no feeling.

I slapped my pocket. "It doesn't even feel strange to have this gun with me. That should bother me, but it doesn't."

Fifi smirked.

The front bell jingled.

We both looked up at the same time. Two thug-types bebopped into the store, dressed in standard street attire. Homeboy jeans, slung so low that their jockey shorts stuck out the top by about five inches, and pure white wife-beater t-shirts. One wore a white nylon windbreaker and a sideways ball cap. It amazed me how such miscreants could wear white clothes and never have a spot on them. When I wore anything white, grime jumped on me as I walked by things like I was a dirt magnet.

The one wearing a sideways ball cap with a flat duckbill brim sidled up to the counter. "Yo, Mama, how's it shakin'?"

Fifi suppressed a snort of laughter and turned her back to the counter. She knew how I felt about disrespectful kids.

I narrowed both eyes into slits and rested my hands on the counter. "I am *not* your mama, and whatever I have shaking is none of your business." Please don't tell me that this little kid had seen my big Jell-O back-side walking down the street.

The other one smiled, displaying a gold-plated front tooth. "Chill. Dial it back, woman, before I feel the need to bounce."

I was just about to reach out and touch someone when he reached inside the windbreaker and pulled out a paper bag.

My hands came off the counter and I backed up, bumping into Fifi. She looked up at me, noticed my big eyes, and turned to face the counter.

"My uncle passed away this week and he left this to my moms, and she's lookin' to sell it." As he talked, he removed a package from the bag.

My heart began to pound. I recognized the wrapping. It was Verlene's book.

I watched his hands unwrap the package.

I glanced at Fifi. She raised an eyebrow. I did a slight nod. My heart thumped against my ribs so hard that I was sure these guys could hear it.

Lightning-fast thoughts raced through my mind. No time to call Justice. No time to call for an RMP. These two would be gone before a motor patrol made it here.

"So?" He glared defiantly. "Your sign says you buy books. Do you want to buy this book?"

I swallowed hard, full of indecision. "What are you asking for it?" I needed a stall, and time to think.

The two guys acted like they had hit pay dirt. Broad grins and fist bumps. Ball cap hitched himself up by the pants and rolled his shoulders as though he were a winning prizefighter.

"We heard that it's worth a lot of money," said Gold Tooth.

"Yeah, boo-coo bucks," crooned Ball Cap.

Gold tooth laid it on the counter in front of me. Neither of these kids were from Fort Greene. Or at least I didn't recognize them, and I knew most of the grown-ups in the neighborhood, and their kids, whether it was just by sight or an acquaintance.

They must hear my heart pounding. I constricted my ribcage trying to make my heart stop the drum roll. I looked at Fifi. She directed her glance down to my side and then back to my eyes. I understood.

I heard the imperceptible tinkle of Fifi's bracelet. Almost in unison, we pulled our guns, and aimed at the would-be felons. Both of them jumped back from the counter.

Fifi's presence bolstered my courage. My hands held steady on my weapon but my elbows were doing a rock 'n' roll. My lungs pushed out breath so hard I could feel the warmth on my upper lip.

Gold Tooth reached for his jean pocket.

His eyes held a glint of danger.

"Don't do it," said Fifi. "I'll blow your hand off, sugah."

His fingers flicked, but he didn't take his hand away. He lowered his head so that his deep-set eyes peered out from the cover of his eyebrows.

"I'll give you to three," she said, calm and collected as could be. From the corner of my eye, I saw her plant her feet.

I stanced, as well, and froze my face into a stern expression, mindful that my face hurt so intensely at the moment that even trying to smile would only produce an even nastier grimace.

His glance traded between the two of us. He stared into Fifi's eyes but still didn't move his hand. His left eyelid twitched.

"One . . . two . . . two and a half . . ."

He lowered his hand. I guess he believed her. I would have too."

The price of this book is probably going to be free, since you stole it," I said, feeling braver every second.

"Yo, we didn't steal nuttin'," said Gold Tooth. A bead of sweat formed on his upper lip below his nose. He sucked in and pushed out his lips a couple times.

"So then you just *borrowed* it to sell. Is that it, sugah?" Fifi glared.

"Yeah, that's how it was." Ball Cap grinned. His feet moved, but he wasn't going anywhere. Gold Tooth backhanded him across the chest with his fist.

I tensed. We had this tiger by the tail, but what were we to do with it now? This was *not* a well-thought-out plan.

Fifi slowly pulled the book out of their reach. Windbreaker guy tried to beat her to it but wound up with his nose only inches from the barrel of her .38. "Don't make me ventilate your face, sugah."

He backed up.

Suddenly they jerked and bolted for the door.

We let them go.

My mouth dropped open and I turned to Fifi. The words came out as a whisper. "Did we just do that?"

She nodded several times, her eyes wide with surprise.

"We really just did that?" I was bouncing from foot to foot and hyperventilating.

She nodded again and grinned.

I screamed and stomped my feet. "We really did that!"

I am woman! thoughts raced through my head.

Fifi wrapped her arms around me, one hand still clutching the book. We laughed until we cried. My tears washed away the sheer terror I had felt. We plopped into desk chairs and stared at the book in her hands.

Fifi raised her eyes, her voice raspy with surprise. "Don't that beat all? We just robbed the *thieves.*" She shook her head slowly. "Well, I never."

"Me either." I perked up. "Auh, breeze! We have to call Griffen Justice. He needs to know that they're in Fort Greene."

Fifi's voice rose an octave and she clucked her tongue. "They won't be in the Greene any longer than they can possibly manage. They may be clear over to Jersey by now."

We roared peals of laughter.

I slipped the gun into my pocket. It no longer felt foreign. It felt comfortable. Like a friend. "When that one character reached for his pocket I thought he was going for a gun."

"Those thugs were only wannabe gangsters. They didn't have any guns or they would have pulled them when we first drew down on them."

I looked at Fifi with a new level of respect. "How do you know that?"

"Me and your ma have been in the business long enough to know which thugs are packin' heat, and which we could just run outta here. That's why I pulled the book out of their reach. You saw the one with the Windbreaker try to grab it. That's when I was sure they didn't have weapons."

Fifi pushed out a sigh and a few more giggles before her face straightened. She looked down at the book in her hands. "I never saw the book before. Are we sure this is Verlene's book?"

"Of course it's Verlene's book. That's the same kind of cloth hers was wrapped in." A nervous laugh jumped from my chest. I pointed at the dark-brown leathery cloth still lying on the counter.

Fifi sat up straight. "Let me get this straight. We just pointed guns at two guys because the *wrapper* looked the same?"

"Well . . . I-I . . . it looks —"

"Sloane! Oh, my goodness gracious! Sugah, are you telling me that we just *robbed* those two guys at gunpoint?"

"Uhm . . . they ran."

"Well, sugah, we *did* have guns pointed at them."

My brain seized. I only saw the book once. What could I remember about it? The cloth. "I remember that *exact* cloth . . . I think."

"Oh, good googa-mooga." Fifi raised the book in her hands. "Tell me something, sugah. Anything."

"I wasn't concentrating on the book. I was

trying not to eat cat food."

"Cat food? What in the world?"

I raised a hand for silence. My life flashed before my eyes as I watched myself being hauled off to jail. My stomach growled. "Food!" I jumped up. "The secret recipe."

I snatched the book from Fifi. *Please God, let there be a secret recipe. Please. Please.* I ran my hand across the leather binding. It felt familiar. My suddenly cold fingers flipped through the pages. What page did Verlene say it was on? Seventy-five? I flipped there. Nothing about secret sauce.

My heart jumped up in my throat. "I don't see it."

The tic started to flick in the top of my cheek below my right eye.

"Give me that." Fifi slid the book onto her lap. Her fingers flipped back and forth between the pages. She gingerly slid a page to the right. Page seventy-one appeared and the handwritten recipe came into view.

The "Hallelujah Chorus" rang in my ears. It was Verlene's book! I wasn't going to jail . . . today, at least. "That's it! Thank you, Jesus."

I wrapped my arms around my braided head. I still had a ton of aches and sore spots, but in the last half hour, I really hadn't noticed any of them. Even my face seemed to be loosening up. Maybe it had something to do with the copious amounts of Advil I had been consuming today. At any rate, I felt a lot better.

"What are you thinking, sugah?" Fifi closed the book and ran her hand over the cover.

"I'm thinking that we need to get that in the floor safe *right now,* and get the security service to come and transfer it to the bank tomorrow."

"I'm on it!" Fifi rose from the chair and headed to the storeroom where the floor safe was hidden. "Are you going to call Detective Justice?"

"Yes . . . as soon as I figure out a plausible story that doesn't involve guns."

Fifi turned at the doorway. "Well, *that's* one that I'd like to hear. Don't forget, you need to call Verlene and tell her that we snatched her book back."

I jumped from the chair. "Great idea."

I snatched up the cordless phone and punched in her number. It rang several times. No answer. I looked down at what I had dialed. I might have keyed it wrong. Hmm, no, the number was right. The phone continued to ring, but the answering machine didn't pick up.

Fifi strolled into the room. "What's the

matter? You look worried."

"Verlene's not answering, and it's not going to her machine."

"Call her cell."

I disconnected, and punched in the number for her cell. "Right to voice mail. It's not turned on." I hung up and drummed my fingers on the counter.

"You're not thinking that she's in any trouble, are you?" Fifi stepped behind the counter.

"I don't know. We don't know if those were the guys who actually stole the book from her. They wouldn't go to her house would they?"

"No! It's broad daylight. They wouldn't be that stupid."

I was getting a bad feeling in my chest again, a sensation I was becoming very tuned into. Even if she were in the backyard, playing with a turkey, she would have her cell phone turned on. "Can I borrow your car? I need to go to Verlene's right now."

Fifi hesitated. "I-I don't think . . ."

I grabbed up my cell phone and keys. "What?"

"There's probably nothing wrong."

"Is this about me driving your car?"

"Well, I don't let anybody —"

"Fifi! This is Verlene." I held out my hand.

"I will not drive like you do. I promise. I just need to be sure she's all right. We have a few more hours till closing, so we can't both go, and I don't want to wait till closing for you to take me."

Fifi screwed up her face but reached in her purse and handed me the keys. "Be careful with my baby."

I tore out the front door.

33

I motored out of the store's parking lot, carefully obeying all the rules of the road that I could remember at the moment. I hadn't driven a car in about four years so Fifi's reluctance to let me borrow it was valid. She'd surely be face-pressed against the front window as I went by, so I resisted the urge to look in her direction. She might have tackled the car and accused me of taking my eyes off the road or something equally as sinister. As soon as I passed outside her field of vision, I floored it.

I had to admit, driving this little sports number was quite sweet. The leather seat molded to my shape, caressing my hips and supporting my back. Funny, I hadn't noticed all this luxury before, while we were careening around corners. I might have to think about getting a car of my own.

I entertained that thought for a good six seconds until I realized that a car would put me square in Verlene's sights. She would expect regular visits and those things called *dinners*. My fantasy of the little blue version of this same model evaporated as I pulled up in front of Verlene's.

Everything *looked* normal. Her car was parked in front of the house. No doors open wide. No shot-out windows. No miscreants hanging around. That alone brought a sigh of relief.

I mounted the steps and rang the bell.

And waited . . . and waited.

I pounded.

I yelled her name. As though she could actually hear me through that old-fashioned five-inch-thick door.

Okay, I must admit that nervous little flutter in the pit of my stomach had returned. I'd talked myself out of it on the way over here. I'd rationalized that nothing bad could happen with my courage pulled together so well. I even had the fallen books as an explanation for the discolored look of my face.

I fumbled for Verlene's key and inserted it in the lock. The door swung open to the usual refreshing coolness of her central air. Her house always smelled of honeysuckle and furniture polish like Mom's used to.

"Verlene! Are you here?"

I walked by the hall table and spied her keys, purse, and cell phone. She had to be here somewhere. Why wouldn't she answer me? I raised my voice again. "Verlene!"

I looked in the library and the living room, and headed for the kitchen. No luck.

A tiny yelp from the rear of the house . . .

Oh Lord, please don't let them be in here.

I pulled my weapon and charged down the hall that opened into the wide expanse of kitchen. I canvassed the room, my weapon trained in front of me.

"Verlene, where are you?" She didn't answer me.

I could make out her form through the sheer curtains on the French doors leading out to the patio. Her arms were raised and it looked like she was struggling with a shapeless form.

I charged through the French doors, my gun drawn, yelling as I went. "Let her go!"

Startled, Verlene swung around to face me with her arms outstretched. The movement pulled the metal rack she was holding out of the brining pot in front of her, dragging a liquid-dripping, untrussed turkey along with it. The bird's legs brushed across the open cookbook lying on the table, covered it in salty water, and pushed it into the tall kettle of hot frying oil sitting on a cooker, next to the table.

The kettle spewed a molten wave of oil bubbles.

Snap!

Crackle!

Pop!

Verlene jumped away from the spattering oil, lost her balance, and let go of the turkey, which jumped legs-first into the same pot as the cookbook, like it was doing a swan dive.

The sudden addition of the turkey disgorged another tidal wave of hot oil that crashed over the sides of the kettle and onto the grass. Verlene stumbled backward and landed on her backside fifteen feet from the pot of oil. Everywhere the oil went, violent flames followed. An angry wall of orange-red flame shot up ten feet in the air and consumed the turkey-frying kettle.

We both screamed. I shoved my gun into my pocket and ran around the inferno to Verlene.

I gripped her under the arms. "Are you all right?"

"I woulda been if you hadn't scared the stuffing out of me."

I dragged her further away. Flames now licked at the side of the young ash tree at the edge of her garden.

I started for the house. "Where's your fire extinguisher?"

"Inside the kitchen, next to the pantry door. Be sure to get the one for oil."

As I ran into the kitchen, I saw Tracie, staring out her sliding-glass door with a cell phone up to her ear. She smiled and waved. That was the oddest thing.

I grabbed the extinguisher and pulled the pin. A fire truck's siren screamed from the next block as the engine pulled out of the station and crossed Willoughby to come in between the buildings from the other end of the street.

I owned up to the fire marshal my role in causing this disaster. By the look on his face, he either thought I was lying or a chip off the old block in my new family role as the next generation of pyromaniacs. I wasn't quite sure which. I was relieved that they didn't issue Verlene another citation.

Verlene surveyed the damage as the last of the firemen grabbed up his turnout gear and departed. "Sloane, what were you thinking coming in here like gangbusters?"

"I'm sorry. I was scared when I couldn't reach you. I thought those thugs might be after you again."

I stared at the ash tree surrounded by a radiating plume of blackened foliage.

Charred plants covered the landscaping around the tree. The smell of burned wood perfumed the air. The poor thing looked a little worse for wear, but a couple more summers and you'd never know the tree did an imitation as a Roman candle one hot, summer afternoon.

Verlene gingerly righted the now-empty turkey fryer. "Why on earth would they return?"

I lowered my voice. "Because they came in my store to sell your book —"

"Yes!" Verlene pumped her fist.

I could feel my face getting warm. "I . . . we . . . me and Fifi held them up at gunpoint and took the book."

Verlene squealed. "You did *not!*"

"*Shh,* we did." I waved my hand. "Keep it down. We haven't even called Detective Justice yet. We wanted you to know first because I was afraid those miscreants might try to take it out on you."

"Now, don't that beat all . . . you give, you take away."

I pulled back my chin. My face smarted from the movement. "What are you talking about?"

Verlene gestured to the oil-logged cookbook lying on the burned grass. "You just made me French fry my personal cookbook.

But on the other hand you reclaimed my *valuable* cookbook."

I stared at the translucent pages of blurred ink. There was no saving it.

"Sloane, don't think this mess has distracted me." She looked at me real serious-like. "What happened to your face, honey?"

I turned to her and the falling book story rolled right to the end of my tongue and hung there like a Post-it note. I couldn't do it. Funny how I never noticed how much she looked like Mom. I could never lie to her either when it came to important stuff. The new confident me told the truth. At least to Verlene.

I lowered my head. "Trey beat me up."

"What!" Verlene started to rant something about geldings.

I grabbed her arm. "He won't bother me anymore. I shot him. Twice."

"Sloane, honey. What did the police do? Why aren't you at the station?"

"We didn't call the police. And I know Trey won't call them, either."

"Did you hurt him bad?"

"I don't think too bad. I hit him in both arms. He seemed to be walking okay when he left the store, and I haven't seen him since."

"You'd better keep that gun with you just

in case."

"I plan to, especially after we robbed your two robbers."

Verlene shook her head. "Look at you. You and Fifi have turned into regular Annie Oakleys."

I snorted a laugh. "More like Lucy and Ethel. But hey! Any port in a storm."

"Did you bring the book with you?" Verlene looked toward the house.

I laughed. "No, I didn't bring it. That puppy is in our store safe, and then it's going to the bank vault for safekeeping until we find you a buyer."

Verlene picked up the oily cookbook with a nearby oven mitt. "Yeah . . . I guess that is a better idea. But I was thinking of maybe keeping it for myself."

"Competitor companies would pay an arm and a leg to get ahold of Sugah's recipe." And I was also thinking that a recipe that important in the hands of someone with Verlene's kitchen skills bordered on culinary sacrilege.

"Yeah, but do I really want them copying Sugah? I mean, he was a legend, and his sauce has remained a secret all these years. I think I should contact Sugah's corporate offices and offer it to them."

I slid my arm around her shoulder. "I wish

all my problems today were that easy to solve."

34

I strolled down the driveway, twirling Fifi's key ring on my finger. At this singular moment in the cosmic reality of my life, I felt pretty good. Things were calming down and working out. And I hadn't even scratched Fifi's car. Two points for me! *Thank you, Jesus, for the answered prayers.*

I began to construct a mental to-do list. Now that Trotter had eradicated the e-mail virus, I wanted to seriously upgrade my computer forensic certifications. My office could be upstairs and maybe I'd dabble as a contract information provider. I'd be out of Fifi's hair and on track with what I am good at.

Speaking of Fifi, her boyfriend, Robby, seemed to finally understand my outright and blatant refusal of Coltrane Realty's proposal. Excellent — one thing done! What can I say? Sometimes I like to put finished tasks on the list, just for the joy and motivation of crossing them off immediately.

And hopefully Trey . . . would stay away. Hmmm . . . the silly rhyming poetry caused me to smirk, which pulled on sore cheek muscles, but it was a smirk nonetheless. "I'm a poet and don't know it" rolled through my mind. Mom used to say that all the time.

Now that Verlene had gotten her book returned, I needed to figure out how to tell Detective Justice, *without* telling him how we pulled it off. And to do it without getting into more trouble since I'm pretty sure he could tell I was lying the last time. That one may take some time.

The afternoon sun blazed a trail down the center of Fulton Street. A wavy haze rippled up from the sidewalk. The heat felt good on my sore cheek. I turned out of the shaded driveway and looked up. I could smell rain, but there wasn't a cloud in the sky. Rain might help to wash away some of the tree charcoal in Verlene's backyard.

Before I could open the door and step into the bookstore, the blare of Fifi's calypso music greeted me with a dull roar. Inside, the blare drowned out even the tinkle of the bell. The rush of air-conditioning washed over me.

I stopped in the doorway and shivered.

Not because of the cold air so much as because of Griffen Justice. He was standing at the counter talking to Fifi.

Thinking maybe I could get out before he noticed me, I backed up and into a hand pressed into the small of my back. I jumped, wheeling to face its owner.

Andreas.

He looked surprised. Well, that made two of us. "Whoa, skittish today, aren't we?"

I felt momentary relief. I lowered my head, allowing the braids to fall across my face. What was I doing that for? He'd already seen the bruises. I met his gaze and shrugged. "Hey, Babe. You scared me. I was deep in thought. So, uh, what are you doing here so soon?"

"I wanted to grab you for an early dinner. Another appointment came up for this evening."

"Let me just see what's going on here, and then we'll go." I already knew he wasn't going to appreciate seeing that Justice was here again. These two had some kind of unspoken something going on that I hadn't quite caught on to yet. All I knew at the moment was that I still had a little attitude about Andreas's controlling behavior earlier.

I moved into the store. Okay, so my "everything is groovy" day had just collapsed into the black hole of "oooh, you're gonna be in so much trouble when they hear what you did" day.

I tried to catch Fifi's attention. Did she call Justice? Had she said anything about Verlene's book?

She wouldn't look at me.

Bad, bad sign. Andreas stopped at the end of the counter and positioned himself between me and Justice. He stared at the detective as though he was sizing up some kind of competition. Ridiculous, of course. But it did a lot for my ego.

"My, my, Detective, you are getting to be quite a regular here. I'm going to have to give you your own Beckham's Books and Brew coffee mug if this keeps up." I plastered a cheesy grin on my face and sauntered around the counter to stand beside Fifi.

Fifi hesitated. "Sugah, the detective has heard from the Interpol team in Egypt."

I looked back and forth between her and Justice. Neither looked happy. "Is someone going to tell me? Did they find Bakari?"

Justice shook his head. "He was dead before they arrived. It was a one-in-a-million shot. He must have raised his hands to shield himself. The bullet hit him on the underside of the arm, in a brachial artery.

He would have bled out in less than ten minutes."

My heart clenched. I didn't know the man, but my mother had. And now another connection to her had also been broken.

More violence.

More death.

I needed to do a better job of Internet investigating these two professors trying to buy that moldy book. I probably should have more respect for it, since its price tag could relieve the debt of a small country.

"I'm sorry;" Justice said, then pulled a notebook and pen from his left inside pocket.

"So am I." I leaned around Fifi and rolled a chair over to me. My knees were shaking. I lowered myself onto the leather seat. At least I could tell that he didn't know about Verlene's book yet or it would have been his banner headline.

Justice clicked the pen. "Look, there's no easy way to approach this, but . . ."

I sank into the chair. *Please, don't bring up Trey around Andreas, please, please.*

"The Brooklyn district attorney's office would like to exhume your mother's body."

Time warped, wrapped around me, then stood still.

My chest tightened. My breathing came

in ragged spurts. "My mom?" Where did this come from?

"You have to be kidding." Fifi stared at Justice.

"I'm sorry, but there seem to be some discrepancies with her tox screen."

"What are you talking about? There were no tox screens. My mom was DOA."

Fifi crossed her hands tightly over her chest.

Andreas moved to my side and slid his hands onto my shoulders. He rubbed his thumbs into the knots forming on the back of my neck. The pain shooting through my shoulders was excruciating. I remained rigid as I waited for an answer.

Justice flipped a couple of pages then looked up. "Apparently, because your mother was dead, they drew blood samples for the phlebotomy students to, uh . . . Anyway, the samples were labeled and stored as part of the, uh . . . I mean their, uh . . ."

"Stop. Stop. I get it. No more." A wave of nausea crept across my stomach and up my throat. Someone stuck a needle in Mom. She *hated* needles. With a passion. "I don't understand what that has to do with her *now.*"

I felt bad discussing Mom like she wasn't

here. But then again . . . she wasn't.

I shut my eyes.

"In their lab class on blood panels, the students found several suspect compounds in your mother's blood sample." Justice flipped another page.

My eyes flew open. I tensed. "Like what?"

Andreas continued to rub my shoulder, pushing his fingers deeper. My muscles screamed. So did my heart.

"Potassium chloride, pancur . . . pancuronium bromide, and thio . . . thiopental sodium."

"What are they?" I wrinkled my forehead. Andreas squeezed a little too tight on my neck muscles.

I winced.

Justice raised an eyebrow. "I'm having a hard enough time trying to pronounce them. One paralyzes muscles, another has the ability to stop breathing, and the other could technically cause a cardiac arrest. The samples were compromised since it was, well . . . suffice it to say just a practice session. The lab would like to run additional tests to be more conclusive."

My head dropped into my hands. A whimper escaped my lips. I had followed Mom's wishes, and now I would never know what happened to her.

Fifi moved to my side, and wrapped both arms protectively around my shoulders, effectively dislodging Andreas from my neck for the second time today. "We can't help you, Detective."

Justice looked confused. "If it's a court order we need, I can get a judge to issue one."

"No . . . you don't understand. We can't help you." I spoke between soft sniffles, as I pointed across the room to the tall, oak bookshelf where recessed lighting pointed at a glass-enclosed case holding a small Ming vase.

Fifi glanced at the case, then at the floor. "Camille was cremated."

Justice stared at the vase for several seconds, closed his notebook, and returned it and the pen to his pocket. "I guess that closes this one. I'm sorry that I had to be the one who opened a painful chapter in your life again. Unless . . ."

I looked up. A tear escaped my swollen eye and rolled down my discolored cheekbone. "Unless what?"

He looked down and fidgeted with his hands. "There is a viable option. The DA wanted direct body tissue contact, so I'm not sure if they're willing to open an investigation on such slim evidence."

372

"What could they investigate?" Andreas laid his hand on my shoulder again.

"The crime scene, for one thing, but the chances of finding anything are slim to none after all this time. It's probably all been disturbed or discarded."

I shook my head. Braids slapped at my face. "No one . . . no one's been in Mom's apartment since she died." The words caught in my throat. "I couldn't bear —"

"This is preposterous." Andreas stepped between me and Justice once again.

I reached out to his sleeve. "It's all right."

His arm went rigid at my touch. "No, it's not. These people are causing you unnecessary pain. They need to let this go."

He was so sweet to be so protective of me. It felt good to have a champion for once.

"I assure you, Doctor, I mean no harm. I was just answering Ms. Templeton's question." Justice readjusted his relaxed posture into a more no-nonsense stance.

But what if Mom *had* been killed like Bakari? It made my insides feel strange to think that Mom might have been murdered over a stupid book. But how could I find out for sure? *Shudder.* Could I keep it under control if I found out someone had hurt Mom?

"Can't you see she's not okay? Camille is

gone, and nothing will bring her back." Fifi glared at Justice.

"I have to agree." Andreas nodded. "This is an exercise in futility."

Justice trained his gaze on me. His voice lowered, softened. "What would you like me to do?"

I stared through Justice for several moments as my thoughts congealed into a solid mass. My hands came up to my face, rubbing away the tears. A shiver rippled down my arms, jerking my head slightly to the side.

What if . . . ?

I pulled my sight into focus and directly into Justice's eyes. "Tell me how my mom died."

Fifi bent down in front of me. "Sugah, are you sure this is what you want?"

I nodded and Fifi brushed the braids to expose my bruised eye. "Then we'll go through that apartment with a fine-toothed comb."

Justice held up a hand. "No! No one can enter that apartment but the forensics team, and that's only if this gets approved. Please, don't compromise evidence by disturbing anything."

Fifi flinched. "Okay, we'll stay away from the apartment."

"So, when can we expect this intrusion?" Andreas glared daggers at Justice.

I had never seen my man so angry. I was glad he didn't know the whole Trey situation. I called that one right. Still, his tone disturbed me, but I couldn't put my finger on the feeling it gave me.

Justice cleared his throat. "I'll have to talk to the DA, but maybe as soon as tomorrow."

I sniffed back a few more tears. This pulled hard on my emotions, regardless of how stoic I wanted to appear. But I was determined. This opportunity would not pass away.

Justice flinched at my last sniffle, almost as if embarrassed that he was causing me to weep. He turned to leave.

I rose and followed him to the front door.

I turned to face Justice as I opened the front door. "Do you really think there was any foul play involved in my mom's death?" The outside air, thick with moisture, invaded the air-conditioned space. The smell of rain drifted in with the heat, closer now.

"I don't know, but there are too many strange circumstances swirling around here lately . . . dead rats, stolen books, *falling* books . . ." Justice made a point of looking directly at my swollen eye.

Ashamed, I diverted my gaze. Why did I feel guilty that I'd lied to him? Because it was to him? Or because of the actual lie?

"Yes, a lot of strange things." The softness of his tone reached inside me and touched something long-ago turned off. My mouth went dry.

Justice tipped his head to get a better look into my downcast eyes. "Listen, I'm here if you need any help."

I nodded, afraid to make eye contact, afraid of what I might say.

A shadow passed across me, breaking the hold the sun had on my face.

I looked up.

He was gone.

I turned to the counter, where Andreas stood, staring.

I trudged toward the counter. Something didn't feel right. "Where'd Fifi go?"

"She went off to help a customer find a book about impressionist art." He looked at his watch then shoved his hand into his slacks pocket. "I'd better get back to the clinic."

"Wait. What about the early dinner?"

"I just got a page." He glanced at his watch again with cell phone in hand.

"Okay . . . so will I see you later tonight?"

Andreas had already moved past me.

I spun to face him. "Andreas?"

"Yes, I'm sorry." He returned to kiss me softly. "I'll call you later tonight." He rushed out the front door.

35

I fiddled with the search parameters again, trying to find more information on the ever-present book, and the two professors who were interested in it. Guilt tugged at me for not doing any work out in the store. It was probably more from embarrassment, but I didn't want to advertise the condition of my face.

"Excuse me."

I flinched, and spun around to face the voice. One of the technicians from Broadview, the Brinks security team, stood at the counter looking sheepish.

"I'm sorry, Ma'am. But when we left earlier today, I forgot to give you the other set of keys." He held out two rings with two keys apiece.

I accepted the keys, and held up the rings to inspect them. "What are they for? You already left me two sets of keys."

"These are for the new front and back

door locks and deadbolts on the second-floor apartment. I'm sorry. I left them in my toolbox when we finished up. I just noticed them when we got back to the garage."

"The second floor? That's my mom's apartment. Who told you to change the locks there?"

"That redheaded woman, Ma'am. She told us to change all the locks and that was one of the keys on the ring she gave us to work from."

I shook my head. "That didn't need to be changed. Mom's de . . . er, gone. But thanks anyhow." I tossed the rings to the rear of the desk. They clunked against the tray where I kept my phone and other keys.

A rumble of thunder.

The Brinks guy looked toward the front windows. "Looks like we're going to get a thunder boomer. We could use it. maybe wash away some of this heat."

His declaration was punctuated by a slash of lightning, a sharp crack, and a sonic boom. The lights flickered. A soft rain slapped against the windows.

He tipped his hat. "Stay dry."

"You too." I smiled, then flinched as another flash of light and a loud clap pierced the air.

People gathered up their possessions, paid for their purchases, and scurried out to beat the deluge.

Fifi charged out of the stockroom and looked around at the empty store. "Man o'livin', Mother Nature is sure mad over somethin'! She was driving away our captive audience too. It's almost closin' time anyway. How about we call it a day, sugah?"

I scrolled through more data on the professors, but it was stuff I'd already found. "I might as well. I'm not getting anywhere here."

Fifi hopped onto the edge of the desk. "What're you tryin' to do?"

"I don't know." I banged on the keyboard in frustration. "I feel useless."

"I don't understand, sugah. Useless how? With the store?"

"No. With figuring out if Mom was murdered."

Fifi's face paled. "Sugah, your momma was a saintly woman who loved everyone and everyone loved her. I can't imagine a single soul who would have wanted to harm a dyed hair on her head."

"I would like to think that too, but we need to look at the facts. Mom wasn't old or decrepit. She was in great health —"

"Sugah, healthy people die every day."

"What about those e-mails? They started when Mom was alive. And we know for a fact that Bakari Ahmed was killed over the book."

"That was some foreigner in a foreign country where they have no respect for life. That could have been about somebody stealing his goats." Fifi's color returned.

My head snapped up. "I'm going to pretend that you didn't just say that."

"Why? It could be just as much the truth as anything else."

"What about the chemicals they found in Mom?"

"I dunno, sugah. I don't understand that either." Fifi shook her head. "We're just gonna have to wait and see."

"This is making me nuts." I ran my hands across my forehead. "One minute, I'm up and happy and feeling confident like I could do anything. The next minute, I'm a mess and thinking I'm so stupid that I can't even do an Internet search right."

"Sugah, maybe it's that time of the month."

My mouth dropped open. "That would be like adding insult to injury right about now."

Fifi tried to hide a giggle behind her hand. "I'm sorry."

"No, you're not. You meant that." I shook my head. Forget that time of the month. Maybe I was reading too much into this, and had to wait for the police to conduct the investigation. "We still haven't 'fessed up to grabbing Verlene's book."

"I say, let sleeping dogs lie for a few days."

"I agree. I think Griffen Justice knows I'm lying about my face being messed up."

"I think that man's taken a shine to you, sugah."

"What makes you say that?"

"Just the way he looks at you. And how his voice gets real soft when he talks to you. Don't think I haven't noticed." Fifi hopped off the desk. "And I think that boyfriend of yours has noticed too."

I raised my head and closed my eyes. "I was hoping that I was wrong about that."

"Well, I wouldn't leave those two alone in a room together."

Another lightning streak and thunder crack rolled through the store.

Fifi grabbed up her bag from under the counter. "Let's blow this pop stand."

"Sounds good to me." I slid the two new key rings to the edge of the desk and reached for my key ring and the other two sets. Only one set lay by the key tray. I moved the tray out of the way.

No keys.

Fifi watched. "What are you looking for?"

"The other set of new keys for my apartment. I threw them both here. Now there's only one." I added the new keys for my apartment and the keys for Mom's apartment to my ring.

"Maybe it slid behind the desk here." Fifi pulled on the corner of the desk but it didn't budge. "We'll move it tomorrow. I don't have time now. There's a hot date waitin' for me."

More thunder, and then the deluge of rain pounded against the front glass. We started for the front door.

"I bet I can guess who that's with," I said.

Fifi grinned. I opened the door. A blast of wind pushed a sheet of rain into the store. Fifi pushed the door shut. "Hold up. You can't go out in that without an umbrella."

"But I want to get wet. It's warm."

She looked at me all disgusted. "I don't care about you gettin' wet. I *care* about you gettin' your momma's gun wet." She tapped my pocket.

I had truly forgotten that it was there. I pulled it out. "I'll leave it here."

"Oh, no, you won't." Fifi tromped behind the counter and shuffled around in a pile of stuff in one of the counter cubbyholes. "We still have an undesirable element out there that you don't want to run into empty-handed."

"I'll get under your umbrella then."

"No . . . Here, use this." She shook open a Ziplock bag and shoved my gun and the nylon holster into it, expelled the extra air, and zipped it closed. "Shove that in your pocket and you're good to go. Just take it out of the bag when you get upstairs, so it doesn't collect moisture."

"Yes sir, er, uh, ma'am." I smirked and saluted.

We locked up and dashed out in the rain.

36

We tiptoed around the side of the building, dodging puddles, then broke into a run. It seemed the faster we moved, the harder it rained. The downpour produced a thunderous roar. Fifi's beach umbrella was no match for the sheets of pelting rain that threatened to collapse it. All it did was slow down her progress to the safety of her car.

I didn't bother. The warm rain felt soothing on all my achy parts. It took about ten seconds for me to get soaked through to the skin, but I refused to run. It made me feel a little daring.

Fifi's hot little sports number swallowed her and the umbrella, and she beeped as she drove by. God bless her soul, she went slowly so as not to splash me with the gushing torrent running down the center of the driveway. In reality, though, I couldn't get any wetter.

I rounded the corner by the Dumpster.

My hand grabbed onto the banister and I swung myself around to the steps. I stumbled back. A hunched-over body sat on the stairs with its head down and arms wrapped around knees that were pulled up tight against the chest. It didn't scare me as much as startle me, especially in this deluge. Yes, I was truly a different person from the one who skulked down these stairs a few days ago.

Rain pelted my scalp like little needles and poured down each of my braids. I leaned over, drawing the waterfall along with me as I reached out to touch the person's shoulder.

Nothing happened.

Don't *tell* me someone's left a body on my steps.

I blinked rapidly to ward off the water running in my eyes. It was starting to sting. I touched the person again, and stepped back. The body didn't tumble over into a puddle, which was a definite plus, and it was warm, so I knew he or she was still alive. Another bonus.

The head rose slowly. Scraggly wet hair plastered tight to the face obscuring it. A hand reached up and pushed an opening in the sheet of hair.

My mouth dropped open, and water immediately rushed in. I spit it out and gasped, then coughed. "Barbara! What are you doing here?" I reached down and helped her to her feet. She staggered, clutching my arm to steady herself.

"I don't know."

"Where's your car?" A stream of water propelled off the ends of my swinging braids as I whipped my head around surveying the lot. Her car wasn't here.

"I-I don't know . . . uhm . . . I don't know. I think-k my husband took i-it."

Her husband? I've never seen her husband. I wouldn't even know how to contact anyone about her. What was I going to do? I couldn't leave her out here, alone. Her speech slurred as though she was drunk. I leaned in closer to shield her. I didn't smell alcohol.

"C'mon, you come with me until we sort this out." I guided her up the slippery stairs.

We stepped onto the second-floor landing. I looked over the railing thinking that from up here I could scope out more than I could down there. It was still the same barren, soggy parking lot, but I could see the puddles better. The lot extended behind several other businesses. There were various employee cars parked in the spaces, but not the light-blue car belonging to Barbara.

She stumbled twice as we climbed to the third floor, but we made it. I fumbled with my newly expanded deadly key bundle, and found one of the new keys. It sure would have been better if I could have figured out the locks while I didn't have water rolling in my eyes. But such is life.

The one key unlocked both the knob lock and the dead bolt. I opened the door and tried to usher the disoriented woman into my apartment.

She pulled away, shaking her head. "It's too dark. Monsters in the dark."

I twisted around and looked at her. I'm going to pretend that I didn't just hear that.

I reached in and flipped the light switches on the control panel. Soft track lighting ran the length of the apartment's open layout and instantly dispelled the encroaching darkness.

Barbara hesitated, then smiled and entered.

We stood on the vinyl kitchen floor shedding copious amounts of water that puddled around us and threatened to run under my refrigerator. I guess I hadn't quite thought out the watering-the-apartment angle of my singing-in-the-rain adventure.

I grabbed a roll of paper towels and made a dam to hold the expanding flood. I love walking in the rain but I'm sure not fond of cleaning up the mess it makes. Sooner or later I needed to learn from the consequences of my silly actions.

Barbara stood perfectly still, her head down and her hands clasped. Her teeth chattered, though it didn't feel cold to me. Then again, I had been running through the raindrops with wild abandon, not huddled in a ball on the steps, imitating a mushroom.

I peeled off my shirt, and stood in front of the sink in my wet Cross Your Heart bra that, cross my heart and hope to die if I lie, had never done a thing for me other than dig into my shoulders. I wrung out the excess water and slipped the shirt over my head.

Lightning crackled. I flinched. A boom of thunder vibrated the walls. The lights blinked off for a few seconds, then returned. Barbara jerked. She gasped and pulled her arms up around her head.

Sheesh, it was only the lights. Lighten up, lady. "It's okay. You're safe in here." I don't have a clue why I said that, but it seemed the right thing to do. She appeared to be soothed for the moment.

She whimpered and lowered her hands, but continued to clasp and unclasp them.

She kept lifting her right foot, as though marching in place.

I kicked off my shoes and removed my slacks and began to wring them out over the sink. My hands ran into the bulge. I angled my back to Barbara, pulled the gun from my pocket, ripped open the baggie, and shoved the weapon into the silverware drawer. She didn't need to think that she was trapped in an apartment with a gun-toting nut job.

Lightning zipped across the sky outside the kitchen window. A boom of thunder exploded in tandem with the light display. The storm must be right on top of us for the two to be that close together and so loud. The lights flicked off again.

Barbara wailed and I reached for her.

She pulled away. Uh-oh, I had forgotten this facet of her behavior, mostly because she'd not done anything like it since that morning I found her. I admonished myself. Don't invade her space or touch her.

"It's okay. They'll come back on." And as I finished the sentence, the lights obliged.

Her shoulders dropped, and she seemed to chill out some.

I remember Mom hadn't been the happiest camper in storms either. But for me, that was one of the few pleasant traits I inherited from my dad. He loved storms, loved to be out in the rain, loved to watch the lightning. As a child, I liked nothing better than to sit in my little rocking chair on the back porch, wearing my raincoat and rubber boots, holding an umbrella and watching the storms.

Lightning and a low roll of thunder rumbled in as the storm moved in. The lights flickered. Barbara clenched and un-clenched her fists. I hurried to the bathroom on this level where my washer and dryer were located and grabbed a stack of fluffy towels. I reached over and shut the adjoining door that led to my office.

"Barbara, would you like to come in here? We can run your clothes through the dryer." I moved outside the bathroom door to motion her in. At least then my furniture would be spared a soaking. Scotchgard was not going to help in this case.

Barbara took a few hesitant steps and stopped. Her head moved in jerky motions as she looked around at her surroundings.

Is she that freaked out by the storm?

I turned on my mommy voice. "Here, let's get you out of those wet clothes." I held out a freshly laundered terry cloth robe. "You can put this on."

She hesitated several times but finally

reached out and took the bathrobe. Her fingers stroked the bathrobe as though she were petting an animal. Very strange.

She made her way into the bathroom. I handed her a couple towels, and shut the door to give her privacy.

I moved around the counter and dropped to my knees with the rest of the towels to sop up the water that was doing a slow ooze under the refrigerator. Lightning flashed, thunder rumbled, and, as I looked up, a dark patch crossed in front of the frosted glass panel in the back door. It was followed by a thump.

I froze.

Was there someone out there?

I watched the door handle. It didn't turn.

I scrambled to my feet and slowly approached the door. Was it Trey, coming after me? Did the book thieves find me? I listened at the door. No sounds. I sucked in a breath. Careful not to make a sound, I slid the chain in place across the door and opened it a tiny piece.

The push broom lay across the doorway. I pushed out a hard sigh. My heart left my throat and returned to my chest. A shiver rolled up my back. No prowlers, just wooden sticks. I almost laughed. Seemed like my world was made up of unstable people, so why should this be any different? I closed the door, pulled off the chain, and flung it open to slide the broom out of the way without standing it up. It would be just like me to trip over it in the dark and propel myself over the banister.

As I shut the door I inspected the new locks. I tried to pull the removable thumb turn out. It wouldn't budge. I grabbed up my keys from the counter and inserted the key into the lock. Turning the tumbler allowed me to remove the thumb turn.

I shut the door and used the key in the now-exposed keyhole to slide the bolt into place. A new bit of calm rolled over me. I hadn't realized that the glass panes had unnerved me that much. I tossed the thumb turn in the silverware drawer and headed for the front door to do likewise. Unless I wanted to switch to doors with no glass panes, using a key was going to be my new reality. I figured a little nuisance was worth it for peace of mind.

As I passed the bathroom door, I could hear the dryer running, and then a gagging sound. I tried the doorknob. It was locked. "How are you doing in there, Barbara?"

The pit of my stomach was fluttering. I didn't even know of anyone whom I could call about her.

"My-y clothes are g-getting dry," said a small gasping voice.

"Do you need help? Let me in." I tried the door again. This was beginning to feel strange.

She mumbled something, but I didn't catch it.

My hand rested on the knob. I was getting a funny feeling. She was acting strange even for her. "But you're sure you are all right?"

A growl emanated from the closed space. "Yes!"

Startled, I moved away from the door. All righty then. She did *not* just growl at me. "Well . . . when your clothes are done, come on out and I'll make you something to eat."

I kept going to the front door and released the thumb turn from the new lock and set it next to the TV. I felt better. I had created my own fortress of safety. I looked toward the bathroom. I was having second thoughts about bringing Barbara up here, but what else could I have done? I couldn't just leave her on the steps.

I stared across the room at the circular staircase, winding down into Mom's apartment, then glanced at the bathroom door. I could go downstairs, fix the locks, and be back up before I heard the dryer stop.

Maybe she's just modest, and doesn't want to come out till she's dressed again. I was getting used to being in wet clothes. Changing could wait a few more minutes.

I finished all the locks and ran upstairs to my bedroom to change into sweatpants and a top. I slowly walked down to my third-floor kitchen.

Fresh clothes, and I still felt just as wet. I was sweating bullets and feeling like I had just gone through the workout from hell. Seven flights of stairs in the last fifteen minutes! Three up from the street and then two flights up and down inside of here from my apartment to Mom's, and then from this floor up to my bedroom and back. My thighs burned like there was no tomorrow. I need an elevator . . . I need an elevator.

But on second thought, all this working out deserved a slice of Red Velvet cake. I stuck my head in the fridge, just like I actually expected to find cake in there. I knew there wasn't any such thing before I opened it; I must be brain dead today. Lightning cracked, thunder boomed, and I whacked my head on the underside of the freezer compartment. I was not going out in this weather for a piece of cake.

I satisfied myself with sandwich fixings — shaved ham, provolone, lettuce, tomato, onion, my favorite honey mustard, and fresh marble rye bread. I spread the feast out on the wraparound counter and reached in for the sour cream macaroni salad. If I couldn't have cake, I sure was going to delight myself with a healthy dose of carbs.

Where was Barbara? The dryer dinged a while ago.

I listened at the door. No movement. What in the world of porcelain thrones did she do in there, pass out? I reached for the knob. A rustling noise sounded from the next room over. I had closed the connecting door when I brought the towels out. I walked into the living room and peered around the corner, into my office.

Barbara was standing at my desk holding the picture that had been sitting by my computer. It was of me with Andreas. Yo, what was she doing, invading my personal space? Not cool.

Be calm. She's not wrapped too tight tonight. On second thought, she's wrapped tight enough to be ready to snap.

A heavy rumble of thunder vibrated the apartment windows.

I strolled into the office. "Hey, Barbara, there you are. Did you get turned around in the bathroom and come out the wrong door?"

She glared at me. Barbara didn't look so good. Her eyes darted around like pinballs. Spittle collected in the corners of her mouth.

I watched in strange fascination as the collection bubbled and grew.

If I didn't know a whole lot better, I'd say that she'd gone rabid.

She didn't speak, just glared. Her rapid breath heaved her chest.

I reached for the framed picture in her hand. She snatched it out of my reach. "You took my husband from me!" she screamed. Her eyes went wild as she backpedaled away from me.

I raised both hands in surrender. "Uhm, Barbara, it's all right. That's my boyfriend. It's not your husband. I promise."

"Liar-r-r!" screeched Barbara. Her voice morphed into a primal sound, wild and scary.

The hairs stood on the back of my neck. Great! What do I do now?

"Barbara," I cooed. The soothing tone had worked before, so maybe it could do it again. "Why don't we go to the living room? You should sit down, maybe. You're not feeling good, honey. Do you know where you are? Do you know who I am?" I inched toward her, a step at a time with small, shuffling steps.

She charged me. I sidestepped and she slammed into the filing cabinet but swung around fast to face me. "I know exactly who you are!" She lunged at me again. "You took my home! My husband! You're the lying, stealing evil —"

"Barbara, please!" She clawed for a handful of braids, but I deflected her blow. Inertia propelled her past me, and I shoved her out of the office and into the open space of the living room. She still had the picture in her hand.

"Barbara, listen to me . . ." I raised both hands, palms facing her, and tried to fill her field of vision. "I own the bookstore downstairs. You made coffee for me. I found you on my steps in the rain. Remember?"

"I'll kill you before I'll let you have him!" She whipped the picture at my head.

I batted it to the side. It hit the coffee table, and the glass disintegrated into hundreds of jagged pieces. I put the table in between us.

Barbara began to rock back and forth as she chewed a tendril of hair.

I need help. Phone! Where's my phone? Oh brother, I don't even remember bringing it upstairs. That's what I get for getting rid of the landline.

The panic button! I had to get to one of the security panels.

Barbara's rocking grew more violent until she fell to her hands and knees in the broken glass. "No. No, no, no." She raked her hands through the shards of glass groping for the picture. Once she had it, she smoothed her hand across the image, leaving smears of blood and glass. She rubbed harder to clean the debris away, which left more blood and led to more frantic swiping. She pressed harder but with each hysterical pass of her hand the glass bits imbedded in her palm snagged and tore the glossy paper. She screamed like a wild animal and began beating her open hand on the floor.

"Watch, you've cut yourself!" I reached out, and instantly pulled back. *Oh, Lord help me. What am I supposed to do?* If I approached her, she'd attack me, but if I let her alone, she was going to turn her hands into hamburger. "Barbara, Barbara! Please, I don't know how to help you. Tell me what you need. Talk to me." With her eyes full of fury, she grunted, and lifted the coffee table.

Run! The front door panel would make me a dead target, so I sprinted toward my office again.

She hurled the table.

I ducked in the doorway.

The frame caught the brunt of the table and the table splintered into pieces. A section of a drawer propelled into the room. I ran through the office, into the bathroom, and out the other door into the kitchen, slamming the bathroom door behind me.

Breathless, I punched the emergency button on the security panel. No light.

Barbara pounded on the door, screamed, and howled.

I punched the button again. And again. Still no light. Stupid! Stupid! I hadn't set the codes and password to activate the system.

I fumbled to unlock the doorknob with shaky fingers. I yanked. It didn't budge. The dead bolt was set. Where are my keys? I couldn't think. Where'd I lay them down?

Barbara wrenched open the door. She passed by the counter, and grabbed up the chef's knife I'd set out for slicing the tomatoes and onions for our sandwiches. I looked helplessly at my options: a locked door or a knife-wielding woman.

With a stomach-curdling scream and the knife held over her head, Barbara charged.

37

The unrelenting rain had turned Fulton into a river. Storm sewers strained to admit all of the liquid rushing down the sides of the street. Cars sent up plumes of road water in their wake as they rushed to navigate. But one vehicle in particular barely made a ripple in the temporary stream.

The black SUV slipped into an empty parking space on the opposite side of the street from Beckham's Books & Brew. It idled for a few seconds before the driver silenced the engine. The black-tinted windows offered observers no hint of who or how many occupants sat within.

Trey Alexander sat in the passenger seat, his nostrils flaring with each breath. He wore a black leather slouch cap, a black nylon Windbreaker over black stovepipe jeans and a black T-shirt, and a stony scowl. The dark ensemble mirrored his mood. His face appeared to be set in a permanent grimace with nostrils flaring with each breath he took.

"Yo, Trey man, why you need to be sittin' here scopin' out this woman?" asked the driver, barely old enough to be called a man.

"Because I said so," said Trey.

"But man, we need to be jackin' up the homey that ventilated your shoulder."

Trey's jaw rolled back and forth like he was grinding his teeth. He didn't answer. He cracked the window a bit to dispel the growing fog.

Thunderous rain pounded on the roof, creating a deafening roar.

The driver swiveled to face Trey. "You know you got backup, man. If you scared to —"

Trey's right hand shot out and snatched him by his t-shirt. "If you ever call me scared . . . of anything . . . ever . . . I'll jack you up, punk." He shoved the boy into the seat and let him go.

The driver smoothed out the grip stretched into his shirt. "Man, I didn't mean to diss you." He grinned, displaying a diamond chip–encrusted front tooth. "I ain't no punk, man . . . I'm a straight-up thug."

"I'm tired of looking at you." Trey stared through the windshield, his eyes trained on the bookstore.

The guy fidgeted in his seat. "What you mean, man?"

"I mean, get out of the car and bounce. Now."

The guy rolled his head into the seat rest. "You don't mean it, man. It's rainin' out there. That ain't right."

Click.

The guy looked down. Trey had inserted a magazine into his semiautomatic handgun.

The guy reached for the door handle.

On the other side of the street, a car rolled to a stop. Andreas Comino exited the car and hurried through the rain to the outside entrance to the right of the bookstore, the entrance to the basement door and the stairs leading up to the apartments.

Trey put his hand across the driver's chest to stop him. "Hang back. I need to scope this out."

"Ain't that the white guy that's been sniffin' 'round your woman?"

Trey briefly left the driver's chest in order to slap him and then returned to keep him still. "Zip it."

The guy recoiled from the hit and pulled himself into the corner against the driver's door. Trey let his hand fall away and continued to watch Comino.

The door opened and Comino entered.

The hall light produced vague shadows through the small diagonal panes of decorative frosted glass. First, Comino's shadow stood on the other side of the glass, then a dark shadow crossed the glass and retreated. There was no longer anyone standing on the other side of the door.

Trey jammed a fist down onto the center console, and then again . . . and then again.

"Sit here and watch my ride," said Trey. He pocketed his gun and zipped up his jacket.

"Where you goin'?"

"To see what he's doing. He got no business going in her basement. He's up ta something."

Trey maneuvered his sore shoulders out of the SUV, forcing the pain down deep where it became fuel for his rage. A flash of lightning lit up the street. He hunched his shoulders against the rain and crossed the street.

Ten feet from the SUV, Greta Feinstein watched out the window as the lightning lit up Trey's face. She'd been monitoring the black-windowed SUV since it pulled up in front of her delicatessen. She pressed a number into her cell phone and held it to her ear, never taking her gaze from the window.

"Hi, Angie, seeing what I'm seeing?" Greta could almost see Angelica Scarpetti's form in the front window of her bakery, next door to Beckham's Books & Brew.

38

I had a death grip on Barbara's hand that brandished the chef's knife. Her breath heaved at my face, assaulting my nose with a powerful sour smell. It made my stomach lurch. My eyes trained on the knife in her upturned fist. Sweat beaded on her forehead as she strained to connect blade to flesh. It had come close to my face several times, but I had managed to push it away. She blinked rapidly, as though she couldn't focus on my face.

The razor-sharp blade aimed at me from her upturned fist. My heart pounded wildly. She kept blinking as though she couldn't focus on my face.

I tried to use that moment of disorientation to clamp my other hand onto her free wrist. I swept my foot out and behind her legs to drop her to the floor. We slammed into the refrigerator.

My foot slipped on the wet floor. Our legs

tangled, and we both went down. I still held off the knife. We rolled and her arm dislodged from my grip. She sprang to her feet like a cat.

Wrenching the other arm free, she crouched and growled at me with her arms spread.

"I'm going to kill you." She lunged. "He's mine!"

Jesus, help me please! I have no idea what this schizo woman is talking about, Lord.

The lights winked out.

Barbara screeched.

I blinked, waiting for my eyes to adjust. It wasn't completely dark outside yet, but the heavy clouds didn't allow much light through the front windows to see by. I had the advantage. I walked around in the dark all the time. My eyes adjusted. I crawled under the dining room table and in silence, skirted around her, as she wildly swung the knife in the dark.

She screamed again. "You will never have him."

I wasn't about to answer her and let her know where I'd gone. What could I use as a weapon? I had thought I could fight her bare-handed but her strength was more than a match for me. What was that all about? I had used every ounce of strength I could muster just to keep her from plunging the knife into me, and I outweighed the woman by at least fifty pounds.

Her strength was not normal, that much I knew. She didn't seem to be part of the drug scene, but at this point, I was willing to bet that she was on PCP. I had seen enough of Trey's drugged-out crowd to know the symptoms.

I couldn't stop it. The prickling sensation ran up my nose. I sneezed. My head hit the table leg and bounced me onto my backside.

She swung around, grabbed the edge of the table, and flipped it against the china closet. I heard the knife hit the floor and skid toward the living room. Glass rained around me, and I threw my hands up to deflect the falling shards.

She growled a throaty guttural sound and pounced. I kicked out with both legs, propelling her back against the counter. She gasped.

I saw my chance.

39

Trey opened the entrance door and moved inside. The hall light had gone out. He flicked the switch on the wall. Nothing happened. A beam of light caught his attention from under the basement door. He slowly opened it and peered down the steps. The beam moved around the basement and went out of sight.

Trey stepped down a step, then another.

The stair squeaked.

He stopped, didn't breathe, didn't think. Waited.

The noise didn't attract attention.

He blew out a slow, quiet stream of air as he moved down another step and craned his neck to look over the banister. He could see into the dark cavern because of the beam radiating from the flashlight in an expanded circle. Andreas Comino stood in front of the fuse box flicking breaker switches.

Comino shut the fuse box door and moved to a junction mounted on the wall, blocking Trey's view. The box was attached to a small beige cabinet with dozens of cream-colored wires snaking from it.

Trey backed up the steps, and out of the doorway. He positioned himself behind the basement door, pulled his semiautomatic from his jacket pocket, and held it to his left side.

Several minutes went by before he heard footsteps on the stairs. He returned the gun to his pocket and moved away so that the door wouldn't hit him. The knob turned and the door swung open. Comino exited the basement and closed the door, exposing Trey.

Trey punched Comino in the side of the face. "I want you out of my woman's life."

Comino stumbled against the steps going up to the apartments. He caught himself with his hands and stood up. "You have no idea who you're messing with, kid." He raised the back of his hand to his jaw and wiped slowly. A trickle of blood played from the corner of his left nostril.

"Why? Because you're some big important doctor, and you *think* you have my honey?" Trey stepped forward and puffed out his chest, crowding Comino's space. "I'm the man in *this* neighborhood and ain't no one gonna invade my territory."

Comino smirked. "You're not a man. You're a hoodlum and a lightweight at that." His fist came up.

Trey blocked and swung with his other arm.

Comino's head jerked. The blow glanced off his temple. He seemed dazed, dropped his chin, and brought his hands toward his face. But then his head and hands came up quick, shoving Trey away.

Trey's body slammed into the closed door. His head whacked against the frame holding the glass panels. A tinge of blood remained on the frame when he moved.

Trey bounced back, circled, and jabbed like a prizefighter. He could wear this old man out. Hopping from toe to toe, Trey watched Comino's slow, unhurried movements. He was getting tired for sure. Trey smiled. This woman-stealing piece of Greek garbage was gonna suffer nice an' slow.

Comino must have gotten his nerve back. He jerked forward a few fake lunges, then followed through.

They slammed into the door, struggled to part, and then rammed into the stairs.

A high, piercing scream echoed down the stairs from the apartments above. They both looked up.

A muffled shot rang out.

40

My strength faltered.

My legs shook. It was probably more adrenaline rush than anything, but I needed a break, a rest, anything. God, please help me.

I tried to wrestle Barbara toward the living room. The amber glow from the streetlights spilled into the room, supplying enough light for her to see me. I had a split-second thought — why were the streetlights on? The storm knocked out the power . . .

Barbara continued to alternate between screaming and wailing.

I couldn't understand most of what she said. It sounded foreign except for *monster, no, dark,* and *kill.* Sounded like a Hallmark card for the Possessed Collection. Sheesh.

She suddenly fell quiet. Uh-oh . . . this probably isn't good.

She lunged at me again, and I used all of my strength to punch her in the face. I expected her to go down. Please . . . let her go down. She shook her head and grabbed me by the throat.

Stars burst in front of my eyes. I raked at her hands. My nails dug into her skin as I tried to pry her hands off my neck. My index fingernail broke her skin. A thin line of blood, reflected in the streetlamp, traced down the backside of her hand. I felt the pain, but it was lost in my desperate struggle to relieve my lack of air. I wrenched my head back and forth, trying to suck in anything. As a last act of desperation, I head-butted her in the face.

She stumbled backward into the flat-screen TV. It rocked and toppled from its shelf. The base snapped off as it hit and rocketed off toward the front window. Weakness overcame my legs and I, too, slumped to the living room floor, gasping for air, my throat raw and bruised.

Barbara scrambled to attack again. With the last ounce of strength I could muster, I reached up on the side table and threw a lamp at her. She tried to slap it aside, but instead she tripped over the fallen TV and spun wildly toward the front door.

The door opened and Andreas stepped in. He raised his hand. There was something in his palm. A semiautomatic pistol. It thudded down on the back of Barbara's head and she collapsed in a heap on the floor.

I burst into racking sobs. Tears rolled down my face. My shoulders trembled as bad as my legs. I used the end table and lifted myself from the floor.

He knelt down beside Barbara and put his fingers to her neck.

"I-Is she dead?" I wanted to run to him but I wasn't going near Barbara. I didn't care whether she was dead or alive.

Andreas stared at her, then looked up at me as he retracted his hand and stood. "She's still alive."

I instinctively backed up another step.

He stepped over her body, and took a couple steps toward me.

I threw myself into Andreas's arms. "You saved me. Thank God. I was so scared. She went crazy," I wailed and clutched at his wet coat.

I buried my head in his shoulder.

His arm tightened around my back. He didn't say anything, just held me.

His calm quiet prompted me to look up at him. To thank him? Kiss him? To —

Andreas's face was blank.

No emotion.

No smile.

No concern.

I had a single moment of clarity.

I pushed away from his chest. "Hon, how did you get in here? I just had those locks changed today."

He didn't answer. His grip on my back tightened. I propelled myself away from him and tripped in the rubble. I regained my footing. "Andreas? Talk to me. What are you doing here?"

A different kind of pounding started in my stomach and worked its way up to my throat.

"I couldn't get in the apartment downstairs, and she was taking too long," he answered flatly. His jaw clenched.

I backed away from him.

He didn't move.

My brain couldn't process that statement. I was too tired. Tears continued to pour from my eyes. "Please. I don't understand what you mean. Please, Andreas. You're scaring me, honey."

He stared at me. The hard lines defining his face made him look wooden in the vague light from the street. He lifted the hand with the gun. "It would have been so neat and clean to have her just go nuts and shoot you. Just be done with it." A scowl crossed his mouth as he waved the gun at Barbara's unconscious body. "But I could never entice one of her personalities to handle a gun long enough to get it on record."

I wanted to slap myself awake. This had to be a nightmare. Barbara must have knocked me out. This can't be happening. I wrapped my arms around myself. I could feel it. I was awake. I backed another step away.

He casually stepped toward me.

"Do you know Barbara?" I kept doing single-step retreats toward the dining room area.

"Of course, I know Barbara, and Tammy, and the rest of her schizophrenic cast of alter egos." He batted at the other end table lamp. It crashed against the wall and slid to the floor. He sighed, "I had this all planned to the last detail." His voice rose. "But, nooo, could I get a break here?" One by one, he batted the framed pictures off the shelf above where the TV had set. "Could I get one" . . . *crash* . . . "single" . . . *crash* . . . "break?" *crash.* "No. Why? Because you're all trying to ruin my life."

I could barely hear him over the pulse pounding in my ears. Granted, I've been known to jump to conclusions before, and I know I've been knocked around a bunch tonight, but after all of this, is he really telling me that I've ruined *his* life?

I had no more energy left to fight. I moved to the dining room, not really caring what happened when my back was turned. Stupid? Sure. But at this point, I wasn't so sure dying was such a bad thing.

"Why do you think I'm trying to ruin your life? I love you." I blinked the tears away so I could see through the blur as we moved away from the light.

"Because . . ." His voice rose, vibrating in my ears. "You won't sell me this stupid building!"

My eyes flew open wide.

"What? What do you have to do with Coltrane Realty?" My mind raced through memories. "Our first meeting at the Concerned Citizens. You supported my position."

From deep within me, anger began to well up. He had played me like an iPod.

He remained silent for what felt like an hour, but in reality could only have been mere seconds. "And that's why you are the stupidest of them all. At least your mother figured it out. The old bat. I *own* Coltrane Realty."

Mom. My heart clenched. Breath came short. "D-Did you hurt my mom?"

"Of course not. The formulas I injected her with are used by our finest prison systems. It's guaranteed to be a painless death."

My head lightened and the room spun. It felt like God had turned up the gravity. I grabbed onto the side of the china closet to steady myself. My shoulders rose. It felt like I had dug my fingers straight into the wood. This can't be happening. Please wake up. Please wake up.

He looked down at the gun in his hand.

I followed his glance. My stomach hollowed out. I couldn't outrun that. *I'm going to die. God, please help me. I'm lost.*

He waved it dismissively, like an "aw-shucks" gesture. "I'm not going to shoot you. It would draw suspicion."

"Thank you." My brow furrowed. "I think." What was I talking about? The shock had numbed me. I forced myself to focus before I slipped into delirium.

I concentrated on controlling my breath until it was even and leveled out.

He slid the gun into his pocket. "I need time to think. It has to look like Barbara has killed you. Maybe we can make it a drug overdose like hers."

I shook my head. "No . . . That wouldn't really work for me. I don't like needles." You idiot! Why are you discussing this with a psychopath?

He moved toward me. My grip on the china closet was like steel. With everything I had in me I pulled on the top of the two-part unit. It tipped, taking Andreas by surprise. He threw up his hands to protect himself but disappeared under the heavy wooden unit. The leading edge hung up on the two chairs that were left after Barbara flipped the table, so it didn't hit the floor flat.

I scrambled up the steps to the fourth floor. Where are my keys? I need them to get out of here. Ugh. I'll never take those thumb turns out again!

I pawed through the wet clothes and towels I had left thrown on the floor. I could hear the keys but I couldn't find them in the mess. My hands shook uncontrollably. Finally, I latched onto the keys, hugged them to my chest, and shoved them into the pocket on my sweats. Now to get out of here.

I started down the steps. My foot stopped in midstride. Andreas struggled and grunted from under the top of the china closet. His head and torso were free. He might be able to reach my legs if I tried to get by him to the rear door.

My only option was to outsmart him. I hadn't done so well up to now, but to be

fair, I hadn't known I should have been trying up until now. Besides, I had new motivation. I knew for certain that he had killed
my mom. Reason and sound judgment were
slowly replacing my fear.

"Sloane! Where are you?"

*Yeah, right. Like I'm going to yell out right
where I am so you can come kill me. Not
today, buddy!*

Dining room rubble scraped the floor as
Andreas rose to his feet.

I needed to hide. The only living space on
the fourth floor was my full bath, bedroom,
and walk-in closet. No places to hide in any
of those. Two-thirds of this floor was storage area that I hadn't been inside for years.
But it was a tangled enough mess that if I
coerced him into there I might be able to
get away before he knew I was gone.

He started up the circular staircase.

I charged down the hall and opened the
door to the storage area. A musty aroma
filled my nostrils. The streetlights in the
front of the building cast a pale glow that
traveled down the two room-length aisles
cut through the mess. Piles of old furniture
and fixtures reached high against the outside
walls. In some places, I couldn't even see
over the mounds.

I started down the left aisle. How had all

this stuff wound up here? I mean, four flights of stairs? Give me a break. I could barely carry groceries up, let alone some of this big stuff. Stairs used to come up to the fourth floor, just like the ones that come up to my third-floor apartment entrance, but the fourth floor set had been gone for at least ten or fifteen years. A large sign, for Kramer's Luncheonette, leaned against an old wooden chifforobe.

I hurried up the aisle, tapping on boxes as I went. Toward the front, up against the wall, one of the boxes sounded hollow. I backed up and pulled on the side. It twisted some. It was a large, heavy, corrugated box about half the height of a refrigerator box, and it was filled with musty brocade drapes.

I scrunched myself sideways into the box, displacing the old fabric. It sent up a mist of dust. I clamped my hand across my nose and peeked out over the leading edge of the end flap. It gave me a perfect vantage point to see when Andreas came by. I knelt down and lost my balance on the disheveled lump. My hand pressed on the backside of the box, and as I bent over, a stabbing pain radiated from my hip.

The killer keys were poking into my stomach. I readjusted where they were, and then on second thought, I pulled them out of my pocket and held the bunch in my hand, positioning several keys to poke out between each of my fingers. The sheer weight of this would give me an advantage as a surprise weapon if I needed it.

"Sloane!" He bellowed. He must be on the fourth floor. "Come out, Sloane. Make it easy on yourself." The echo told me he was looking in the bathroom.

Sure, any time now I'm just going to stop ruining your day and let you kill me. The anger that had built mimicked a second wind, almost an adrenaline rush for survival.

"You should have sold me the building, Sloane. If you had, the others would have too, and this deal would have been done!"

The makeup mirror in my walk-in closet smashed to the floor. He was getting closer.

"Come out, Sloane, wherever you are," he singsonged.

That in itself unnerved me, that he could be so cool and calculated while seeking me out to kill me, like it was a game.

That taunt came from the doorway.

"I could have gotten my money and returned to Greece where women know their place and obey their men." He was coming up this aisle.

He banged on boxes as he moved closer to my hiding place.

Please, God, hide me. Please, God. And then it happened. His hand slapped on my box. His footsteps stopped. I froze. My grip tightened on the keys and I held my breath, ready to swing out at any second. *Please, please, please.*

Now that I had sucked in air, I couldn't let it out with him standing there. My head started to get dizzy. My lungs burned and felt like they were going to burst.

He moved on. I slowly let out the air. The pounding in my head intensified. *Thank you, Father.*

If I could somehow tell when he was on the other aisle, I might be able to sneak out. How would I know though? I needed him to talk some more. *Lord, I know I've asked for a lot, but is that too much to ask for?*

"I even tried to make it a beautiful ending for you. A limo and a picnic. I wasted a whole dose on a dessert that you never ate." He had tried to poison me with Red Velvet cake. I would never look at it the same way again. A loud thud. He punched another box.

But I knew where he was. Now was my chance. I pulled up on the flap so that it wouldn't scrape the floor, and quietly poured myself out of the box. I tiptoed on bare feet down the aisle and out the door, throwing the hasp across the lock hanger. But there was no lock — never had been.

I scrambled down the stairs. As soon as my feet hit the stairs, he slammed against the closed door. Two hits and the doorjamb splintered. I ran for the rear door. He had already hit the stairs.

Keys! Finding the right one in full light was hard enough. I strained to identify them in a shaft of light coming in off the street into the back window.

He hit the bottom step.

I dropped the keys and wrenched open the silverware drawer, grabbing up my gun.

He snatched me by the back of my shirt.

I spun around with the gun raised.

He backed up. "You've actually got some fire in you."

I lowered my voice. "I can't believe I loved you."

"I can't believe I stood for your incessant whining all this time."

I wanted to pull the trigger so bad. But something held me back. "You're slime. Even Trey is better than you are." Did that just come out of my mouth?

"True. That degenerate actually liked your fat body, and how you were always stuffing that lousy cake in your face, and wearing all those baggy misshapen clothes."

My lip quivered.

"And while we're at it, you'd never make it in the computer field. That Asian guy knows a lot more than you do."

I didn't know what to say. It was like he had punched me in the gut.

He nodded, head cocked to the side and looking down, as though contrite. "Yeah. You're probably right about the Trey thing." He blew out a heavy sigh, the kind people give when resignation hits. "You know what else? Trey is a lot deader than I am too." He moved a step forward, his chagrined affect dropped off so fast that I could feel a bit of a breeze. Now he looked flirty, boyish, and charming, with that little smile he used when he wanted to snuggle. "I bet . . ." He cast a coy glance at the ceiling then back at me. "That you . . ." He stepped closer and rolled his bottom lip against his teeth. "Can't. Shoot. Me."

I gulped and backed away. I hadn't realized how close he'd come. Both my hands wrapped around the grip of my gun. My hands started to tremble. "You sure don't want to find out." I backed up a step.

His mouth curled into an ugly sneer. "Let's see what you've got."

I backed up another step and hit into the door. There was no place else to go.

"You've run out of room." He stepped forward again.

Now he was about four feet from me. My heart was pushing on my chest, creating a rhythm in the movement of my arms. "Don't come any closer, or so help me, Andreas, I will shoot you."

"I bet you won't."

A shot rang out.

Andreas spun to the right and dropped to the floor almost at my feet, grabbing at his left shoulder.

"Well, if she won't shoot you, I sure will," said Fifi.

Fifi, Greta, and Angelica tromped through the living room mess and into the dining room with their guns drawn.

Fifi stepped over his fallen form. She looked at him for a second then looked up at me. "Your ma never liked him anyway."

I looked at my gun and dropped my arms to my side. "And unfortunately she was never wrong, but I learned that too late." My head lowered. *Thank you, Jesus.*

Suddenly the lights blazed to life. Fifi looked up at the track lighting. "That would be compliments of Gus. He's down in your basement."

"Watch out!" I pointed. "Barbara is back there by the front door passed out."

"Yeah, we saw her. Stavros has that under control."

They moved to the side and I could see him kneeling beside her.

"Be careful. I think Andreas must've filled her full of PCP or something. She's real whacked out." I laid my gun on the counter, and then on second thought put it in my pocket. "We need the police."

"Taken care of, sugah. They're on the way," said Fifi looking rather proud.

Andreas moaned and moved a bit. Angelica shoved her .45 Long Colt in his face and declared, "Make my day."

I grimaced. "I think you'd better call her off, Fifi. So we don't have to explain a corpse."

Fifi snorted. "This is one corpse I wouldn't mind explainin'."

Greta stood beside Angelica, gun in one hand, flashlight in the other. "Yeah, make our day," she said, waving the flashlight.

I looked at Fifi. "Why is she threatening him with that little flashlight?"

Fifi raised her chin and put her hand on her hip. "Hey, Greta, show Sloane how your flashlight works."

Greta touched it to Andreas's leg. His body vibrated and convulsed onto his side.

"Stop!" I yelped.

Greta moved away.

"What in the world?" I stared at Andreas. A small thread of drool rolled from the side of his lips as his legs quivered.

Fifi snorted. "That's Greta's stun flashlight. Ain't it a pip?"

"A pip! Stun guns are illegal in New York City. What is she doing with that?"

Fifi raised her hands. "Hey, sugah, she's a little ol' lady. I ain't tellin' her what she can and cannot have."

"For crying out loud, get that put away before the police arrive." I rolled my eyes up to the ceiling and then squeezed them shut. What a night.

Greta frowned and shoved it into the big quilted bag that was hanging off her shoulder.

Sirens and flashing lights stopped in front of the building.

I reached out and hugged Fifi. "I have never been so glad to see anyone in my entire life. How did you know?"

"I had a date with Robby, remember?"

"Yeah. So?"

"We went to dinner up at Cristos, and we're sitting there talking and he tells me that he can't help me find an apartment because he quit his job," said Fifi. "So I'm thinking, great, so he's gonna be tellin' me that he's broke and I need to pay for this fancy dinner. But instead, sugah, Robby tells me that he quit 'cause he done found out who owned Coltrane Realty."

We both said it in unison. "Andreas Comino."

Fifi's jaw dropped. She touched my arm. "Sugah, you knew?"

"Yeah, for like the last ten or fifteen minutes. He taunted me with it."

"Well, anyway, just about that time, Angelica calls up to tell me that both Andreas and Trey have come into this buildin' and haven't come back out, so we hightailed it up the street."

I looked at Angelica. My angel, for sure.

"When we arrived here, Trey was dead downstairs." She pointed at Andreas. "And this one was nowhere to be seen. So I called the cops."

I looked at the four of them. "But how did you get in here?"

Fifi held up the keys to Mom's apartment. "You left these on the desk in the store. I had figured on sneakin' up the circular stairs from her apartment to see what was goin' on up here, but then I saw the post-Colonial, neo-chaos redecorating you'd been workin' on and decided to join the party."

A knock at the front door announced the police. Gus stood and approached the door. He looked befuddled trying to figure out how to open it.

I tossed Gus my keys. "The one to unlock it is in there somewhere."

My knees gave way and I slid to the floor.

Fifi rushed to my side. "Oh, sugah. Are you gonna be all right?"

"Yeah. Sure. Don't you recognize this?"

Fifi squinted.

"It's how I celebrate the conclusion of all my just-escaped-my-third-homicidal-maniac-this-week position."

EPILOGUE

Two weeks later . . .

Calypso music drifted in from the kitchen. Fifi sashayed in carrying two sandwiches on plates and a bag of potato chips jammed under her arm. She plopped down on the rug without losing a thing.

"Here ya go, sugah. Sustenance to tide us over till dinner," said Fifi as she tore open the bag of chips and dug in.

I sat cross-legged in the middle of the large, lime green shag rug, sipping on a bottle of black cherry carbonated water. I buried the fingers of my right hand into the soft fibers as I leaned back and supported myself on that arm. I didn't know that they even made shag rugs anymore, let alone that anybody would use one.

I looked around the room. Stacks of boxes littered every available space. "It's going to take you a month of Sundays to get this stuff all unpacked."

Fifi leaned back with both hands resting on the rug. "Yeah, but I figure since I don't ever have to move again, I have plenty of time."

"Don't *even* look at me! I'm *not* coming down here every day to help you get this stuff put away. You're on your own."

"No, sugah, we'll never be on our own again. We have each other."

I grabbed up a half of sandwich. "If you're all right with living in Mom's apartment after what the police found, then so am I."

"Sloane, sugah, me and your momma spent a lifetime as friends. I feel her in every room of this apartment."

"When I think about it now, I still get shivers. If he hadn't actually needed me for the building, he would have killed me that same day," I said.

"What do you mean?"

"I didn't remember it until Griffen talked about Andreas's confession, but when I found Mom, he was just suddenly there . . . behind me. I was so distraught at the time, and so glad to have him to lean on, that I never questioned it."

"He was already in the apartment?"

"Yes. Can you imagine that? I didn't even realize. Apparently, he was repositioning Mom's body to make it look natural and

433

knocked the drug vials and needles behind the headboard. He was trying to retrieve them when I came in."

Fifi shivered. "Ugh."

"Griffen pointed out that if I had let Andreas help clean this place like he offered, he would have found the evidence and then had no more use for me. He would have killed me."

"God was watching over you, sugah."

I swallowed the bite of sandwich and looked into space. "You're right."

"I know I'm right. Do you realize the list of coincidences that had to come together for him to get caught?"

I shook my head. "No coincidence. Only the hand of God."

Fifi looked at me. "I'd sure say that your momma was right on target about that man. And I think she'd have liked this particular change in events very, very much, sugah."

"What change of events?"

Fifi rolled her eyes and batted her lashes furiously. "Griffen this and Griffen that."

"Don't be silly. He said I could —"

A knock sounded on the door.

"Hold that thought." Fifi scrambled to her feet and opened the door.

Griffen Justice stood there in a casual shirt, blazer, and tan Dockers.

"Well, Detective Justice, do come in." Fifi grinned broadly as she turned her head in my direction.

I looked down and brushed the crumbs off my shirt. Auh breeze, I'm such a slob.

"Ladies, please," said Justice, holding up a hand. "I'm off duty. Call me Griffen."

I smiled and nodded.

He held my gaze.

I felt self-conscious and diverted my eyes to the sandwich still in my hand. Why am I holding this? I set it on the plate, and brushed my hands together to get rid of the crumbs.

Fifi scrambled from the kitchen with a folding chair. "Have a seat, *Griffen.*"

I rolled my eyes at her deliberate accent on his name. Big deal. He had told me to call him by his first name last week when we spoke about the case.

Griffen sat down on the chair. His heady sandalwood cologne drifted across my face.

"The guy down in the store said that I could find you ladies up here."

"What brings you to our domain today, sugah?" Fifi had taken a rug seat next to me.

"With succeeding interviews and his lawyer's cooperation, we've gotten more details." Griffen leaned forward, resting his elbows on his knees.

"Lawyer cooperation? What does that mean?" I asked.

"It means that Comino has plea-bargained himself into a lighter sentence."

Fifi slapped her hand on her knee. "Are you kidding me? He murdered Camille. How can this happen?"

Griffen clasped his hands together, and looked down at the floor. "It was the DA's decision. There were other people involved and the prosecution got him to roll over on them for a deal."

I felt a lump forming in my throat. "That hardly seems fair to my mom."

"Or to Mr. Mastronardi."

"What?" I looked into Griffen's eyes and saw sadness.

"Comino's henchman killed the old guy right before your mother, in a bid to get control of the largest part of the property."

My hand went to my throat. "That poor old man."

"It's just sad that your momma and poor Mr. Mastronardi had to die for his greed," said Fifi.

"Sad for Mom, but I don't know about old lady Bianca. She mourned him for a hot five minutes and is still on a cruise to Sicily. I don't think she's missed a beat since he died." I grabbed up some chips to push down the lump. This was not the time to cry.

"Are you all right?" asked Griffen. "We don't have to talk about this. Now or ever. You tell me what you need, and I'll do it."

I swallowed the chips and the lump, and huffed a sigh. "Yeah, it's just hard to digest." I didn't mean the chips. "Did they kill Mr. Mastronardi the same way as Mom?"

"They contacted the wife, and she allowed a disinterment so they could do another autopsy. They traced the drugs from the autopsy to Andreas. Something about the drug batches having chemical markers so that they can tell who they were issued to."

I sat up straight. "So he's as good as done, right? The papers say he's looking at several lifetimes in prison for all of this."

Griffen raised the left side of his mouth. "Well, not with the plea deal."

"What? How long will he get?" Fifi scrunched up her forehead.

"Not sure," said Griffen. "He embezzled almost five million dollars from his company. They're willing to forgo charges if they get the bulk of their money returned."

My mouth dropped open. "Don't forget they caught him dead to rights for killing Trey and drugging poor Barbara."

Griffen nodded his head, sending more musk in my direction. "The DA is taking all that into consideration."

"What about poor Barbara? She's certainly not my favorite person, but I sure don't wish her harm," said Fifi.

"They've involuntarily committed her for thirty days, so her system can absorb the drugs. They'll do a psych evaluation to see if she's fit for outpatient care after that," said Griffen.

"No thanks to Andreas . . ." The name rolled a shiver up my spine. "He tried to make that poor woman a psychotic." I hung my head.

Griffen shook his head. "Apparently she has a multiple personality disorder that he was using to his advantage."

"And all this was because he needed this block to put the embezzled money back into before the audit discovered that it was missing." I grabbed up a burned potato chip. I loved the burned ones. *Great. I'm munching like a cow in front of Griffen.*

Griffen sat up and slapped his hands on his knees. "Yep. That would be the crux of it."

"Yeah, well, we still have the e-mails and the rat that are unexplained," said Fifi.

"Couldn't they prove that any of that was

attributed to him?" I nibbled on a potato chip.

Griffen shook his head. "No, and he didn't admit to any of it either."

"I guess it's all over, till we hear something to the contrary." Fifi shrugged.

"That would be my take." Griffen rose from the chair. "Ladies, I should be going."

I raised the side of my lip. "I —"

He turned from the door. "Yes?"

"Um, nothing . . ." I shook my head. What was I thinking? "Thank you for the information . . . Griffen."

He smiled, nodded, and was gone.

I watched the door.

Fifi made kissy faces at me.

I shot a glance in her direction. "What?"

Fifi covered her mouth. "It looks to me like you and Griffen Justice might be turning into an item."

"Don't be ridiculous. He's not my type."

"Yeah . . . right, sugah. I know that look."

"We're just lucky that the timing was right when we told him what we had done about Verlene's book. We could have wound up in big trouble for hindering an investigation." I grabbed a gulp from my bottle of black cherry water.

Fifi wiggled a finger at me. "I'd say part of that luck came from Verlene's *friend,*

Derby, being Griffen's partner."

"Besides, I heard how smooth your voice got when you were talking to him. Uhm, huh!"

I cut my eyes at her. "Did *not!* I can see that you're going to be the bane of my existence now that I can't get rid of you. Aren't you?"

Fifi put her finger to her chin. "Let's see . . . I own the bookstore and you own the building. Yep . . . you're stuck with me forever."

"Mom knew what she was doing all the way around, didn't she?"

"Are you really okay with it, sugah?" Mom's will had stipulated that I sell Fifi at least controlling interest in the store if I wanted to remain involved. We could have avoided all the angst if I had just gone through the paperwork sooner.

"Yeah, I'm fine with it now. Honest, that's why I sold you the whole thing. A lot has happened in the last few months. Mom will always be in my heart, but I need to get on with my life, and that is *not* as a bookstore owner. That's your gig."

"I think your momma realized that books weren't your thing a long time ago. She was a very smart woman. And to think that I fought with her about that book purchase."

440

Fifi shook her head.

"Well, we should finish up with that next week. It's a little strange that both doctors agreed to put the auction off a week. I get the strange feeling that they are going to purchase it together. I'll just be glad when it's over. That whole deal was starting to make me feel nervous."

Fifi picked a few stray crumbs from the rug and set them on the edge of her plate. "Did they ever find out why that Bakari —"

"I don't know, and I'm sorry but I don't want to know. I've had enough death and drama for a whole lifetime."

"I agree. But ya know something, sugah? With the kind of money we're going to get for the sale of that book . . . Well, I really hate to bring it up, but did you call the lawyer about your ex-husband yet?"

"Yeah, right . . . like when have I had time to think about him?"

"Well, I just don't want you to wind up having to face him in court. I think your momma's will gives you a way out. She must'a been thinking about somethin' like that when she drew it up. She always dotted her I's and crossed her T's."

"Thanks to Mom, we will have a lot to share."

Fifi looked sad. "I would gladly give it all

up if we could have Camille back."

I rubbed her shoulder. "Believe me. I know where Mom is, and I'm absolutely positive she would not come back for all the tea in China."

"You think so?"

"I know so," I said as I looked at my watch. "Our lunch break is over. We need to get downstairs and see what damage our — correction — *your* new assistant has wrought in our absence."

We walked into the store together and were greeted by Rolling Stones music blaring from the sound system. Fifi screwed up her face like she had just eaten three lemons.

"Gabi!" she yelled over the music. "Turn that racket down."

I burst out laughing. "Boy, does that sound familiar."

Fifi charged to where they had moved the counter, and reached behind it to flick off the stereo. "That boy is going to be the death of me yet."

"Yeah, but that boy graduated at the top of his class with a degree in Hungarian Literature from Pratt," I said. "You two are a match made in heaven."

Gabi Fabian, my former hairdresser, strolled out of the stockroom with a load of new books. "I couldn't heart you from in there."

"*Heart* me? What are you talking about, heart me?" Fifi glared.

I snorted with a laugh that, if I let it out, would cause Fifi to belt me. I could see the look in her eyes.

"Dude! Heart replaces the word *hear,* because you should be listening with your cosmic heart rather than your natural ears."

Fifi shut her eyes.

I had to turn away from both of them. I had lost a hairdresser, but gained a comedy team.

I could hear Fifi giving him a piece of her mind as she followed him to the bookshelves.

"Hello, can you tell me where I can find Sloane Templeton?" asked the deep, delicious voice.

I turned to the counter with my best smile pasted on.

Before me stood a black Adonis.

"I'm Sloane Templeton." I managed to say without drooling on myself.

His chiseled jaw showcased the large hazel eyes rimmed by long, thick lashes. His shirt looked painted onto the bulging biceps straining to release themselves from the confines of the soft fabric of his silk shirt that was tailored all the way down to his trim waist.

"Hi, I'm Danny Kellogg. I'm a fireman at the station up the street from your Aunt Verlene. I saw you at the turkey fryer fire, and Verlene said you might be available for a date.

My brain seized right up.

Actually, it shouted a hallelujah chorus, and when the chorus was done, the pipe organ exploded and pieces of it shot through every brain cell I owned.

My track record jumped up and slapped me in the head. Every one of the last three men that I had picked had been based on their outstanding good looks and muscles that apparently were only in their heads and not their hearts. My overwhelming lesson had been that I did not need a man to validate me . . . at least, not one who wanted to kill me.

I shook my head. I was *not* going to be led by eye candy ever again!

I needed a vacation from boyfriends for a season . . . a man-cation.

"I'm sorry, Danny. I'm sure you are wonderful, but my aunt was mistaken. I'm off the market indefinitely."

DISCUSSION QUESTIONS

1. Why do you think someone like Sloane keeps getting into destructive relationships?
2. Did Sloane have the right to flee from the relationship with her husband? And for either position, why do you feel that way?
3. Fifi felt that helping people was a "social services" problem. What do you think?
4. How far should Sloane have gone to defend herself from Trey?
5. How would you have handled Sloane's abusive situations?
6. Why do you think Sloane would not admit the abusive relationship with Trey to Fifi?
7. Has your nurturing spirit ever gotten you in trouble with a particular person whom you have chosen to help?
8. How can God use each of these situations to teach and grow us as Christians?

9. Why would conducting verbal conversations with God make you feel closer to Him?
10. What lessons should Sloane learn from these recent brushes with disastrous men?
11. How would you describe Sloane's spiritual journey?
12. What evidence did you find to support or deny that Sloane understands true love?